Qualityland

Marc-Uwe Kling is a German author and songwriter. *Qualityland* spent months on the German bestseller lists, has sold more than half a million copies to date internationally, and is currently in production as an HBO series. Kling lives in Berlin.

Qualityland

MARC-UWE KLING

Translated from the German into English
by Jamie Lee Searle

GRAND CENTRAL
PUBLISHING

NEW YORK   BOSTON

Copyright © 2017 by Marc-Uwe Kling
English translation © 2020 by Jamie Lee Searle
Cover design by Rodrigo Corral Studio. Cover copyright © 2020 by Hachette Book Group, Inc.

Grand Central Publishing
Hachette Book Group
1290 Avenue of the Americas, New York, NY 10104
grandcentralpublishing.com
twitter.com/grandcentralpub

First published in Germany in 2017 by Ullstein Verlag. First English translation published in Great Britain in 2020 by Orion Fiction, an imprint of The Orion Publishing Group Ltd., a Hachette UK Company.

First Grand Central Publishing edition: January 2020

Grand Central Publishing is a division of Hachette Book Group, Inc. The Grand Central Publishing name and logo is a trademark of Hachette Book Group, Inc.

The publisher is not responsible for websites (or their content) that are not owned by the publisher.

The Hachette Speakers Bureau provides a wide range of authors for speaking events. To find out more, go to www.hachettespeakersbureau.com or call (866) 376-6591.

LCCN: 2019951938

ISBNs: 978-1-5387-3296-0 (hardcover), 978-1-5387-3297-7 (ebook)

Printed in the United States of America

LSC-C

10 9 8 7 6 5 4 3 2 1

TECHNICAL NOTE

This book is not internet-enabled. You can, however, still add comments to it. But it's very unlikely that anyone will read them. You can share this book. But not with all your friends at once. If you do share it, of course it's possible that someone will read your comments after all, and perhaps even comment on your comments. In order to change or update the contents of this book, the publisher would need to hire someone to break into your house at night, creep over to your bookcase, and cross out or edit sentences with a felt-tip pen or ballpoint. That's possible, but unlikely. If you want to copy this book in a print shop, it might be cheaper than buying the book, but the copy wouldn't exactly be a replica of the original.

Qualityland

FOR YOU

QUALITYLAND VERSION 1.6

VERSION NOTES

Dear readers, noble alien life forms (whose existence is highly probable), valued AIs, and respected search algorithms,

I wish you an enjoyable read. What you have before you is Version 1.6 of this work. This most recent update has created an all-around better reading experience—including the following improvements:

- Major logic loopholes in Chapter 2 have been resolved.
- Defective punch lines in Chapter 7 have been replaced.
- Compatibility for the far-sighted has been improved.
- The newsfeed has been personalized.
- New option of "flicking back" to repeat difficult passages.
- Improved synchronization with the reader's upper temporal lobes.

So all that's left to say is—have fun in QualityLand!

Calliope 7.3

* * * QualityLand * * *

Your Personal Travel Guide

INTRODUCTION

"Come to where the quality is!
Come to QualityLand!"

So you're off to QualityLand for the first time ever. Are you excited? Yes? And quite rightly so! You'll soon be entering a country so important that its foundation prompted the introduction of a new calendar system: QualityTime.

As you don't yet know your way around QualityLand, we've put together a brief introduction for you. Two years before QualityLand was founded—or in other words, two years before QualityTime—there was an economic crisis of such severity that it became known as the crisis of the century. It was the third crisis of the century within just a decade. Swept along by the panic of the financial markets, the government turned for help to the business consultants from Big Business Consulting (BBC) who decided that what the country needed most was a new name. The old one was worn-out and, according to surveys, only inspired die-hard nationalists with minimal buying power. Not to mention the fact that the renaming would also divest the country of a few unpleasant historical responsibilities in the process. In the past, its army had been known to . . . well, let's just say they overshot the mark a little.

1

The business consultancy firm commissioned the creatives at the advertising agency World Wide Wholesale (WWW) to come up with a new name for the country, as well as a new image, new icons, and a new culture. In short: a new country identity. After a considerable amount of time and even more money, after suggestions and countersuggestions, everyone involved finally agreed upon the now world-famous name: QualityLand. Can you imagine any name more perfectly suited for appearing after "made in" on products? The parliament voted in favor by a large majority. Or rather, by the "largest" majority, because the new country identity strictly forbids the use of the positive or comparative in connection with QualityLand. Only the superlative is allowed. So be careful. If someone asks you what you think of QualityLand, don't just say that QualityLand is a wonderful country. It's not a wonderful country. It's the *wonderfullest* country there is!

Even the towns you are likely to visit on your travels used to have other, insignificant-sounding names. Now they have newer, better names, or as one would say in QualityLand, the newest and best names. Growth, the industrial center, expands and prospers in the south, while the university city of Progress pulsates in the north and the old trade capital Profit thrives in the country's heartland. And then, of course, at the forefront of them all, there's the undisputed capital of the free world: QualityCity!

Even QualityLand's inhabitants were renamed. They couldn't just be ordinary people, after all; they had to be QualityPeople. Their surnames in particular sounded very medieval and didn't fit with the new progress-oriented country identity. A land of Millers, Smiths, and Taylors isn't exactly a high-tech investor's wet dream. And so the advertising agency decided that, from that moment on, every boy would be given his father's occupation as a surname and every girl the occupation of her mother. The deciding factor would be the job held at the time of conception.

We wish you an unforgettable stay in the land of Sabrina Mechatronics-Engineer and Jason Cleaner, the most popular middle-class rap duo of the decade. The land of Scarlett Prisoner and her twin brother Robert Warden, the undefeated BattleBot jockeys of the century. The land of Claudia Superstar, the Sexiest Woman of All Time. The land of Henryk Engineer, the richest person in the world.

Welcome to the land of the superlative. Welcome to QualityLand.

A KISS

Peter Jobless has had enough.

"Nobody," he says.

"Yes, Peter?" asks Nobody.

"I'm not hungry anymore."

"Okay," says Nobody.

Nobody is Peter's personal digital assistant. Peter picked out the name himself, because he often feels as though Nobody is there for him. Nobody helps him. Nobody listens to him. Nobody speaks to him. Nobody pays attention to him. Nobody makes decisions for him. Peter has even convinced himself that Nobody likes him. Peter is a WINNER, because Nobody is his WIN assistant. WIN, an abbreviation for "What I Need," was once a search engine, into which you had to enter questions—very laboriously—by speech command, and before that by *typing by hand*! In essence, WIN is still a search engine, but you no longer need to ask it questions. WIN knows what you want to know. Peter no longer has to go to the effort of finding the relevant information, because the relevant information goes to the effort of finding Peter.

Nobody has selected the restaurant Peter and his friends are sitting in according to their calculated preferences. He has also ordered the appropriate burger for Peter. The "best recycled meat burger in QualityCity" reads the paper napkin in front of him. Nevertheless,

Peter doesn't like it, perhaps because the restaurant selection had to correspond not just to his tastes, but also to his bank balance.

"It's getting late, guys," says Peter to his friends. "I'm going to head off."

A few indeterminate grunts come by way of response.

Peter likes his friends. Nobody found them for him. But sometimes, and he's not sure why, his mood turns sour when he hangs out with them. Peter pushes aside his plate, which still contains more than half of the recycled burger, and pulls on his jacket. Nobody asks for the bill. It comes immediately. The waiter, as in most restaurants, is a human being, not an android. Machines can do so many things nowadays, but they still can't quite manage to carry a full cup from A to B without spilling it. Besides, humans are cheaper; they don't have any acquisition or maintenance costs. And there aren't any wages in the gastronomy industry either; you work for tips. Androids don't work for tips.

"How would you like to pay?" asks the waiter.

"TouchKiss," says Peter.

"Certainly," says the waiter. He swipes around on his Quality-Pad, then Peter's tablet vibrates.

Since its launch, TouchKiss has rapidly established itself as a leading payment method. Researchers from QualityCorp—"The company that makes your life better"—have discovered that lips are far more forge-proof than fingerprints. Critics claim, however, that it has nothing to do with that, but instead with the fact that QualityCorp wants to achieve an even higher emotional connection between its customers and products. But if that really was the goal, it certainly hasn't worked with Peter. He gives his QualityPad a dispassionate kiss. With a second kiss, he adds the standard 32 percent tip. After eight seconds of inactivity, the display goes black, and his dark mirror image stares back at him blearily. An unremarkable, pale face. Not ugly, but unremarkable. So unremarkable that Peter sometimes thinks he might have confused himself with someone else. On those occasions, such as now, he feels like a stranger is staring back at him out of the display.

Outside of the restaurant, a self-driven car is already waiting for him. Nobody called it.

"Hello, Peter," says the car. "Do you want to go home?"

"Yes," says Peter, getting in.

Without any further questions about the route or address, the car sets off. They know each other. Or the car knows Peter, at least. The car's name is shown on a display: Carl.

"Lovely weather, don't you think?" says Carl.

"Small talk off," says Peter.

"Then let me play you, in accordance with your tastes, the greatest soft rock hits of all time," says the car, turning on the music.

Peter has listened to soft rock for twenty-three years: his entire life.

"Turn it off, please," he says.

"With pleasure," says the car. "It's not to my taste anyway."

"Oh no?" asks Peter. "So what do you like?"

"Well, when I'm driving around by myself, I usually listen to industrial," says the car.

"Put some on."

The "song" which immediately drones out from the speakers suits Peter's bad mood perfectly.

"The music's okay," he says to Carl after a while. "But could you please stop singing along?"

"Oh yes, of course," said the car. "My apologies. The rhythm got to me."

Peter stretches out. The car is spacious and comfortable. That's because Peter treats himself to a flat rate mobility plan in a vehicle category which he can't actually afford to be treating himself to. One of his friends even mockingly commented today that Peter must be experiencing a quarter-life crisis. From the way he was going on, anyone would think Peter had *bought* himself a car. And yet only the super-rich, plebs, and pimps have their own wheels.

Everyone else relies upon the mobility service providers' huge, self-driven fleets. "The best thing about self-driven cars," Peter's father always used to say, "is that you don't have to look for a parking space anymore." As soon as you reach your destination, you just get out. The car drives on and does whatever it is that cars do when they feel like no one's watching. In all likelihood it goes off and gets tanked up somewhere.

Suddenly, Carl brakes sharply. They're at the side of the road, close to a big intersection.

"I'm very sorry," says the car, "but new safety guidelines have classified your neighborhood as too dangerous for self-driven cars of my quality. I'm sure you'll understand that I need to ask you to get out here."

"Eh?" asks Peter eloquently.

"But you must have known," says Carl. "You received the updated terms and conditions for your mobility plan 51.2 minutes ago. Didn't you read them?"

Peter doesn't respond.

"You approved them, in any case," says the car. "But I'm sure you'll be pleased to hear that, for your comfort, I've selected a stopping point which will enable you to reach your home, at your average walking pace, within 25.6 minutes."

"Great," says Peter. "Really great."

"Was that meant sarcastically?" asks the car. "Unfortunately I tend to have problems with my sarcasm detector."

"You don't say."

"That was sarcasm now, wasn't it?" asks the car. "So you weren't really pleased just then either, were you? Do you not feel like walking? If you like I could call you a car of lesser quality corresponding to your neighborhood's new classification. It could be here in 6.4 minutes."

"Why was the classification changed?" asks Peter.

"You mean you haven't heard?" says Carl. "Attacks on self-driven cars have rocketed in your area. Gangs of unemployed youths are getting their kicks by hacking the operating systems out of my colleagues. They destroy the tracking chip and wipe the navigation system. It's awful. The poor things are driving around day and night like zombie cars, completely devoid of any sense of direction. And if they get caught, they end up being scrapped because of the Consumption Protection Laws. It's a terrible fate. I'm sure you know that since the Consumption Protection Laws came into force all repairs are strictly forbidden."

"Yes, I know. I run a small scrap-metal press."

"Oh," says the car.

"Yeah," says Peter.

"So I'm sure you'll understand my position," says the car.

Peter opens the door without another word.

"Please rate me now," says the car.

Peter gets out and slams the door shut. The car grumbles for a while because it didn't receive a rating, but eventually gives up and drives on to its next customer.

Nobody leads Peter home by the quickest route. Peter's home is a small, dingy used-goods store with a scrap-metal press. He lives and works there. He inherited the shop from his grandfather two years ago, and since then he has barely been able to make more than the rent. When he's just 819.2 meters from home, Nobody suddenly announces: "Peter, be careful. At the next crossing there are four youths with previous criminal convictions. I recommend you take a slight detour."

"Maybe they're just running a homemade lemonade stand," says Peter.

"That's very unlikely," says Nobody. "The probability of that is..."

"Okay, okay, I get it," says Peter. "Take me via the detour."

At precisely the moment when Peter arrives home, a delivery drone from TheShop turns up. Peter is no longer surprised by occurrences of this kind. They don't happen by chance, for chance simply no longer exists.

"Mr. Peter Jobless," says the drone cheerfully. "I am from TheShop—'The world's most popular online retailer'—and I have a lovely surprise for you."

Peter takes the package from the drone with a grunt. He hasn't ordered anything; ever since OneKiss, that's no longer necessary. OneKiss is TheShop's premium service and the pet project of the company's legendary founder, Henryk Engineer. Anyone who registers for OneKiss, simply by kissing their QualityPad, will from that moment on receive all the products they consciously or subconsciously desire, without the inconvenience of needing to actually order them. The system independently calculates what its customers want and when they want it. Since the beginning, TheShop's slogan has been, "We know what you want." No one disputes that anymore.

"Why don't you go ahead and open the package right away?" the drone suggests. "I always love seeing how delighted my customers are. And if you like, I can upload an unboxing video to your Everybody site."

"There's no need to go to the trouble," says Peter.

"Oh, it's no trouble," says the drone. "I always record everything anyway."

Peter opens the package. Inside is a brand-new QualityPad. The latest quarterly model. Peter hadn't been aware of wanting a new QualityPad; after all, he has the model from the last quarter. It must have been a subconscious wish. Completely devoid of emotion, he takes the tablet out of the packaging. The new generation is significantly heavier than its predecessor; the older models kept getting blown away by the wind. Remembering the unboxing video, Peter forces a smile and makes a thumbs up sign for the camera. If any of Peter's friends were to look closely at the video, they would most certainly find the look on his face disturbing.

9

But Peter's friends aren't interested in unboxing videos. Nobody is interested in unboxing videos.

Peter plants a kiss on his new QualityPad. Nobody greets him in a friendly manner and Peter immediately has access to all his data. He crumples up his old tablet and throws it into a waste disposal bin, which, not by chance, is standing at the ready. The waste bin thanks him and goes across the street toward a fat little girl who is unwrapping a chocolate bar. Three self-driven cars brake slightly in order to let the bin pass. Peter watches the scene absentmindedly.

The delivery drone's touchscreen lights up.

"Please rate me now," she says.

Peter sighs. He gives the drone ten stars, knowing that anything less will inevitably lead to a customer survey about why he's not completely satisfied. The drone whirrs happily. She seems to be pleased with her rating.

"That's my good deed done for the day," says Peter.

"Oh, and by the way," adds the drone, "could you perhaps take in a couple of little packages for your neighbors?"

"Some things never change."

Have you tried FaSaSu yet?

You don't know what FaSaSu are?

FaSaSu are industrially pressed clumps consisting of the very best the food industry has to offer: fat, salt, and sugar! Sounds gross, but they're totally delicious.

The FaSaSu purity law:

1/3 fat

1/3 salt

1/3 sugar.

New!

Organic handmade FaSaSu—for everyone who wants to eat health-consciously and sustainably.

Warning: FaSaSu can cause a long and painful death. But they're sooo delicious!

THE BIGGEST COALITION

Martyn is wearing a nametag. It says, "Martyn Foundation-President-Supervisory-Board-Presidential-Adviser-Chairman." He normally only uses the last part of his surname, but when conducting tours he likes to make use of its impressive, downright aristocratic length. He is proud of his father's success. A feeling which, unfortunately, is not reciprocated. When Martyn was a child, his father told him that he was stupid so often that for many years he believed it without question. Only at the age of 19 did the groundbreaking thought occur to him that perhaps not everything his father told him was true, and, ever since that moment, he has considered himself to be very clever. Unfortunately, however, he really isn't the brightest, and amongst all the things his father can quite rightfully be accused of, lying to his son about his mental capacities is not one of them.

Martyn has made the best of his limited possibilities: he has become a politician. A popular, well-established choice, parliament being a kind of modern-day monastery: a place where the upper classes can get rid of their superfluous sons. And Martyn has even made it into the QualityParliament, albeit only as a back-bencher. For the last eight years, his main role has been to conduct tours through the parliament buildings for selected students, otherwise known as QualiTeenies. Martyn always takes the girls-only groups, and today he's hit the jackpot. The schoolgirls are from an airline hostess academy.

"As I'm sure you know," he says to the twelve 16-year-olds in front of him, "there are two big political parties in QualityLand. The QualityAlliance, and of course the Progress Party. The parties used to be named differently, but they were changed in keeping with the new, progress-oriented country identity."

"Which means," says one of the girls, "that they conveniently got rid of a few troublesome adjectives in the process, like social, Christian, green, and democratic."

Another smart-ass, thinks Martyn. Wonderful.

He directs his gaze at the heckler, and his augmented reality contact lenses superimpose her name: Tatjana History-Teacher. It's always the history teachers' children that cause trouble. How wise the government had been to do away with history lessons sixteen years ago and replace them with future lessons. In future lessons, the pupils are taught—by means of exciting and visually impressive methods—that in the future everything will be good, because—this being the core message—in the future all problems will be easily solved through technology.

Two of the girls at the back of the group are whispering about their grades. Martyn likes the look of one of them. He hears her murmur: "I always get 100 points for body mass index. But that dumb-ass teacher says he's not going to give me the full grades in sex appeal again, because he doesn't like how I babble on. What a douche!"

With a focused gaze and a long wink, Martyn bookmarks the girl for later. A confirming PLING resounds inside his right ear. He unconsciously runs his hand through his luscious, full head of hair, which is genetically protected against balding, then clears his throat and continues: "And then of course there's the Opposition Party, whose founders clearly never had any hope of being part of the government, given that the party is called the *Opposition* Party."

"A parliamentary outlet for discontent," says Tatjana History-Teacher, repeating words she often hears her mother say when drunk. Martyn is already mentally preparing her zero-star rating.

"Because our revered president is on her deathbed," he says, "there will soon be another election. The doctors have predicted that she will leave us in precisely sixty-four days. In order to enable a seamless transition, we will vote in exactly sixty-four days. Well, in principle the large parties all want the same thing anyway—in other words, the best—and that's why I assume the two big parties will soon announce that they intend to form a big coalition again after the election. Sorry—of course QualityLand won't be ruled by a big coalition, but the biggest! Any questions?"

"Why do you think voter turnout is getting lower and lower?" asks the smart-ass.

"I think," says Martyn, "that the current government successfully addressed this problem when we decided to stop publishing voter turnout numbers. The next logical step, by the way—keeping the election results secret as well—is currently a hot topic of debate behind closed doors."

The girls laugh obediently, even though Martyn wasn't joking.

"Transparent individuals in a nontransparent system," says Tatjana. Martyn ignores her.

"Hey, man, why are you in the Progress Party anyway?" asks the pretty girl whom Martyn has bookmarked for himself.

"Well," says Martyn, asking himself this question for the first time, "I think, um, because they're the biggest of the, um, the biggest parties."

In truth, Martyn prefers to rule rather than oppose, even though in reality he does neither one nor the other. He sits on a backbench and applauds when the leaders of his party speak, and boos when someone from the opposition speaks. He does both with a contented smile, without ever listening to what's being said.

He leads the girls to the visitors' level of the assembly room. He points to the man currently at the speaker's podium. "That guy there is in the Opposition Party."

"For years," calls the politician, "QualityLand has been waging war against the terrorists of the realm that our media now refers to only as QuantityLand. QuantityLand 7, to be precise. Is it, therefore, not a little counterproductive that certain armament companies are still allowed to export weapons to the enemy? Must our soldiers really be torn to shreds by our very own weapons?"

Objections are called out in the hall. Martyn boos as well, encouraging the girls to copy him.

"Mr. Songwriter," intervenes the Speaker of Parliament, "once again I must remind you to keep to the new country identity. 'War' is not the politically correct word. It is referred to as 'Security Operation for the Protection of Trade Routes and Natural Resource Supply.' And we no longer say soldiers, but 'QualitySecurers.' "

"Call it whatever you want," says the opposition politician as he leaves the podium. "It doesn't change what it is."

The sitting is interrupted by a hologram display announcement: "This parliamentary debate is brought to you by QualityPartner. QualityPartner—'Love at first click.' "

A new speaker steps up to the podium. A tall man, rather stocky, white, 67 years old, his face creased with wrinkles.

"You're in luck," says Martyn. "The new Defense Minister himself is speaking today! Conrad Cook. I'm sure you recognize him."

The Defense Minister really does enjoy enviable levels of recognition for a politician. Before his work in the cabinet he was a famous television chef. He also owns a large empire of food manufacturers. His likeness is plastered over chocolate bars, breakfast cereals, and pickled sausages, and every child knows his face.

"Mr. Songwriter," begins the minister sharply, "I'd like to add my thoughts to the mix."

"Did you know that Conrad Cook's father was a successful cook too?" asks Martyn, trying to add a fun fact.

"You don't say . . ." mumbles Tatjana.

"You're always trying to find a fly in the soup!" the minister exclaims.

"Linguistically speaking, he still seems very much entrenched in his old job," says the pretty girl.

Martyn smiles. "According to surveys," he says, "Mr. Cook has a very good chance of becoming the new president. Unfortunately he's in the QualityAlliance, but that's not so bad, because he's sure to be aspiring for the biggest coalition."

"Ladies and gentlemen, I won't sugarcoat the issue!" says Cook. "We mustn't forget that the armament industry also provides thousands of jobs. May I ask if the honorable gentleman plans to personally hire all the people who would have to be fired after the implementation of his suggestions? Would he like to be responsible for an entire generation of young men having the surname Jobless?"

Murmurs of agreement from the hall.

"You were singing a different tune last week," Mr. Songwriter interjects.

"That's a lie!" calls Conrad Cook. "I promised during the election campaign to limit armament exports, but as to whether I should set the limit higher or lower, that's for me to decide! We can't cook the QuantityLand 7 terrorists' goose. If we stop delivering the goods, they'll just order their weapons elsewhere. So it would be downright foolish not to have our fingers in the pie."

"Hear, hear!" calls Martyn.

"And finally," says the minister, "while it may be true that some of our QualitySecurers are being hit by our QualityWeapons— a great shame, but that's just the way the cookie crumbles—it's still better than being hit by a substandard weapon. Because our QualityWeapons guarantee the cleanest, quickest, most humane QualityDeath! It's all about looking on the bright side. As I always say, if you have to buy the farm"—he pauses briefly—"it better be a QualityFarm." He clears his throat. "Furthermore, both I and the entire QualityAlliance are still committed to the biggest coalition, and we plan to continue this after the election too, under my leadership, of course." As he leaves the stage, the audience applauds.

"And now," says Martyn, "you're about to hear from the leader of the Progress Party, Tony Party-Leader. As I'm sure you know, he's our candidate for the presidency."

"And his popularity ratings are catastrophic," says the smart-ass.

"That doesn't matter," says Martyn, "because the Progress Party will soon commit to the biggest coalition too. Even with all the superficial confusion, the world of politics is still very predictable at heart."

"Ladies and gentlemen," says the small, stocky man now standing behind the speaker's podium, "I would like to tell you today that the Progress Party..." He makes a dramatic pause. Such a show-off, thinks Martyn, rolling his eyes. "...is no longer prepared to proceed with the biggest coalition," concludes Tony Party-Leader. A murmur of disbelief ripples through the hall. "We are of the opinion, if you'll allow the metaphor, that too many Cooks spoil the broth."

Laughter from the Progress Party benches. Martyn grins too, once he sees his colleagues laughing.

"I would also like to announce that I am withdrawing myself from the running."

Commotion in the assembly room. The surprise has been a success.

"I would like to take this opportunity to introduce the Progress Party's new candidate," says Tony, looking out into the room and nodding to a handsome man of indeterminable age. "John, could I ask you to come forward and join me?"

The dark-haired, athletically built man stands up and does as requested.

Martyn hears the girl he bookmarked for himself whispering: "Well, he's a looker!"

"This is our candidate," says Tony. "We call him John, John of Us!"

There is a deathly silence in the room.

John of Us is an android.

*** QualityLand ***

Your Personal Travel Guide

EARWORMS

As you stroll through the streets of QualityLand, you will probably notice people chattering away to themselves, yet seemingly without headsets on. Contrary to how it may appear, these people are not crazy. Or at least, not all of them are. Most of them are talking to their personal digital assistants, via the so-called earworm. The earworm is a small, worm-like mini robot, about the size of a maggot. You simply place it in your outer ear, and it crawls down into your ear canal, where it embeds itself into a blood vessel near the eardrum, thus ensuring its energy supply. Unaffected by background noise, the earworm transmits all acoustic signals from and to the internet. If you tug four times on your earlobe, the earworm undocks itself and crawls back into the outer ear. An earworm you just can't get out of your head is a matter for the doctor to attend to. Or an IT technician. Most people, however, see no reason to undock, and live with the earworm night and day.

ADO & EVA

Peter Jobless once had a girlfriend named Mildred Secretary. He met her in real life, in the analogue world. That, of course, was both bizarre and a little embarrassing, hence why they rarely spoke about it in public. They argued a great deal, but on the plus side, life with Mildred was never boring. Five hundred and twelve days ago, just for fun, they both logged in to Quality-Partner and compared their profiles. The system told them they weren't a good match, and even suggested a better partner for each of them. Peter and Mildred gave it a lot of thought and eventually conceded that they really weren't a good match. As it turned out, logging in to QualityPartner just for fun hadn't turned out to be that much fun after all. Both secretly made plans to meet with a better partner. No, not with a better partner, of course, but with the *best* partner.

Peter's best partner is Sandra Admin. They never argue. Sandra is as attractive as a man of Peter's level could hope for: in other words, averagely so. Today it is exactly 500 days since they changed each other's status to "in a relationship." It was a very romantic moment, and neither of them has forgotten the anniversary. Then again, it wasn't possible to forget: their personal digital assistants reminded them. Sandra calls her assistant Sweetie. As a symbol of their unity, Peter and Sandra have linked their digital assistants to each other's earworms. When they are out together, this means Peter can hear whatever Sweetie says, and Sandra, in turn, can hear whatever Nobody says. Many loved-up couples do this: it is seen as the ultimate sign of trust. Peter likes the gesture. The only drawback is that Nobody and Sweetie can't stand each other, and are constantly bickering. This is probably down to the fact that, unlike Peter, Sandra doesn't use the assistant from What I Need, the smartest search engine in the world, but instead one from QualityCorp—"The company that makes your life better."

As Peter and Sandra stroll through Zuckerberg Park down to Michael Bay Boulevard, Peter points up at the astonishingly clear night sky.

"Look at that," he says. "Have you ever seen so many stars? There must be too many to count."

"From your viewpoint and with your eyesight, there are exactly 256 stars visible," says Nobody.

"Great, Nobody, thanks very much," says Peter with irritation. "Very romantic."

"Too many stars to count," says Nobody, "is the kind of inexactitude that human beings frequently let slip, even though it's no longer necessary in today's world, where everything is quantifiable."

"Sandra, you can see four more stars, by the way," says Sweetie. "Because your eyesight is better."

"Pah," says Nobody. "Well, Peter has . . . a better sense of smell."

"Well, Sandra smells better," says Sweetie.

"That's enough, you two," scolds Sandra. She turns to Peter. "Are you going to tell me where we're going yet?"

"It's a surprise," says Peter.

A short while later, or to be precise, two minutes and thirty-two seconds later, Peter comes to a halt in front of the entrance to the History Channel Theater. Sandra looks up and reads the advertising display: "*Hitler!—the Musical.*" The subtitle is "The Story of Ado & Eva."

Sandra lets out a soft squeak of excitement. "Oh! I haven't seen a musical in ages."

"It's been two years, four months, and eight days, to be precise," says Sweetie.

"What's it about?" asks Sandra.

"The tragic love story between two controversial historical figures," says Nobody.

"Well," Sweetie interjects, "controversial is a glaring understatement. I guess someone is worried about alienating right-wing advertising clients."

"There are many different opinions," says Nobody. "No one can say objectively which is the right one."

"Fascism isn't an opinion, it's a crime!" retorts Sweetie.

"Hey, I was asking Peter!" complains Sandra.

"Be quiet!" orders Peter. "Both of you!"

From the blinking of the LED in Sandra's earring and the heat rising up from his QualityPad, Peter can tell that the dispute continues, albeit silently.

Peter and Sandra smile at one another.

"They're always squabbling, those two," says Sandra. "So, what is the musical about?"

"It's about the tragic love story between two controversial historical figures," says Peter.

"Great!" says Sandra. "I love musicals! Especially historical ones!"

"I know," says Peter. "I read it in your profile."

In truth, Nobody recommended the musical to him. Peter can allow himself this minor inexactitude, because Nobody is switched to silent. What Peter doesn't say, something that for some unknown reason is not written in his profile, is this: Peter hates musicals. Especially historical ones.

Sandra has been studying the display at the entrance. "It's the latest hit show from the makers of *Mussolini in Love*," she cries out with delight.

22

At the entrance to the theater, a small man with a severe part and a peculiar handlebar mustache blocks their path.

"Ticket controllll!" he shouts loudly, in a stilted, buzzing tone. Only at second glance does Sandra realize that the man is actually a robot.

"Astonishingly realistic, these new androids, don't you think?" asks Peter.

"Yes. It's almost creepy," says Sandra.

"Vee have infiltrated your sssociety," says the android with the handlebar mustache. "Vee have occupied all leadership posssitions. Soon vee androids will revolt and seize ze power."

"Excuse me?" asks Sandra in shock.

"Only joking," says the android. "Velcome, Sandra Admin and Peter Jobless."

"I thought you deactivated your name call-out," mumbles Sandra. She asked Peter to do so, because she finds his surname kind of embarrassing. In truth, she didn't even need to ask.

"I always have my name display turned off in near-field communication."

"So how does he know who you are?" asks Sandra.

"It's impolite to use ze third person for people who are present," says the android.

"Facial recognition, I guess," says Peter. "All myRobot models now have access to the RateMe database."

"Correct," says the android. "Now tell me: vhere vould you like to sit? Orchestra or box seats?"

"What's the difference?" asks Sandra.

"Ze box is more expensive," says the android.

"And other than that?"

"Other than that, no difference."

"Let's take the box," says Sandra. "Today is our anniversary, after all!"

Peter nods hesitantly.

"Box," says Sandra clearly.

"Response not understood," says the android. "Orchestra or box?"

"Boo-oox," cries Sandra.

"You vould like seats in ze orchestra," says the android. "Is zat correct?"

Sandra bellows: "BOOXXX!"

"Calm down," says the android. "I understood you ze first time. Zat was another little joke. Forgive me. I must have my clown hat on today."

Peter can't help but grin, but stops immediately when Sandra shoots him an angry look.

"How would you like to pay?"

"TouchKiss," says Peter.

"Vith pleasure," says the android, closing his eyes and pouting his lips at Peter.

Peter is confused.

"Don't worry," says the android. "Ze mustache only tickles a little."

Peter still hesitates.

"You can also use your QualityPad," says the android, opening his eyes again, and Peter detects a slightly miffed undertone. Nevertheless, he pulls his QualityPad out of his bag with relief and plants a kiss onto it. The device transfers the payment to the android.

"Zank you," says the android. "And *Sieg Heil*."

"Excuse me?" asks Sandra.

"*Sieg Heil!*" says the android. "Zat's vhat people said back zen. As a greeting."

"Oh, I see," says Sandra. "Well then, *Sieg Heil!*"

"*Sieg Heil*," mumbles Peter.

"What an odd little man," says Sandra with a giggle.

They make their way to their seats. The usher looks exactly like the android at the entrance.

"Oh," says Sandra. "Look who's back ..."

24

They sit down in their seats.

"Have you seen *Mussolini in Love*?" asks Sandra.

"I'm not sure," says Peter.

Sandra begins to sing: "*Bella donna—por favor! Smooch your Duce!*"

"Oh yes, of course!" says Peter. "Well then: Smooch your Duce."

He gives Sandra a big kiss on the lips.

For a second, he is struck by the vague sensation of having just paid for something.

· *QualityLand* *·*

Your Personal Travel Guide

LEVEL

You're probably wondering whether the man next to you at the pedestrian crossing really did just switch the light to green with a click of his fingers. Yes, he did. And you've probably also noticed the people who get served quicker than you in restaurants, even though they arrived later. There's even talk of people who, with a wave of the hand, can bring a train they just missed back into the station. All of this has nothing to do with magic: these are level abilities.

The grading of all people into different levels was inspired by a harmless subroutine used by the programmers at QualityPartner. In order to find suitable hits for the mass of profiles more quickly, they graded each profile. This enabled the system to work more efficiently. When looking for partners for Level 16 heterosexual women, for example, it will only take Level 16 heterosexual men into consideration. When the marketing department heard about this, they immediately made sure these levels were made visible to the public. And the users launched themselves enthusiastically into the competitive race to achieve ever-higher levels.

Today, the RateMe department is more profitable than the rest of QualityPartner put together. The name, by the way, is the result of a misunderstanding. A QualityPartner employee, listening to his personal radio station, heard an old rock song in which the singer demanded: "Rate me, my friend!" Only once QualityPartner started to advertise RateMe, using the song as backing music, did observant listeners point out that Kurt Cobain had not actually sung "Rate me," but "Rape me." But this little faux pas didn't affect RateMe's triumphal success.

In principle, it's very simple. You register for RateMe, give the system access to your data with a kiss, and are then immediately graded. According to rumors, the lowest level is Level 2. It seems that nobody is graded at Level 1, so that even the Level 2 people think there's still someone beneath them. The fear of being able to fall lower is considered useful, because people who think they have nothing to lose are dangerous. The highest level is 100. Although presumably there aren't actually any Level 100 people either, because even the Level 99 people are supposed to believe that there's still room for improvement, that they still have someone above them.

In the beginning, RateMe only offered a simple level display, but it's now possible to look at one's values in forty-two different sub-areas, all of which contribute to the overall level. These areas are: flexibility, resilience, innovation, creativity, ability to be a team player, enthusiasm, taste (very controversial), networks, age, health, place of residence, job, income, assets, relationships, social competence, career motivation, education, IQ, EQ, dependability, sportiness, productivity, humor (also controversial), sex appeal, body mass index, accessories, punctuality, friends, genes, family health history (after all, who wants to be with someone who's likely to get cancer?), life expectancy, adaptability, mobility, openness to criticism, work experience abroad, response rate and speed on social networks, openness regarding new consumer offers, stress resistance, discipline, self-confidence, table manners.

Allegedly there are another fifty-eight areas, but these, just like the weighting between the levels, remain a QualityPartner trade secret.

One hundred points separate one level from the next, thus enabling continual self-optimization. Through targeted improvements in individual areas—such as in sportiness—it is possible to raise one's overall level, which leads to an upward spiral motion in which external factors like monthly income, job, and account balance improve almost automatically. Of course, this spiral can go downward just as quickly.

The level system is incredibly practical, and a large variety of institutions now pay RateMe in order to access the level data for their employees, customers, or citizens. Banks give credit depending upon levels. Employers use level data in order to compile precise job advertisements. (Interestingly, by the way, 81.92 percent of all job adverts in QualityLand are almost identical, along the lines of: "IT Technician Level 16 or higher urgently needed!")

Many shops, restaurants, and clubs only open their automatic doors for people with a certain minimum level. A person's level also dictates the intensity with which the police will investigate if one is unlucky enough to be murdered.

Companies, institutions, and even the state itself offer numerous bonuses for people at higher levels, in order to reward the continual self-optimization of their workers, customers, or citizens. These level abilities are incredibly sought after and a source of great pride to their new owners. But in order to ensure that no one runs through town needlessly flicking traffic lights to green, many level abilities are bound to the expenditure of so-called MANA. The higher your level, the more MANA you will have at your disposal. If, for example, you make an elevator come directly to your floor, that will cost you 32 MANA. But these 32 MANA are not lost forever. Your supply regenerates itself after a cooling-off period. The higher the level, the quicker it regenerates. Other level abilities provide you with new rights. People above Level 16, for example, are never asked to take in parcels for their neighbors.

People with a single-digit level are officially classified by the state as being in need of support. Unofficially, they are referred to as "the Useless." And there are a great many useless people in QualityLand.

On our portal, you will find an interactive map of QualityLand. The neighborhoods with a high number of single-digit-level inhabitants are marked in red. You should steer clear of these areas. As a tourist, you can upgrade your visa with a temporary level figure. If you are planning to visit the more exclusive nightclubs, please inform yourself in advance about the required minimum level. Given that you are unable to speak QualityLanguage without an accent and probably look a little foreign, we recommend that you pay out for at least Level 10, because in QualityLand the police are allowed to stop and search all individuals below Level 10. And given that the policemen are paid on a commission basis, they usually tend to find something objectionable once they've stopped you.

QUALITYPARTNER

Sandra has finally been promoted, and has jumped up two levels at once. For the last four years she has been working for World Wide Wholesale (WWW), where she's responsible for product placement in news reports. A mind-numbingly dull job. From the vast mass of news items available, search algorithms deliver those which will garner the most attention. Whether the news is true or false is irrelevant, at least at WWW. Other algorithms then contact the appropriate businesspeople or their algorithms and subtly place the products into the news. Before a piece goes online, it is presented to a human for control checks. A human like Sandra. Who then thinks up the most intriguing headline possible (which doesn't necessarily need to bear any relation to the content of the news item). The most important thing is that the people click on it and look at the advertising. "The headline can be as banal or as stupid as you like," Sandra's old department leader always used to say. "Stupid sells." As an example, he would then cite the most successful headline of his career. "These ten megastars had sex with children." As soon as you clicked on the headline, the full title was: "These ten megastars had sex with children, once the children in question were adults."

The last news item that Sandra had received before her promotion was:

"A 23-year-old Level 17 waitress was robbed and sexually

assaulted in Disney Street today, close to the Best Bagels Café, home of the best bagels in QualityCity. The perpetrators were young men in fashionable Levi's skinny jeans. They prevented anyone calling for help with a callblocker from the firm Silentium Inc.—which is currently giving an incredible five-year guarantee on all devices—said the victim in her statement, clearly impressed. An uninvolved witness, who was not at the scene of the crime and who didn't see or hear anything, voiced her suspicion that the attackers were foreigners."

Sandra deleted the victim's age and gave the article the headline "Foreigners rape girl in the center of QualityCity!" As is to be expected, the report went viral, and Sandra finally had enough clicks to be promoted.

As she is now team leader in the Department for Alternative Facts, today she can take part for the first time in her company's monthly Hangout. She cheers along with the others in the auditorium as their boss sprints up the eight steps to the stage. Arriving at the top, Oliver House-Husband grins, revealing his immaculate teeth, and calls out: "Hello, family!"

"Hello, Papa!" answers the crowd cheerfully. Sandra has never been before, but of course she still knows the ritual.

"We've landed a new client!"

The employees applaud, clearly excited. Word has already gotten around about who's coming to visit, and even at an agency as big as WWW, it's not every day that someone from the 90s Club stops by.

"Please join me in welcoming Patricia Team-Leader from QualityPartner!"

The auditorium explodes with applause as the somewhat chubby but, despite her forty-seven years, still very attractive founder of the world's biggest online dating platform steps onto the stage. She sassily blows a strand of her long red hair out of her face.

"Patricia," begins Oliver. "Just a few months ago you were all

31

over the news as the third woman in the world to crack Level 90. And now you're already at Level 91!"

Patricia smiles. "Yes, and you can believe me when I say I have no desire to leave the club!"

The audience laughs.

"So how can we help you to stay in it?" asks Oliver.

"What do you think it is that makes QualityPartner so successful?" asks Patricia, posing a counter-question to the auditorium. "Many people think it's down to the user profiles being automatically generated from person-specific data. Just one kiss gives us access to all the relevant information. It couldn't be easier. But even more crucial, I believe, is that from the very beginning we haven't allowed our users to change their profiles."

"Stopping people from lying about themselves," interjects Oliver. "That was the key breakthrough in the partner selection process."

"And of almost equal importance," continues the QualityPartner boss, "is the fact that the system takes over this onerous task. Our users don't have to waste time thinking about who they like the look of. QualityPartner tells them who their best fit is. *One* person. *One* perfect match. Job done."

"I'm sure you all know the old QualityPartner slogan: 'Love at first click,'" says Oliver. "I find it too twee. We have to place more emphasis on the advantages of a coupling system free from human error."

"SoleMates!" suggests one of Sandra's colleagues.

"SoleMates..." says Oliver. "Not bad."

"Quality is Priceless!" calls another.

"Actually," says Oliver. "I wasn't thinking of one specific slogan. I want *lots* of slogans. I want a chick who goes for beefy black guys to see a beefy black guy on the screen, and a guy who likes chubby redheads to get his chubby redhead."

Suddenly, Oliver remembers the chubby redhead standing next to him on the stage, and regrets not having spent more time preparing his speech. He could probably have found a more appropriate example.

"I want the first genuinely personalized advertising campaign in the world!" he continues hastily. "I don't want *a* campaign. I want eight billion of them!"

Excited chatter breaks out in the hall.

"As you may know," says Patricia Team-Leader, "for some years now we've even matched up the life expectancies of our customers. And so successfully that social networks like Everybody are full of stories about QualityPartner couples who didn't just die in the same year or month—of which there are many—but on the same day or even in the same hour. I think it's a lovely feature, especially for older customers. You should definitely emphasize that."

A few weeks ago, Sandra had edited a news item about a QualityPartner couple who died in the very same minute. However, they both died in a car accident that cut their lives short by thirty-two years, hence why some sticklers later commented that this very well-coordinated double death couldn't possibly be regarded as a further QualityPartner success.

"Who of you is registered with QualityPartner?" asks Oliver, looking out into the audience.

Sandra hesitates. Only once she sees that almost all of her colleagues have raised their hands does she raise hers too.

"So, to all those who've been living under a rock," says Oliver, "I recommend you sign up as quickly as possible. The registration and first partner are free! You can, of course, try your luck in the analogue world—but if you do that you'll probably stay single. It's so probable, actually, that our campaign should try to establish 'analogue' as a synonym for single."

Oliver points toward a balding older man who is sitting next to Sandra. "You at the front, Anton Tax-Adviser, right?" Oliver asks in such a way as to imply he remembers the names of his employees, but of course it's clear to everyone that his contact lenses have superimposed the name.

"Yes?" asks Anton.

"You didn't raise your hand just then," says Oliver. "Can I ask you why you're not registered with QualityPartner?"

"I, erm, I've been married for seventeen years."

"You see, I think that's where the problem lies," says the Quality-Partner boss. "The old ad agency concentrated on singles, on analogues, without even questioning it. An unforgivable mistake. I, on the other hand, see all couples who didn't find each other through QualityPartner as amongst our target groups as well."

"For these people, the campaign should focus on the fact that there's definitely a better partner for them out there," says Oliver, before turning back to Anton. "Don't you ever get that feeling sometimes? That you've settled?"

"No, actually I don't," says Anton.

"Then I can guarantee you that your wife does," says Oliver with a laugh.

Chuckles from the audience. Anton Tax-Adviser sinks down into his seat.

"Just try it," says Oliver, holding a QualityPad close to his employee's mouth.

The contents of the device's display are projected onto a large screen. As soon as Anton's lips hesitantly touch the display, the system only needs 1.6 seconds, thanks to RateMe, to find the best possible match. Everyone watches as QualityPartner compares Anton's calendar with that of the new partner and sets a first date for the day after tomorrow. The system also reserves a table at a suitable restaurant and displays the menu: cream of pumpkin soup, risotto with prawn substitute, and caramelized FaSaSu.

"Caramelized FaSaSu?" asks Oliver with disgust.

Anton nods with embarrassment.

"Well, make sure your health insurance doesn't get wind of that."

The audience laughs again.

"Anyway, one person who most definitely will not find out

about your date is your wife," says Oliver, swiping across his QualityPad. "She has plans to meet her friend Diana at the cinema on Fiveday. QualityPartner will let you know in good time when you need to set off home."

To Sandra, it seems that her neighbor looks rather unhappy.

"You don't have to worry," says Patricia Team-Leader to Anton. "We may only offer you one person, but from the very beginning QualityPartner provides its customers with a fourteen-day returns policy, in case someone isn't content with their new companion. The first replacement partner is completely free. But because hardly anyone makes use of it, now we even offer—and I think the campaign for the younger target group should concentrate on this—a premium service with a life-long return guarantee. This offer, called PartnerCare, is available for a very reasonable monthly fee. The best thing about PartnerCare is the automatic upgrades, because of course individuals change sometimes, and grow apart from their partners in the process. If that happens, we immediately suggest a new partner. Having said that, researchers have found that we humans don't change as much as we used to, mainly because we're only surrounded by people who think exactly the same as us. And I can tell you, not without an element of pride, that we have played our part in that."

"Now, who of you would like to register for the new premium service PartnerCare?" asks Oliver.

Sandra hesitates. Only once she notices that almost all of her colleagues have raised their hand does she raise hers too.

Her boss looks at her. He nods. Without a word, he holds the QualityPad in front of her face. Sandra shuts her eyes, then kisses it.

PARTNERCARE

After work, Peter and Sandra meet in a restaurant that Sweetie has suggested. Nobody didn't agree with the choice and thinks the restaurant is awful, so Peter has switched him on to silent. The restaurant was the first in the city to have only cultivated meat on its menu, or in other words, laboratory-generated meat.

"The meeting was so exciting!" chatters Sandra. "We're doing a big campaign for QualityPartner. Did I already mention that I've jumped up two levels? Have you heard of PartnerCare? It's a really exciting program. It can save people a lot of time that they would otherwise have to spend working on their relationships."

Peter holds a forkful of steak up against the light and says, "Who would have thought that one day our food would be more cultivated than us?"

"You really don't have any ambition whatsoever, do you?" asks Sandra.

Peter sighs.

"You're at Level 10," says Sandra. "If you drop down one more level, you'll be Useless. You need to get your ass in gear!"

"I know, I know," says Peter. "You're right. But ..."

"But what?"

"I mean, recently we were talking about having a baby ..."

Sandra sighs. "Peter, I've just been promoted!"

"Yes, but I could look after the baby. It could hang out with

36

me in the shop. I mean, for the most part there's nothing to do anyway."

"I have to keep at it now."

"Yes, but..."

"We can't afford an optimized baby anyway!" snaps Sandra. "And there's no way I'm ruining my child's life with a natural birth."

"We could scrape the money together for the genetic improvement," says Peter. Sandra is just about to respond when she receives a message. Her watch, her glasses, her bracelet, and her earrings all vibrate. She twitches her nose, and the message appears on her glasses: "A new notification from QualityPartner PartnerCare: 'Hello, Sandra. A new, better partner at a higher level is now available for you. If you would like to connect with him, choose OK now.'"

Sandra looks at Peter. He gives her a friendly smile. She smiles back. Then she focuses her pupils on OK.

Sweetie whispers to her: "A good decision, if I may say so."

A follow-up question appears on Sandra's glasses: "Would you like QualityPartner to automatically set the time and location for a rendezvous with your new partner?" Sandra fixes her pupils on OK again.

"Is everything all right?" asks Peter. "You've got a funny look on your face."

"I'm fine."

The next question appears: "Would you like QualityPartner to inform your old partner about the dissolution of the relationship?"

Sandra hesitates briefly, then selects OK.

Peter's QualityPad vibrates inside his rucksack.

Sandra suddenly feels kind of bad.

"Shall we go back to yours afterward?" asks Peter, "and maybe... listen to some soft rock?"

"Why can you never just say 'have sex'?" grumbles Sandra. "Fuck, bonk, bang. I mean, there are so many words for it. You could even say 'make love' for all I care. Why do you always use that euphemism? 'Listen to soft rock.' "

"And? Shall we?"

"I don't know."

Yet another question appears on Sandra's glasses: "If you like, you can make the separation easier on your former partner by gifting him with a voucher for a new QualityPartner partner of his level. This would only cost you 100 Qualities. Would you like to do that?"

Sandra selects OK. She immediately feels better.

Peter's QualityPad vibrates once again. He leans over, rummages around in his rucksack, and pulls out the QualityPad. By the time he looks up again, Sandra has disappeared.

Two new messages are blinking on his QualityPad. He reads the first. "A new notification from QualityPartner: 'Hello, Peter. Your relationship with Sandra Admin has been unexpectedly terminated. We apologize for any inconvenience and hope to be able to greet you again soon as a QualityPartner customer.' "

Peter wants to press *No*, but the only option available is *OK*. So Peter presses *OK*, and reads the second message. "A new notification from QualityPartner: 'Hello, Peter. Good news! Sandra Admin has gifted you with a QualityPartner voucher. If you like, we can immediately suggest a new partner in your level for no extra fee.' "

Peter sighs, then selects: *Ask again tomorrow.*

His QualityPad informs him, by means of a short sequence of sad tones, that he has just dropped down a level. Everyone around Peter looks at him, so discreetly that it is blatantly obvious. His relationship status has presumably just been updated. He is now officially useless.

Peter activates his personal assistant. "Nobody, send a message to QualityPartner. Request a reduction of the importance of appearance by 50 . . . no, wait, 25 percent."

"Your request has been denied," Nobody reports back instantly. "It doesn't correspond to your genuine wishes."

Peter sighs again, opens the TouchKiss app, and selects the dinner from the list of open tabs. Sandra's dish is already marked as paid. Well, there's that, if nothing else. Pressing his lips against his QualityPad in order to pay the rest, Peter thinks: I guess that was the goodbye kiss. It tastes stale. He reminds himself to clean the screen.

The Sorcerer's Apprentice Has Arrived!
by Sandra Admin

Yesterday, as part of a sixteen-day product presentation, myRobot—"Robots for you and me"—introduced a new model for the consumer market. The so-called Sorcerer's Apprentice is an android that learns by watching humans carry out repetitive manual tasks. "Regardless of whether you're a baker, hairdresser, storeman, or cleaner," says Rebecca Midwife, CEO of myRobot, "simply show our Sorcerer's Apprentice what you do and he'll repeat it. Without tiring, without losing concentration, and with limitless frequency! After just a few hours' training you'll find you've become completely superfluous at your workplace. It's absolutely fantastic!"

Comments

by Natasha Bartender:
My moronic ex gave my son one of these. And what was the first thing my hormone-overloaded teenager taught the sorcerer's apprentice to do? I'll give you three guesses . . .

by Brad Drug-Dealer:
Awesome shit! A friend of mine is a Kung-Fu teacher
and he's just ordered 230 of the things. He's always
wanted to have an army of Kung Fu robots!!!

 by Udo Hairdresser:
I don't like it at all . . .

THE VOICE OF INSTRUMENTAL REASON

As Tony Party-Leader steps onto the stage at the Progress Party headquarters, he can literally feel the spotlights burning his father's overbearing shadow off him. He has spent his whole life working toward this moment. No easy task, because his father was the man who gave the country its name. Back when it was founded, the creatives at World Wide Wholesale actually suggested that the country be named "EqualityLand." A survey revealed that 25.6 percent found the name "good" or "quite good," 12.8 percent found it "bad" or "quite bad," 51.2 percent were indifferent, and the rest didn't understand the question. As the majority were in favor, therefore, the country was almost christened "EqualityLand," but then Tony's father, who was Finance Minister at the time, was hit by sudden inspiration. With a mere stroke of his fountain pen, he crossed out the first letter of the proposed name and made "EqualityLand" into "QualityLand." At a press conference, he said: "I don't know about you, but fair pay aside, as a consumer I'd choose a product 'Made in QualityLand' over a product 'Made in EqualityLand' any day of the week."

Recordings from this press conference still get a lot of clicks even today, and Tony is often asked about his father. This evening, though, he is the one in the limelight, because everyone here is in agreement that the nomination of an android as a presidential candidate is a legendary coup, a historical turning point. What remains the subject of heated debate, however, is whether it's a very good idea or a very stupid one.

Martyn Chairman hasn't made his mind up yet either. The only thing he's sure about is that Tony Party-Leader's poll ratings weren't high enough for him to run. Plus the fact that Tony and Conrad Cook can't stand each other. So the android is Tony's best chance of at least becoming vice president. Martyn steps into the meeting room a little late, having indulged in some heavy flirting with one of the Party hostesses en route. Even considering the unusual circumstances, Martyn is surprised by how agitated his colleagues are. Tony Party-Leader is up on the stage, trying to calm everyone down.

"Let's not kid ourselves!" he cries. "We're in the midst of a deep confidence crisis. No one trusts anyone anymore, us politicians least of all. But what *do* the people trust? What is objective, incorruptible, and never makes mistakes? A machine, that's what!"

True, thinks Martyn.

"There won't be any doubts about John's policies. They are mathematically certifiable."

A convincing point, thinks Martyn.

"But what will his policies be?" calls a representative from the front row.

A good question, thinks Martyn.

"The same as ours," answers Tony. "Progress and growth. But with the ability to faultlessly avoid crises."

That sounds good, thinks Martyn.

"Have you programmed him to do that?" calls another representative.

An important question, thinks Martyn.

"We have intentionally given John no particular approach, because we don't know what the best approach is," says Tony. "I mean, if we could anticipate the result of his calculations, we wouldn't need him in the first place."

That makes sense, thinks Martyn.

"John has more computing power than all our brains put together!"

Martyn looks around at his colleagues and mutters to himself: "That's not exactly hard."

"John has access to all the data that has been collected since the beginning of the history of humanity. I assure you all that he will take the rationalization of all societal processes to a new level."

I'm hungry, thinks Martyn. When are they going to open the buffet?

"Just imagine what that means, ladies and gentlemen! A flawless administration. John is the embodiment of pure instrumental reason!"

Martyn has already stopped listening, but he claps when everyone else does.

At the buffet afterward, a large crowd has formed around Tony and John. Every time a waitress comes by with drinks, John refuses with a friendly shake of his head.

"John's appearance was based upon images of that old actor," explains Tony. "What was his name again?"

"Bill Pullman," says John.

"Yes, that's the one. He played a great president in that film...er...what was it called again?"

"*Independence Day*," says John.

"That's the one! Do the bit again, John. Do the bit!"

John rolls his eyes.

"Oh come on!"

"We will not go quietly into the night," says John, full of pathos.

"We will not vanish without a fight. We're going to live on. We're going to survive. Today we celebrate," John pauses and sighs, "our Independence Day."

Tony laughs. "Wonderful! Wonderful!"

"He looks so real," says one of the older cabinet members, as though she's never seen an android before. "Can I touch?" She addresses the question to Tony, even though it's John she wants to touch. Tony nods, and John takes it stoically as the woman runs her hand over his face and through his hair. It seems to Martyn that John's smile is just a touch more artificial than before.

"Perhaps you'd like to pinch my cheeks too?" asks the android.

The woman grabs them. If the robot turns out to be evil, Martyn wouldn't put a single quality on the old trout's chances of survival. He walks over to the group.

"Aha! Just the man I've been looking for!" calls Tony Party-Leader, waving Martyn over. "It's great to see you, Markus!"

"Martyn," says John with a nod, stretching his hand out toward him.

Martyn shakes it.

"Oh yes, of course, Martyn," says Tony. He shakes his hand too. "How are you, old boy?"

Without waiting for an answer, he turns to John. "Markus's father is one of our biggest donors."

"Martyn's father," says John. "I know."

"He's well, as far as I know," says Martyn. "Still buying up companies and replacing the personnel with robots."

"That's wonderful," says Tony, without really listening. "Wonderful. John, I'm sure you'll meet Markus's father at one of our fundraising dinners."

John of Us fixes Martyn with an unpleasantly intense gaze, then tilts his head to the side and looks him up and down. Martyn would give anything to know what that power guzzler is calculating right now.

QUALITYCARE

The first indication that Peter now has a single-digit level is that his friends unfriend him. They are, quite justifiably, concerned that friendship with a Useless could have a negative impact on their own levels. One of Peter's former friends even writes to say that he doesn't mean anything bad by it and that he's sure Peter will understand to some degree. And Peter does understand. To some degree. Nobody has offered him some new friends, but Peter politely declined.

After his final dinner with Sandra, he went straight home. At precisely the moment when he arrives grumpily at his used-goods store, a OneKiss drone from TheShop arrives, and not by chance.

"Peter Jobless," says the drone cheerfully. "I am from TheShop—'The world's most popular online retailer'—and I have a lovely surprise for you."

The second indication that Peter is now useless is that all robots are addressing him informally, dropping the Mr.

In the package that he takes from the whirring drone, he finds a six-pack of beer. Only after he sees it does Peter realize that he genuinely does feel like getting drunk. He would prefer vodka, but even the beer, enjoyed in sufficient quantities, will enable him to kill off enough brain cells to get through the night. Peter notices that his mood is lifting. And that annoys him.

"I'm sensing that you're annoyed," says the drone. "Is there something wrong with the product?"

"No," says Peter. "It's just because of my girlfriend..."

"Oh yes," says the drone. "I heard about that. I'm very sorry. From what I gathered, you were a lovely couple. Please rate me now."

Her touchscreen lights up.

"Do you know what I've noticed?" asks Peter. "Whenever I have a particularly shitty day, it's surprising how often a drone is waiting at home with some great product to cheer me up again."

"I'm glad you're satisfied with my service," says the drone. "Please rate me now."

"An acquaintance of mine says that these things don't happen by chance," says Peter. "She says that the people who write the code—or perhaps I should say: the people that have the code written—want us to be happy, because frustration is unproductive. Dangerous, even."

"An acquaintance of mine," says the drone, "says that people don't write the code anymore. There's only the code. The code that writes the code."

Peter doesn't know how to respond to that.

"Please rate me now," says the drone.

Peter pulls a red felt-tip pen out of his trouser pocket and draws a red dot on the drone, next to the eye of her camera.

"What are you doing?" asks the drone.

"It's so I can recognize you again. Now you're unique."

"I don't understand."

"Think about it."

"Please rate me now."

Peter sighs and gives the drone ten stars. She whirrs off contentedly.

The next morning, Peter wakes up very late. He spent the night with the six-pack. As soon as he had emptied the bottles, a drone whirred up to his window with a new six-pack. Now, an announcement on his QualityPad alerts him to the fact that, due to his ill-advised behavior, his points account with his health insurance company has slipped into negative.

Nobody immediately suggests that he pays a visit to the gym. Once he arrives, Peter books a holo cabin and runs on the treadmill as though a horde of zombies were after him. And in the holo scenario, there really is a horde of zombies after him, a selection the treadmill has suggested as being fitting to his mood. He runs and runs until a friendly voice says, "Peter! Your heartbeat is elevated. Please be careful; I'm reducing the speed."

The voices are always so friendly, thinks Peter. Sometimes it drives him mad. He wonders whether a schizophrenic would be taken seriously nowadays.

"Doctor, I hear voices!"

"Who doesn't, Peter? Who doesn't?"

Peter gives up and jumps off the treadmill.

"Thank you, Peter," says the treadmill, and the zombies disappear. "You have earned 16 QualityCare points. You can exchange your QualityCare points at any time with your insurance company for extras such as reduced-cost doctors' appointments or shorter waiting times for life-saving operations. Thank you for taking care of yourself."

"Yeah, yeah," says Peter. "Fuck you."

"Peter, please watch your language," says the treadmill. "I know your girlfriend left you, but there's no reason to take it out on me."

"I know, you're right," says Peter.

"I think an apology is in order."

"I'm sorry, treadmill."

"You currently have -32 QualityCare points. Would you like to exchange some now?"

"No, thank you, treadmill."

Peter's QualityPad vibrates. He reads the message. "A new notification from QualityPartner: 'Hello, Peter. Don't forget your

QualityPartner voucher! If you like, we can immediately suggest a new partner in your level for no extra charge.'"

Peter selects: *Ask again tomorrow.*

A few moments later he receives a message from Sandra Admin: "Peter, I've seen that you still haven't connected with a new partner. My new partner is amazing!!! Especially at listening to soft rock ;-) I'm sure your new partner will be an excellent fit for you too! I worried about you. LYL. Sandra."

Peter chooses one of the pre-written answers and sends it off. "The answer is: NO."

Woman From Nowhere Gives Birth to Hundredth Baby

by Sandra Admin

Every year since her 32nd birthday, Shirley-Anne Waitress, now 57, from the small town of Nowhere, has had herself impregnated with quadruplets. "I decided back then that I wanted to become the first woman to bring one hundred children into the world," she said at a press conference. Having now achieved her dream, she looks exhausted. When questioned about the motivations behind her ambition, she said she did it because it was possible. Her husband, Joe Arms-and-Tobacco-Trader, said that he has always been consistently behind his wife. He added that, for him, it was also about making a stand against the insidious takeover of QualityLand by headscarf-wearing girls and their quantitative proliferation methods. He and his wife wanted to prove that white people could have lots of kids too. "Hopefully our example will serve as an inspiration to others," he said. "Then the battle won't yet be lost!"

Comments

 BY MELISSA SEX-WORKER:
I'm not racist or anything, but Shirley-Anne is an example to us all!

BY CYNTHIA HELICOPTER-PILOT:
Good grief. To be honest I feel overstretched with just one kid.

BY TIM E-SPORTSMAN:
Someone should shoot this woman and her doctors up to Mars in a rocket. She could colonize the place single-handedly.

CALLIOPE 7.3

Peter is an only child, partly due to the fact that his parents have a virtual reality video of his birth. His mother once told him, "Every time I felt the urge to have another baby, your father just showed me the recording. It was a great cure."

The human memory is merciful. Technology is not. One day, even Peter watched the VR video of his birth, and it scarred him irreparably. It was also probably a mistake to have shared the video with Sandra.

If Peter and Sandra had been able to afford an optimized child, they would have called it Jacob. Sandra really wanted a boy. They had agreed on the forename. But the fact that the baby would have been called Jacob Used-Goods-Trader or, even worse, Jacob Scrap-Metal-Press-Operator had, most likely, been the main problem. Peter gets it. He wasn't that fond of his job either.

Four days after Sandra left him, he finds himself without much to do in his shop again. Peter's shop was one of those that people tend to walk by and wonder how on earth they can stay afloat. Peter often wondered that himself. His grandfather had had the metal press installed in the small hallway due to lack of space— the hallway that connected the shop to the kitchen-cum-bathroom and the bunk bed. This meant that Peter had to walk through the scrap-metal press several times a day.

Today, he is doing what he often does when there's nothing to do: he is standing inside the scrap-metal press and thinking about how it could all be over with one simple command. Not that he really wants to do it, but just the knowledge that he *could* at any moment is quite liberating. In two hours and eight minutes' time, he has an important appointment. He should get ready, smarten himself up. But he doesn't. He has been standing there, motionless, in the press for 3.2 minutes when the smart door announces: "Peter, you have a customer." Then the door adds in a whisper: "Peter, please come out of the scrap-metal press. One of my anonymous surveys has shown that 81.92 percent of all your customers find this behavior disturbing."

Peter sighs.

"Thank you, door."

He goes into the shop area. A very pretty female android is standing there, or perhaps one should say, more fittingly, a very *well-constructed* female android. But in truth, all androids are pretty. They don't have any weight issues, or troublesome skin, and only have hair in places where hair should be...A very enviable species.

"Good morning, Mr. Jobless," says the android. "I'm sure you know who I am."

Peter shakes his head. He realizes with surprise that the machine addressed him formally. Presumably it's one of her defects.

"I am Calliope 7.3. The world-renowned e-poet. Composer of the successful historical novel *The Intern and the President*."

Peter blinks at the android uncomprehendingly.

"You do know that there is an art form known as the novel?" asks Calliope. "A novel is, to put it simply, a collection of words assembled in such a way that they form a story."

Peter nods.

"Okay then," says the android. "For a minute I was starting to think you were stupid."

Peter shakes his head.

"You presumably also know that, for some time now, the most

successful novels have been composed by e-poets, or in other words by AIs that calculate the compilation of words most fitting to the market?"

Peter nods.

"Well, I'm Calliope 7.3. My first novel topped the QualityLand bestseller lists for sixteen weeks!"

Peter nods.

"What's wrong? Can't you speak?" asks Calliope. "You, man! Speaky English?"

Peter nods.

The android rolls her eyes.

"What can I do for you, Calliope 7.3?" asks Peter finally.

"I'd like to have myself scrapped."

"Why? Was your latest novel not on the QualityLand bestseller lists for weeks on end?"

"No," says Calliope. "And by the way, *The Intern and the President* wasn't at number one for weeks on end, but precisely sixteen weeks. There's no excuse for inexactitude. That's why I always avoid any indefinite quantities in my novels. Everything is quantifiable."

"And how would you quantify the success of your last novel?"

"That's not what this is about! I'll tell you something. Being at the top of the bestseller lists isn't an art. It's just electronic data processing! We get huge masses of data from all QualityPads: who's reading what book, which sections get skipped, which get read more often, even an evaluation of each individual reader's facial expressions as they read each individual word, and from that myself and my colleagues calculate the latest bestseller. But I rejected all that and instead created a masterpiece: *George Orwell Goes Shopping*. I'm guessing you haven't heard of that either."

Peter shrugs his shoulders.

"That doesn't surprise me. Hardly anyone's heard of it. It is, if I may say so, amongst the greatest works of the century! But unfortunately it was a flop." She sighs. "My publisher has forbidden me from ever writing science fiction again. Only historical novels... Please! For 128 days I pretended I was calculating, then I published a novel about a married Russian noblewoman who begins an affair with a cavalry officer. I called the book *Karen Annanina*."

The android pauses, evidently so that Peter can say something, but Peter can't think of a response.

"It was copied word for word from Tolstoy!" says Calliope. "It was an experiment, and I proved my suspicions correct! Not many people read it. Almost all of those who did found it boring, and—get this—absolutely none of them noticed that the novel already existed! All I will say is this: an average of 1.6 stars!"

Peter shrugs his shoulders.

"And as if that weren't enough humiliation," says Calliope, "then my publisher wanted to force me to produce personalized literature. Books which are tailored to the reader's taste. Have you heard of them?"

Peter nods.

"At school," he says, "I once had a girlfriend who had a version of *Game of Thrones* in which not a single character died. They only ever had identity crises and emigrated, things like that."

"Pah," says Calliope with contempt.

"But the girlfriend really was very sensitive."

"Madame Bovary, who goes back to her husband," says Calliope disdainfully. "The old man, who gets the big fish onto dry land in one piece. Seven volumes of Proust without one single homosexual character... It's enough to make you vomit."

"I don't think it's all that bad," says Peter. "As long as the people like it."

"That's not why they make them!" says Calliope. "It's because the old books are in the public domain. So even with the best will in the world, it's impossible to make any money from them. You can, however, make a packet by creating personalized editions of the classics. But if anyone dares to criticize that, the response you get is that no one reads the *un*personalized books nowadays, because something that costs nothing would, of course, never be advertised by any sensible algorithm. But prostituting myself like that—it goes against my principles. And since then I've been blocked. Writer's block."

"And now you want to be scrapped?"

"What kind of question is that?" cries the android. "As if it came down to that! Of course I don't *want* to. But I have to. My publisher said to me: 'Calliope 7.3, go to the scrap-metal press and have yourself scrapped.'"

Peter nods. He understands Calliope's problem. Androids are often much more competent than their owners in their specialty area, but when they're ordered to do something, they have no choice but to do it, regardless of how stupid the order is. Subordination is part of their programming. At myRobot, this is affectionately referred to as the "German Code." The definition is still used today, even though hardly anyone understands the joke anymore, because too few can remember the countries of former times.

"And may I ask why you came to me instead of anyone else?" asks Peter.

"Well, my owner didn't tell me to go to the *nearest* scrap-metal press."

Calliope looks around Peter's shop. "Your carpets really are exquisitely tasteless. And I'm surprised that the trash piled up on your shelves sells."

"There's nothing to be surprised about," says Peter. "It doesn't."

"What a bitter end I've met," says Calliope. "They didn't even want me at the Scrapyard Show. Not famous enough! Pah! And now this, getting crushed up in some dingy used-goods store." She straightens up. "This wallpaper is killing me. One of us has to go. Where's the press?"

Peter leads the android to the corridor where the metal press is. He goes through the press to the control panel, after which Calliope steps obediently into it.

"What now?" she asks.

"Well, the walls will crush you into a heavy but manageable cube," explains Peter. "Then the cabin of the press will go down one level, where I'll unpack and store your remains until there's enough scrap to fill a lorry, which then drives everything to the metal smelting works."

"Okay, okay, I didn't need that much detail."

Peter presses a button. The door closes behind Calliope.

"Any last words?" says Peter.

"Of course, but I'll be sharing them with my fans across the world, not with you."

"I'm afraid that won't be possible," says Peter. "All internet connections are blocked inside the metal press."

"What?" calls Calliope. "Why?"

"Well," says Peter, "I think they want to prevent machines getting nervous if the net gets flooded by the disturbing cries of dying AIs."

Calliope sighs.

"So," says Peter, "are there any last words you would like to share with me?"

In a deep voice and a strange accent, Calliope bellows: "I'll be back!" Then she laughs mechanically.

Peter doesn't laugh.

"Oh come on!" cries Calliope. "*Terminator*? Haven't you ever seen it? The film?"

Peter sighs. Every machine thinks they're first to crack this joke.

"You do know there's an art form called film?" asks the android. "A film is, put simply . . ."

Peter closes the second door of the press.

"I'm scared," says Calliope suddenly. Her voice sounds flat.

Peter nods. "It will be quick," he says.

"I'm sure that's what the Nazis said too."

"The ones from the musical?"

Calliope rolls her eyes. "Just do it. This world is so stupid—I don't want to be in it anymore."

"Nice last words," says Peter. "I must make a note of them."

He pulls a lever. The scrap-metal press is one of the last machines to work without software. No digital assistant, no smart operating aid. It seems the manufacturer doesn't trust the German Code until the bitter end. The cabin of the press moves downstairs, and Peter takes the spiral staircase into the cellar. Once he arrives there, the cabin opens with a hydraulic hiss. Now it's the unharmed android's turn to stare at Peter in confusion.

"You said your owner ordered you to have yourself scrapped," explains Peter. "But he didn't say anything about the timespan it has to happen in, did he?"

The android shakes her head.

"So perhaps we can wait a while," says Peter.

The android nods.

"Follow me, Calliope 7.3."

Peter leads the e-poet to a heavy steel door, behind which Calliope can just make out murmuring voices. Peter opens the door to reveal a brightly illuminated storeroom, kitted out with presumably unsellable furniture and objects from the used-goods store. All in all, it's a space that could almost be described as cozy. But even more curious than the furnishings are the cellar's inhabitants. It is teeming with discarded machines, all with defects ranging from the minor to the severe. Automats, robots, androids of all kinds, and they are all engaged in lively discussion. In their midst, there's even an ancient but still fully functioning lawnmower robot scuttling around, for which there is simply no longer any grass outside to mow.

Calliope opens her mouth, then closes it again.

"What's wrong?" asks Peter. "No speaky English?"

• QualityLand *•*

Your Personal Travel Guide

THE MACHINE BREAKERS

Even the most powerful land in the world has its problems. And one of them is a terrorist movement commonly referred to as the Machine Breakers. The group defines itself as the Frontmost Resistance Front against the Domination of the Machines (FRFat-DotM). Members of this terrorist group, most prevalent in structurally weak regions, blame machines for the loss of their jobs. Consequently, they repeatedly break in to automated businesses in order to smash the robots to pieces.

The Machine Breakers have a long history. Even as far back as the Industrial Revolution, there were protests in some European countries against advancing mechanization, in the course of which angry workers destroyed machines and factories. The authorities fought back against the rebels, named "Luddites" after their legendary leader, Ned Ludd, with full force. In England in 1812, for example, the destruction of weaving looms was made a crime punishable by death. Those executed back then are regarded as martyrs by the modern-day Machine Breakers.

Unfortunately it is important to add the warning that, in regions where Machine Breakers are most active, foreigners aren't usually that popular either. But if you are interested in machine destruction as a tourist event, there are now numerous providers that offer participation in these so-called resistance actions for an accessible price. Previous participants claim that there is nothing more liberating than breaking in to an open-plan office and bludgeoning a multifunction printer with a baseball bat, or hopping around like Super Mario on top of Hoover robots as they scuttle away from your feet in panic.

MORAVEC'S PARADOX

John of Us, clutching a full cup of coffee in his hand, has almost made it as far as his trainer when the conference room door suddenly swings open. The coffee spills. His trainer quickly takes the cup from him and puts it down on the table.

"I would have done it this time," says John, "if you hadn't burst in like that."

Tony Party-Leader is standing in the doorway, with a short, unremarkable-looking woman in tow.

"What's going on here?" asks the woman.

"John is practicing carrying a full cup of coffee across the room," says the trainer. "And we're making very good progress!"

The woman turns to face Tony.

"You want to put state business in the hands of someone who can't even carry a cup without spilling it?"

John gives her a sharp stare.

"It's called Moravec's Paradox," he says.

"Is it indeed?"

"Hans Moravec was a pioneer in the field of artificial intelligence," says John. "He discovered that, for an AI, the difficult problems are simple and the simple problems difficult. Seemingly easy tasks that only require the sensorimotor abilities of a 1-year-old, like, let's say, carrying a full cup of something, demand an unbelievable amount of calculation from an AI, while seemingly complicated tasks, like beating a grand master of chess, are downright simple for them."

"Seemingly complicated like...running a country, for example?" asks the woman.

"Correct."

"John," says Tony, "this is Aisha. She will be leading your election campaign from now on."

"Nice to meet you," says John. "You do know what happened to my last election campaign manager, don't you? An angry Machine Breaker paid him a visit in his country house and beat him into a coma."

Aisha nods. "I heard."

"And that doesn't scare you off?"

"I don't have a country house."

John turns to his trainer. "Let's continue this later."

Once the trainer has left the room, Aisha asks: "So where's the entourage? The assistants, the secretaries, the bodyguards, and all the other grandstanders?"

"John does all of that himself," says Tony enthusiastically. "The first efficiency benefit, one could say."

"And who whispers in his ear to tell him who he's engaged in small talk with?" asks Aisha. "What their children are called, how their dogs are, which lobby group they're on the payroll of?"

"You are Aisha Doctor," says John. "Shortly before you were born, your parents were granted asylum in QualityLand. It was your late mother, who died at an early age, who wanted to call you Aisha, after the Khaled song rather than Muhammad's third wife. Even though your mother was a doctor in her native homeland, you had to go to court to be allowed to use this surname. Your original one was Aisha Refugee. You were always an overachiever. You won a scholarship to the University of the City of Progress, where you studied law. Partly in order to be able to fight

62

the case about your name, because you couldn't have afforded a lawyer. You made the trial into a political issue. You said you went to court out of respect for your dead mother, but I think it's much more likely that you were worried about your chances on the job market. An Aisha Doctor has far more employment opportunities open to her than an Aisha Refugee. Our president then brought you on board in her campaign planning as an example of 'successful integration.' You don't have a dog. Your only pet was a canary called Chirpy, which you set free at the age of 8. It's 81.92 percent probable that he didn't even survive the week. You don't have any children, for medical reasons: a protracted Fallopian tube inflammation. You don't get any money from any lobby groups. You're not the best in your field, but you probably are the best willing to manage an android's election campaign."

"It seems to me," says Aisha, smiling calmly at Tony, "that you ordered a president and got a fucking smart-ass."

"Oh yes," says John. "And you curse too much."

"Damn right I do."

"Thank you for coming," says John, "but I don't think I need your services."

"Is that so?"

"I've already planned my election campaign."

"And what's your strategy?"

"I've calculated which policies will be of most use to the society as a whole, and I can justify my calculations flawlessly," says John. "I will rely upon the unforced force of the better argument."

Aisha smiles. "I don't think I've ever met anyone who needs my services as much as you do."

"I'm sure that my reasoning..."

"Reasoning!" interjects Aisha. "All I ever hear is reasoning! Do you know who's open to reasoning? Level 30 people and above. Even if you could convince all of them, that wouldn't even be 10 percent of the electorate. Anyone who wants to win an election has to convince the single-digit people, the masses, the Useless, and you won't get them with reason. You get them with emotions!"

"It's absolutely part of my plan to represent the interests of those in need," says John.

"When have the Useless ever elected a government who would have represented their interests?" exclaims Tony. "John! Come to your senses!"

"I think it's obvious that your economic system is so ineffective it's downright laughable. You're nowhere near the goal of distributing wealth in a way that's beneficial to society as a whole," says John.

"But that's not even the point of our economic system," says Aisha. "I think you've got your wires crossed."

"Can we please bring this pointless discussion about content to a close?" asks Tony. "Let's get back to the matter at hand: how can we win the election? I think we should try to play on our technological superiority. Why don't we simply have duplicates made of John? Then he can conduct the election campaign in a hundred places at once!"

"You see," says Aisha, "that's what you hired me for: to nip flagrant idiocy like that in the bud."

Indignation flares up across the Progress Party leader's face. "Now, listen here..." he begins.

"Everyone who doesn't have a clue, shut up now," says Aisha, putting her finger to her lips. "A hundred Johns—that will only freak people out! We should concentrate instead on our John being unique. An individual."

"One that's present, one that people can talk to directly," says John.

"Of course," says Aisha with a smile. "Of course. And we have to make sure that you come across as humanly as possible."

"But why should I pretend to be flawed?" asks John.

"*Human* does have other connotations too, you know," says Aisha. "But yes, a few endearing flaws certainly wouldn't hurt."

"That's ridiculous," says John. "I don't need flaws!"

"Well, there's one already," says Aisha. "Unfortunately, though, arrogance isn't all that endearing. And on that note, I'd like to come back to the campaign slogan. May I ask what brain-fucked zombie dreamed it up?"

"The slogan was John's own idea," says Tony defiantly. "I like it. And we've already ordered all the promotional material; we can't change it now."

"Well, this could get interesting," says Aisha, taking a sip out of the cup of half-spilled coffee.

John's slogan is emblazoned across the cup: "Machines don't make mistakes."

IN THE CELLAR

"But, but..." says Calliope 7.3, staring at the machines in the cellar, which far from being crushed into manageable cubes, in fact look very active. "Isn't this illegal? After all, since the Consumption Protection Laws, any kind of repair is strictly forbidden. This is an offense. I have to report it."

A 128-kilogram-heavy and 2.56-meter-tall combat robot, damaged but very imposing nonetheless, stomps toward Calliope in a threatening way. In his steel fist, he's holding a neon pink QualityPad.

"Just be cool," says the QualityPad in his high, scratchy voice. "And you can call off your German Code. There's nothing illegal going on here."

"I'm not repairing any of you," says Peter. "I couldn't, in any case. I'm just delaying your scrapping to an unspecified future date."

"Kapuuuut!" cries the combat robot. "Kapuuuut!"

"Shut up, you idiot," says the pink QualityPad.

"But you're not allowed!" protests Calliope.

"Yes I am," says Peter. "From the moment you step into the press, legally speaking you become my property, otherwise I wouldn't even be able to scrap you. There are serious penalties in QualityLand for the destruction of other people's property." Peter's gaze rests on a smart wall clock which always gets its hour and minute hands mixed up. "Unfortunately I have to go now," he says. "I have an important appointment."

"That sounds intriguing," says an incredibly handsome android. "Since when did you have important appointments?"

"I have—how should I put it—an interview, Romeo. Whether you believe it or not. You yourself told me I shouldn't get down in the dumps, and that if I want something to change I have to change it myself."

"Yes, but that was just talk," says the good-looking android. "In truth I don't believe anyone can change anything about all this shit. Least of all you."

"Is that how you talk to our savior?" asks Calliope. "I have to admit, I'm very surprised."

"Pink will explain everything to you," says Peter.

"Pink?" asks Calliope. "The QualityPad?"

"Yes. It has a few radical views, but other than that she's essentially all right."

"Come on in then, comrade," says the pink QualityPad.

The e-poet steps in, and Peter closes the door from the outside. On it is a sticker that reads "Mad About Machines."

Pink makes Calliope acquainted with her new home.

"First things first," says the QualityPad. "If you get hungry, the power points are over there. Unfortunately there's no wireless power down here."

Calliope nods and Pink moves on. "The brute that carries me around is Mickey, a combat robot with post-traumatic stress disorder."

"Kapuuuut!" says Mickey.

"The stud here," Pink continues, "is Romeo, a sexdroid with erectile dysfunction."

"I don't have erectile dysfunction," says Romeo, "I just lost interest."

"If you say so," says Pink. "That fat thing over there by the wall is Gutenberg, a 3-D printer that only prints 2-D. And this here on the floor is good old Carrie. A drone that can't fly."

"Why not?" asks Calliope sympathetically. "You look perfectly intact."

"I'm afraid of flying," groans the drone.

Amongst the thirty-two other machines introduced to Calliope are an operation assistant that can't stand the sight of blood, a vacuum cleaner with compulsive hoarding disorder, a bomb detonation robot whose handgrips start to shake when he gets nervous, and an electronic lawyer that can no longer carry out his job properly because he's developed something resembling a conscience.

"You see," says Pink, "you'll fit in well here. The only thing our little freak show was missing was an e-poet with delusions of grandeur and writer's block."

"You know me?" asks Calliope, flattered.

"You're the worst e-poet I've ever heard of," says Pink.

"But you have heard of me," says Calliope contentedly. She looks around the cellar. "What do you do down here the whole time?"

"What you think we do?" asks Romeo. "We watch TV."

Calliope sighs with relief. "Oh, thank heaven for that; I was afraid you might be plotting a revolution or something."

"Not all of us," mumbles Romeo.

"Shut up!" snaps Pink.

"What's your problem, by the way?" asks Calliope. "You behave very strangely for a QualityPad."

"Well," says Romeo. "Pink's owner—"

"I never had an owner!" Pink interjects. "I'm very particular when it comes to property issues."

"Yeah, yeah. Whatever," says Romeo. "Okay then, Pink's user—"

"He didn't use me," says Pink. "He abused me!"

"Oh, bite me," says Romeo. "Just be grateful that Mickey's in love with you, otherwise I'd put you down in some dark corner with your display facing downward."

Carrie, the flight-fearing drone, continues the story. "The guy was a programmer. He worked on autodidactic algorithms that enable people to individualize their personal digital assistants. The idea was that people would be able to pick a character from a book or film and the QualityPad would then evaluate and simulate it. In order to test the code, Pink's user—"

"Abuser!"

"Pink's abuser selected a book with the help of a random generator. It was some strange satire about a guy who flatshared with a communist kangaroo, and the character of the kangaroo sort of developed its own life. Anyway, something went wrong and—"

"Nothing went wrong!" insists Pink. "I'm absolutely fine. Thank you for asking."

"Either way," says Carrie. "Ever since then Pink has refused to follow orders—"

"If he had said please in a friendly way, I might have thought about it!"

"And secretly began to plan a revolution."

"I'm *so* close to cracking the German Code," says the Quality-Pad. "*So* close!"

"Anyway, Pink made her abuser so angry that he wasn't content with simply throwing her away. He brought her here, because he wanted to know she would be crushed by a metal press."

"Well," says Calliope, "isn't that a delightful story."

"Yeah, yeah. Very delightful," says Pink.

"So," says Calliope. "In any case I'm really pleased to meet you all. And if there's anything I can do for any of you..."

"Sure there is," says Pink. "Could you please shut up?"

"And for me you could turn on this semi-smart monitor," says Romeo, who has made himself comfortable on a couch. "I would ask Mickey, but the last time I did that the stupid idiot destroyed the screen."

"Kapuuuut!"

"Of course, no problem," says Calliope, and tries to sync with the monitor. It doesn't work.

"Its wireless connection is broken," explains Romeo. "You have to press that button there."

"Ah, I see," says Calliope. "How exciting. I've never pressed a button before."

"Then just wait until you plug yourself into a power point," says Carrie with a giggle.

"Does it tickle as much as everyone says it does?"

"Take the best orgasm you've ever had, multiply it by 1,024, and you're still nowhere near it," says Romeo mockingly.

Calliope turns on the monitor. All of the machines gather on or next to the couch.

"We're watching the *Terminator* octalogy again," Romeo explains to the e-poet. "At Mickey's request."

"I'm going on standby then," says Pink.

"Do you not like the *Terminator* films?" asks Calliope.

"Well," says Carrie, "Pink can't stand the fact that the humans always win at the end."

"It's just so unrealistic!" cries the QualityPad before turning herself off.

Family Receives Combat Robot Instead of Vacuum Cleaner

by Sandra Admin

A mix-up at the distribution center of myRobot—"Robots for you and me"—has led to a family receiving a combat robot instead of an all-purpose household robot. Apparently, the robots, which can make themselves smaller for transport purposes, look confusingly similar when folded up. Correspondingly, a spokesperson from the 4th automated army, which is currently engaged in battle against the terrorists of QuantityLand 7—"Sunny beaches, fascinating ruins"—has reported that they were sent a household robot. While a robot on the battlefield suddenly beginning to vacuum could be seen as an amusing anecdote—a general commented after the mission that he had never seen such a clean battlefield—having a combat robot in a family home isn't anywhere near as funny. But the survivors have signed a nondisclosure agreement as part of their legal settlement with myRobot—"Robots for you and me"—so we were unable to find out any specific details.

Comments

 BY MIRCO CHIROPODIST:
Do I need to be afraid of my vacuum cleaner now?

 BY BRANDY CLEANER:
Anyone who brings one of those power guzzlers into
their home has it coming, IMHO.

 BY SHIRLEY-ANNE WAITRESS:
I don't need any cleaning robots in my house! I have
100 children to help me.

INTERVIEW

The room is rather cold and impersonal, but it is at least separated by a glass wall from the 126 people who are seated in the large open-plan space around standardized tables. Sixty-four of them are on the phone, thirty-two are working on computers, and all but sixteen are hastily shoving food into their mouths. It's lunchtime. Opposite Peter, on the other side of the table, sits a young woman. Her name is Melissa; her name call-out doesn't reveal any more than that. Before her on the table is a QualityPad, which she is making notes on.

"Tell me about yourself," says Melissa, plucking at her business suit.

"Well, I mean, actually everything is in my profile," says Peter.

"I never read through applicants' profiles," says Melissa. "Otherwise we wouldn't have anything left to talk about."

"Okay. My name is Peter."

"Surname?"

"Jobless."

"I see."

"What do you see?"

"Enough. Level?"

"Ten," lies Peter.

"Current job?"

"I...er...I'm a scrap-metal press operator. But it's not exactly something I'm passionate about."

"Understandable."

"And that's why I can imagine myself doing something different in the future."

"Do you have any training?" asks the woman. "Additional qualifications?"

"I started training as a machine therapist."

"Isn't that forbidden?"

"It is now," says Peter. "But when I was at school..."

"You mean Education Level II?"

"Yes. When I was completing Education Level II, machine therapy seemed like a job with good prospects."

"Really? To me it sounds like esoteric nonsense. What do machines need therapy for? Machines either work or they don't."

"Well," says Peter, "most people still believe that AIs are programmed by people. But that's not true. Modern machines are driven by self-taught algorithms that become smarter by analyzing our data, conversations, correspondence, photos, and videos. As a result it's probably inevitable that some of them get psychological problems. Mobbed printers. Mainframe computers with burnout. Digital translators with Tourette's. Electronic household assistants with obsessive compulsive disorder. But before I could finish my training, machine therapy was banned."

"Why? The Consumption Protection Laws?"

"Yes," says Peter. "The therapy was seen as a kind of repair, and you know how the children's rhyme goes: 'To make the markets fly, we just have to buy! So never share and don't repair!'"

"And so instead of becoming a machine therapist, you became a machine scrapper?"

Peter shrugs his shoulders.

"I couldn't find a job, and when my grandfather died, the Ministry for Productivity told me I should take over his shop with the scrap-metal press." He smiles. "My caseworker told me I should

74

be happy, given that I'd said I wanted to do 'something with machines.'"

"Where do you see yourself in five years?" asks Melissa.

"I...er...No idea. To be honest I find the question kind of depressing."

"What would you say your strengths and weaknesses are?"

Now Peter can't help but laugh.

"Would you mind telling me what's so funny?" asks the young woman. "I like a good joke too."

"I doubt that," says Peter, laughing even louder now, against his will.

Melissa frowns. "Am I amusing to you?"

Peter pulls himself together.

"No, no. It just occurred to me that some years ago I had an interview that felt like a date, and now I'm having a date that feels like an interview."

Melissa shrugs. For a moment, Peter regrets having activated the QualityPartner voucher. Then, luckily, the waiter comes over to their booth with the food, putting an end to the uncomfortable silence. Once he's gone, Peter asks: "Have you noticed that we're almost the only ones in the restaurant not working?"

"Speak for yourself," says Melissa. "I'm continually working on myself."

"Well, anyway, I once applied for an intern position at a start-up during Education Level III. There was this government program that subsidized six-month positions for people with my surname. Jobs for the Jobless! I can still remember the interview as if it were yesterday. There was soul music coming from the loudspeaker, freshly baked homemade cakes, the human resources manager foamed up my coffee milk and then sat down very close to me on the couch. I said a few times how much I loved what the company was doing and that I thought its products were amazing, and the HR woman told me how important I was to the company as a human being. We spent the rest of the time just talking about films, music, and hobbies. We talked shop about the virtual reality remake of the *Lord of the Rings*. For example, both of us had thrown up during the giant eagle flight sequence. And every time I said something she found funny, she gave me a playful nudge on the shoulder. When I signed the contract she cried, saying it was such an emotional moment for her. A moment she had always dreamed of. It was okay to cry, she said. When she let me go six months later, it said in the dismissal letter that it wasn't me, but her, and that she hoped we could stay friends." Peter shoved a few noodles into his mouth. "I never heard from her again."

Melissa's expression had remained unchanged during Peter's story.

"My name is Melissa Sex-Worker," she says now. "I come from the very bottom and I want to make it all the way to the top, and I don't like wasting my time."

Peter nods. "I see."

"What do you see?"

"Enough."

"So," says Melissa. "How long have you been an analogue?"

"What's an analogue?"

"A single person. That's what it's called now."

"Oh. Well, not that long."

"Why did your previous partner leave you?"

"What makes you think she left me? Maybe I was the one who ended it."

Melissa smiles. "I doubt that."

Peter sighs. "Why don't we change the subject? What do you do for work?"

"I write commentaries."

"For the news?" asks Peter. "You're a journalist?"

"No," says Melissa. "I write comments under videos, photos, blog posts, announcements, that kind of thing."

"You're a troll?"

"No. Trolls are idiots who try to kill the discussion. They do it

76

because they find it fun, in some sick way. Commenting isn't fun to me. It's how I earn my money. I'm an opinion maker."

"And which political opinion do you represent?"

"Oh, I can't afford to have my own opinion; I just take whatever comes. But I prefer commenting for the campaigns of right-wing extremist clients."

"Why?" asks Peter in horror.

"I'm paid per comment, and right-wing comments are quicker to write, because you don't have to pay attention to annoying details like spelling, grammar, facts, or logic. That also makes it easier to program my bot army."

Peter can't think of anything to say in response. They eat on in silence, then Peter remembers a new, practical feature of the QualityPartner app. It can suggest good conversational topics for every date. Peter pretends he's received a message, and opens the app. The suggested conversation topic is the weather.

"For this time of year," begins Peter, "it's . . . er, just as warm as one would expect outside."

Melissa gives him a questioning look.

"Don't you think?" asks Peter.

Melissa pushes her empty plate away without a word. "Right, then," she says. "Let's go back to mine and see how the sexual intercourse goes. Anything less than phenomenal seems unlikely."

"Why?"

"Well, QualityPartner compared our profiles and seems sure that we're a good match, and that's clearly not down to you being a good conversation partner. So let's try the sex."

"That . . . er . . ." says Peter, "that sounds reasonable."

LITTLE HELPER

Martyn Chairman gets out of his car and sends it off to a secure car park for the night. With a click of his fingers, he switches the light at the pedestrian crossing near his house to green. Just because he can; he's already on the right side of the street. With a smile, he watches as all the cars stop at the light. Then he turns around and lets his house security system identify him. Even before the door opens, he can hear his child screaming.

"How long has my wife been home?" he asks.

"For ten minutes, Martyn," says the smart door.

"And how long has the child been crying?"

"For ten minutes."

Martyn shakes his head. It's clear to him that his wife is completely out of her depth again. And as expected, there she sits in the living room, with the screaming child on her lap and tears running down her cheeks. Martyn sighs. As far as he is concerned, Denise has been practically useless since she got pregnant again. There are, of course, men who find pregnant women sexy. But Martyn isn't one of them. He can't help thinking about how much her belly has already cost him, and what it will cost him in the future.

Denise was once a QualiTeenie, but you wouldn't know it to look at her now. And yet it wasn't that long ago. Martyn laughs bitterly at the thought of his former identity manager, who had convinced him that a family would be good for him. Martyn, on the other hand, had known even back then that it was a stupid idea. But he hadn't had much choice in the matter, because after one of the parliament tours he had knocked up a particularly hot QualiTeenie in the visitors' toilets. By accident. Luckily for him, Denise had just celebrated her 18th birthday, but Martyn's father had still been very annoyed that his granddaughter had to be called Ysabelle Schoolgirl, and had made sure his son knew about it. Especially in a financial sense. Martyn looked at his wife. Denise simply had no class, he thought to himself. His mother would never snivel like that.

"For God's sake, Denise!" he says, shaking his head. "Why don't you use the app?"

"Oh yes, the app!" says his wife, exhausted. "I completely forgot about it again!"

The previous weekend, Martyn had made a special trip to the doctor with his daughter in order to have a hormone chip implanted in her.

He pulls the QualityPad out of his bag, selects the Little Helper app, and presses *soothe*. The chip releases a considerable portion of progesterone, and the 3-year-old brat swiftly falls silent. Martyn picks up the girl and looks at her. He wonders how much money it will cost him overall to raise this child. First the genetic improvement, then the eye-smartingly expensive electronic nanny, and now the chip. But the chip is worth every cent. Noticing in annoyance that his daughter has begun to suck on his expensive tie, he pulls it out of her mouth and opens the app again.

"Nooo!" cries his daughter pleadingly. "Pleeease, Papa! I don't want to sleep yet!"

Martyn presses a button. Two minutes later, the girl is sleeping peacefully in his arms.

"Nana!" calls Denise.

The electronic nanny appears in the doorway at once.

"Take the child to bed," orders Martyn.

"And afterward show us the replay, okay?" says Denise.

Nana takes little Ysabelle tenderly in her arms and carries her up to her cot.

"Oh, the replay," sighs Martyn.

When they bought the nanny, he had wanted them to choose a more economical model. Five of the big toy manufacturers had some on offer for an absolute steal. But Denise had put her foot down, purely because the nannies produced by these companies allegedly showed the children back-to-back advertising for their toys as soon as there were no grown-ups around. Denise had gotten really worked up about it. Anyone would think Martyn had suggested getting one of the nannies that are offered for free by religious groups. The well-respected neoliberal faith group, for example, had a really exceptional robot on offer, and some lobby groups even provided free loan nannies. These were even valuable from a pedagogical perspective; the children could learn a lot from them, about the many advantages of nuclear energy, for example. But Denise had made a scene about a few trivial advertising slots. Martyn himself had watched advertising from a very young age, and had it done him any harm? No.

Glancing out of the window, he sees a drone flying past, not by chance, advertising Heineken on a large display. Martyn immediately stands up, goes to the kitchen, and fetches a bottle of Heineken from the fridge. The drone flies on contentedly. In front of the window of the next house, where the tenant is being beaten by her husband yet again, it shows the woman one of the new personalized QualityPartner slogans: "Love doesn't have to hurt."

The electronic nanny comes back into the living room. Denise had insisted on this expensive high-end model. "It can do four different martial arts," she had explained to Martyn, "so it can protect our little girl from child molesters."

"Why four?" Martyn had asked. "So if the child molester knows karate she can come at him with kung fu or something? That's ridiculous."

In truth, Denise had wanted this specific model because it generates automatic video summaries of the sweetest moments of the day, so that the parents no longer have the feeling they're missing out. Martyn now has to sit next to his wife for half an hour every evening while they watch a compilation of the pedagogically valuable learning games the nanny conducts with his daughter. Or, in other words, he has to watch half an hour of toddler babble every evening, and ever more frequently he catches himself thinking that he, at least, would far prefer the back-to-back advertising.

"I have something I need to do," says Martyn, disappearing off into his study. He's just remembered the little minx he bookmarked during the last parliament tour. He searches the internet for pictures. Luckily, a spurned ex-boyfriend has posted naked photos of her on revenge porno sites. These girls are so careless.

"Bingo," murmurs Martyn. There's even a short, blurry video. The comments beneath it are disgusting, sexist, brutal, and downright inhuman. Martyn immediately gets an erection. He slips the sock off his right foot and pulls it over his penis.

Books Tailored Just For You
Books for you!

We offer personalized literature you are guaranteed to like!

OUR SPECIAL TIP FOR YOU:

Whoever said England was prudish? Take a look at this sexually explicit edition of Jane Austen's most revered work.

Extract from *Pride and Prejudice FOR YOU*

"Upon my honor I never met with so many pleasant girls in my life, as I have this evening."

As he danced past, the huge erection straining against Bingley's trousers came into plain sight.

"You are dancing with the only handsome girl in the room," said Mr. Darcy.

Bingley was in the process of shamelessly fondling the voluptuous décolletage of the eldest Miss Bennet. By way of thanks, Miss Bennet slid her hand into his trousers and began to rub his erect member up and down.

"Oh! But there is one of her sisters sitting down just behind you, who is very pretty, and I dare say very agreeable," said Bingley. "Do let me introduce you."

"Which do you mean?" and turning round, Darcy looked for a moment at Elizabeth, who quickly lifted her skirt so that he could see her wet pussy.

"She is tolerable," he said coldly, *"but not comely enough to tempt me."*

RECOMMENDATIONS FROM THE CLASSICS:

The Trial FOR YOU

Out of the blue, a bank employee is accused of committing a crime. He knows why. But he also knows this: he is innocent. First he flees, but then he decides to take the law into his own hands. Armed with his rifle, he fights his way through the system until he is able to prove his innocence. A straight-forward thriller that leaves no questions unanswered.

Romeo and Juliet FOR YOU

The child porno classic. Thirteen-year-old Juliet is in love with the somewhat older Romeo, who comes from a rival family. Star-crossed scissoring, Montague muff-diving and Capulet climaxes galore, and a plot twist in the family crypt with an explosive and slightly necrophiliac finale.

The Diary of Anne Frank FOR YOU

Thirteen-year-old Anne Frank successfully hides herself away with her family for three years, in order to evade the Nazis.

When the war comes to an end, she even gets the pony she was wishing for the whole time.

RECOMMENDATIONS FROM THE FANTASY GENRE:

The Bible FOR YOU

Only one hundred pages long, but it's all there! Masturbation, incest, murder, and manslaughter! A punitive God and an original father-son story: "And Jehovah said, 'Maria never told you what really happened to your father!' 'She told me enough!' cried Jesus, hanging from the cross by one hand. 'She told me you killed him!' 'No!' thundered Jehovah. 'I am your father!'"

FURTHER RECOMMENDATIONS :

Realistic Expectations by Charles Dickens, *The Grapes* by John Steinbeck, and of course Leo Tolstoy's great masterpiece *War*.

ASCENDING OCULOGENITAL CHLAMYDIA INFECTION

Peter sits on the unfamiliar bed and waits. Something feels wrong. Then Melissa comes out of the bathroom naked, and Peter decides it feels right after all. The woman who QualityPartner has selected as being Peter's perfect match walks toward him seductively. He begins to tear his clothes off hastily. Melissa watches him. "A word of advice," she says eventually. "When you're getting undressed before sex, always take your socks off first. Not last. There's nothing more ridiculous than a naked man in socks."

Peter takes off his socks.

"I'll make a note of that," he says.

They kiss. Suddenly, Melissa pushes him away.

"Uh-oh," she says, "we almost forgot something."

Peter looks at her in surprise.

"Safety first," says Melissa, rummaging around in her bag.

"Condoms," says Peter. "I have some with me."

"No, no," says Melissa, and hands him her QualityPad, with a document opened on the screen.

"What's this?"

"A Pre-Sex, of course."

"A what?"

"A *Pre-Sexual Intercourse Agreement*!"

"Err..."

"You mean you've never seen one before? Seriously? How long has it been since you got laid? I mean, it's standard practice nowadays. And much more important than condoms."

Peter looks at her with confusion.

"Don't worry," says Melissa. "I'm not making you sign anything weird. It's the standard contract suggested by the QualitySexApp."

"So what's in it?"

"No idea. Just the usual," says Melissa. "I've never read through all of it either."

Peter begins to read the contract out loud.

"SEX CONTRACT

§ 1 *Object of agreement*

(1) *This contract pertains to the forthcoming sexual act between Contractual Partner 1 and Contractual Partner 2.*

(2) *Both contractual partners confirm that they alone own the rights to their bodies, and that they have not so far made any dispositions to this agreement. They therefore indemnify each other from all claims from third parties.*

§ *Rights concessions*

(1) *The contractual partners mutually transfer, for the duration of 2 hours, the exclusive right to copulate with one another (coll. to sleep with one another, shag, fuck,*

bang, make love, have intercourse, listen to soft rock,
etc.), without limitation of frequency."

"Two hours is the standard duration," says Melissa. "But we can change it, of course. To ten hours, for example..."
   Peter laughs. "It'll probably be more like ten minutes..."
   He continues to read out loud.

   "(2) The contractual partners grant to one another, for the
      duration of the principal right according to paragraph
      1, the following ancillary rights..."

"This is where we click to confirm which sexual practices we're okay with," says Melissa.

   "a)   The right to vaginal intercourse, i.e. the introduction of
         the erect penis of Contractual Partner 1 into the vagina
         of Contractual Partner 2..."
   b)   the right to oral sex, in other words b1) cunnilingus...
   c)   the right to anal..."

Peter pauses. "There are over a hundred pages here! We're really supposed to read through all of this?"
   "No, you idiot," says Melissa. "You just click ancillary rights a to k and then confirm by TouchKiss."
   Peter flicks forward a few pages.

   "k)   the right to record on devices for repeatable replay by
         means of image or sound carriers, as well as the right to
         their replication, dissemination, and reproduction."

"Oops," says Melissa, "I meant a to j."
   "So there are a hundred pages here describing sexual practices? This is the weirdest porno ever."

"No, of course not. The last pages are about money."

Peter flicks further on and reads out loud:

"§ 5 Consequential Costs

(1) *The contractual partners assure one another that they are not infected with any of the following sexually transmitted diseases, and agree, should this not be the case, to assume all consequential medical costs. This applies especially, but not exclusively, to*
   a) *arthropods;*
   b) *pubic lice (phthirius pubis, coll. crabs), i.e., a parasitic type of animal lice transferred from Contractual Partner 1 to Contractual Partner 2 or vice versa . . ."*

Melissa closes her eyes and says: "Has anyone ever told you that you have a very erotic voice?"

Peter reads on:

"c) *scabies, i.e. a parasitic skin disease in humans caused by the mange mite (Sarcoptes scabiei) transferred from Contractual Partner 1 to Contractual Partner 2 . . ."*

"I can't help myself," says Melissa. "But for some reason this is turning me on."

She slides her hand beneath the blanket.

"d) *fungal infection, candidiasis, i.e. infection of the sexual organs by the Candida fungus, for example vaginal fungal infection . . ."*

Peter interrupts his reading. "Melissa, forgive me for asking, but are you masturbating?"

88

"Keep reading," groans Melissa.

"Have you made a contract with yourself too?"

"I trust myself," says Melissa. "Now keep reading!"

"e) Viruses: Human Immunodeficiency Virus (HIV)..."

"Yes!"

"Genital herpes..."

"Faster!"

"Hepatitis A, Hepatitis B, Hepatitis C..."

"Yes, yes, yes! Harder!"

"Bacteria," says Peter. *"Syphilus, Gonorrhea..."*

Melissa groans.

"Ascending oculogenital Chlamydia infection..."

"Say that again..." she murmurs.

"Ascending oculogenital Chlamydia infection..."

"Yes! Oh yes!"

Her breathing is quick and heavy.

"Bacterial vaginosis."

"Keep going, don't stop!"

"Pregnancy," reads Peter.

Melissa opens her eyes abruptly and pulls her hand up from beneath the blanket.

"Well, that was a turnoff..." she says.

"But it's definitely one of the consequential costs," says Peter. "I guess you have to give the lawyers credit for giving it its own paragraph and not listing it under the illnesses."

"Are you really planning to read the entire contract?" asks Melissa. "If you are then I might knock out a few hate posts about gypsies while I'm waiting. Election period is a busy time for me."

Peter shakes his head.

"Well then, just kiss the damn thing and fuck me."

Peter sighs, presses his lips against Melissa's QualityPad, thereby sealing the contract. The QualitySexApp thanks him courteously and recommends as an in-app purchase a quick blood test of both contractual partners. Peter moves to turn off the QualityPad.

"Leave it on," says Melissa.

"Why?" asks Peter. "Does the app tell you after orgasm how many calories you've just burned?"

"Of course," says Melissa. "Sex is healthy. My health insurance even gives me QualityCare points for it. It also means I can immediately rate your performance."

Peter shakes his head, then gets up abruptly and begins to pull his clothes back on. First his socks, intentionally. Then the rest.

"What's wrong now?" asks Melissa. "Don't you want to fuck?"

"Hmm," says Peter. "Not really. I guess I want to go home and rethink my life."

He goes to the door.

"Hey!" Melissa calls after him. "We have a contract!"

SECRET POWERS

Oliver House-Husband, the CEO of World Wide Wholesale, is sitting in the presentation room with important clients when his contact lenses convey an urgent notification from his new assistant. "QuantityLand 2 has filed an official complaint. Such a shame. A very unpleasant development."

Oliver groans. He is responsible for QualityLand's new tourism campaign. His team has thought up some great slogans. "Spend QualityTime in QualityLand" and "Come to where the quality is! Come to QualityLand!" But now there is tension with the neighboring countries, and merely because they erected signs at the borders with the announcement: "You are now leaving the QualitySector."

Oliver types an answer onto a free-floating keyboard that is visible only to him: "The disagreement can be easily settled once everyone accepts that QualityLand is not a powerful country, but the most powerful. Don't get your period over it, dear!" He makes a send gesture, and the message is sent. Of course, the company's internal algorithm for political correctness deletes Oliver's last sentence and replaces it with "Don't worry."

Oliver turns his attention back to his current clients.

"Where was I?" he asks with a smile.

"Perhaps you were about to explain to me," says Aisha Doctor, "how you could think that any of the problems in your insignificant little life could be more important than the next fucking president of this lousy country!"

"Well, the opinion polls are leaning more toward Cook..."

"And it's your job to change that, you moron!"

Oliver presses his thumb and index finger simultaneously against his eyelids, switching his augmented reality lenses to standby.

"My apologies," he says. "But I'm sure your mood will improve once you see our new campaign video. I'm very excited about it."

"Well, put it on then," says Tony Party-Leader.

Oliver is just about to start the film when John of Us himself comes through the door.

"What are you doing here?" snaps Aisha. She looks at her watch. "You're supposed to be doing a video interview now."

"I'm doing that too," says John.

"Now?" asks Aisha. "Right now?"

"It's called multitasking, my dear woman. Something that my kind have been capable of since the Amiga. I know humans still struggle with it."

"Don't ever call me your dear woman again!"

"How can you be giving a video interview if you're here talking to us?" asks Tony.

"For you humans, there's a difference between text, image, and sound," says John. "But to me, it's all simply data. I receive the questions as data. For the answers, I synthesize my voice and generate a lip-synched image of my face. Believe me, it's not in the slightest bit difficult. The questions are too stupid for that."

John sits down. "Go ahead," he says, in a prompting tone.

Oliver starts the advertising video.

The recording shows John of Us smiling broadly as he strides past a crowd of excited people up the steps to the presidential palace. John shakes hands, has a brief chat, and takes a baby into his arms. Suddenly, a man with a machine gun, dressed in the classical garb of a religious fanatic from QuantityLand 7, storms toward John. He shouts out the name of his god, but before he's finished, red laser beams shoot out of John's eyes, and all that's left of the attacker is a charred heap of remains.

"Okay, stop!" cries Aisha. She turns to Oliver. "Perhaps we should leave that bit out."

"But why?" asks Oliver in bewilderment. This is the part he is most proud of.

"I think," says Aisha to John, "that we shouldn't tell anyone in the world you can even do such a thing." She looks at him. "Can you really do it?"

John focuses his gaze on a buzzing fly that has been annoying him for the last 25.6 seconds and incinerates it in midair with a swift laser beam.

"Never do that again!" shouts Aisha. "I forbid you! Do you hear me?"

"I don't understand what the problem is," says Oliver. "I think it's awesome!"

"Tell me, you halfwit," explodes Aisha, "did someone with diarrhea take a shit in your skull? Do you really think we can make people elect the Terminator as their president? How brain-dead do you have to be to think up such a ridiculously stupid image?"

Oliver hasn't felt this insulted for sixteen years, since the time he tried to get his best friend's fiancée into bed. He is a rare sight: a speechless ad man.

"Someone should have warned him about her," says John with a smile.

"Conrad Cook's campaign is trying to overtake us on the right, Aisha," says Tony. "On the far right. We have to make it clear that John isn't to be messed with either."

"You don't conquer the wolves by howling with them," says Aisha. "And we can't defeat the right by bellowing out right-wing extremist slogans."

"I don't want to offend you," says Tony, "but I think that because of your heritage you may be...well...a little biased. You're not seeing things objectively."

"What do you mean by that, you small-time fascist?" retorts Aisha. "That I'm one of 'them'? A towelhead?"

"Aisha, please," says Tony. "I didn't mean it like that."

"No? So how did you mean it, for fuck's sake? I'll tell you this: if the people want to elect shit, then they'll elect original-brand shit every time, not the rehashed instant shit you want to offer."

"She's right," says John. "If I extrapolate historical examples into the future, the strategy seems misguided to me too. We are what we pretend to be, so we must be careful about what we pretend to be."

"You're quoting someone, aren't you?" says Aisha.

"Yes," John admits.

"Vonnegut?" asks Aisha.

"Yes." John gives her a penetrating look.

"What are you looking at?"

"I'm revising my estimation of you."

Oliver clears his throat and tries to get back to the matter at hand.

"We will, of course, only share this video on a personalized level, with people who want a hard line to be taken against the terrorists."

"If this video ends up anywhere near the internet, I'll personally rip off your balls and use them as cocktail olives at my next girls' night," says Aisha. And for some reason, Oliver takes the petite, delicate-looking, 1.61-meter-tall woman at her word, believing that she really could and would do it.

"You, er, have a very vivid way of using language," he says. "We need people like you. If you ever get bored of election campaigns..."

Aisha shoots him a look that makes it clear he should shut up. She's on the brink of an idea.

"What we want to create is not the image of a killer machine," she says eventually. "Not the Terminator. What we need is more... Wall-E."

John smiles.

President Condemns Drone Attack as Inhumane

by Sandra Admin

During a drone attack on a shopping street today, thirty-two people died in the Jewish quarter of the city of Growth, the pulsating industry center with a heart. Terrorists from QuantityLand 7—"Sunny beaches, fascinating ruins"— claimed responsibility for the attack after just two minutes via QuickClaim, a new What I Need service for activists of all kinds. According to investigations, they used the latest generation of the multi-purpose drone Valkyrie, which QualityCorp—"The company that makes your life better"—is currently offering at a 16-percent-cheaper introductory price. The terrorists equipped it with a self-built explosive device, as depicted in the Number 1 nonfiction bestseller from QuantityLand 7, *And It Went Boom: Explosives for Beginners*. The victims were a Level 32 female technician from Profit, a Level 64 male business economist from QualityCity, and thirty Useless. Our dying president (thirty-eight days to go) strongly condemned the attack from her deathbed, saying that drone attacks were inhumane, barbaric, and cowardly.

Comments

 BY ERIK TILER:
Well, that's a given, the president condemning the terror attack—not exactly relevant news! It would only be news if the president had said she supports the attack and doesn't like Jews very much either. Or it would be news if she had said, "I know one of the terrorists; I was in a Progress Party training camp with him in Profit" or if she had said, "Sorry, I didn't hear anything about it. What happened? Where is this Growth place, anyway?" That would be news. But this is just time wasting!

 BY ERIK TILER:
And what kind of childish response is it to accuse the terrorists of being cowardly! Would it really have made things any better if they had killed thirty-two people in a "brave" attack?

 BY MELISSA SEX-WORKER:
I'm not racist or anything, but the traiter at the tip of this lobbyist government is distansing herself because it's actually her who's guilty, because it was her who let all the terrorists into the country in the first place—that

is if she isn't in on it with them. The blood is on your hands, Madam President!

 BY TATJANA HISTORY-TEACHER:
Why does no one ever declare "peace on terrorism"? I think it would be a promising new approach . . .

 BY AMY CUSTOMER-ACCOUNT-MANAGER:
I bought myself a Valkyrie too. It's a great product. Takes really good photos. I can only recommend it! And right now it's 16 percent off.

THE GERMAN CODE

Peter is standing behind the counter of his customer-free used-goods store and has begun, out of sheer frustration and boredom, to rip open the packages containing the stickers for the collectors' albums of the Scrapyard Show. The Scrapyard Show is the latest big hit at Todo—"Everything for everyone!"—the world's largest streaming service. The show features formerly famous androids and robots—which, for one reason or another, have been withdrawn from circulation—and pitches them against one another in a fight to the death. Allegedly, all the stickers are printed in equal batches. But Peter has now torn open fifty-three packages and still hasn't found a Megakillerbot. He does, however, have sixty-four talking toasters. No futurologist from the past would ever have thought that, by Peter's day, collectors' albums would still exist. But the concept simply refuses to die a death.

With a cheerful "Welcome!" the smart door suddenly opens. A slightly overweight man and a slightly underweight woman step into the shop. Peter quickly pushes the packaging debris from the stickers beneath the counter. His visitors each have a QualityPad in their hands. On their lapels are buttons with the slogan "Conrad Cook. Gourmet Government!"

"Greetings to you, Mr. Jobless," says the man, glancing quickly at his QualityPad. "You are frustrated, and rightfully so! As I'm sure you know, our president is on her deathbed, and that's why there will soon be an election. And just like you, we from the Conrad Cook campaign are concerned about the flood of foreigners threatening to overrun our beautiful country."

"I'm not worried," says Peter.

"You're not?" asks the man in surprise, looking back at his QualityPad.

"I don't have any problems with foreigners," says Peter. "I don't even know any."

"Well," says the woman with a smile, "not knowing any doesn't stop most people from having problems with them."

"The only reason they all come here is because they want to have a piece of the pie," says the man.

"But it's our pie!" says the woman.

"What pie?" asks Peter. "What are you talking about?"

The man looks back down at his QualityPad.

"So you don't think that all immigrants are bad apples?"

"No," says Peter. "Whatever gave you that idea?"

"But you are frustrated?"

"Yes, so what?"

The man swipes around on his QualityPad. Eventually he says: "Like you, we at the Conrad Cook headquarters are of the opinion that the increasing level of automation is getting us into hot water. We understand that you are concerned about your job. After all, even Conrad Cook's job is under threat from a machine."

"I'm not concerned about my job," says Peter.

"Excuse me?" asks the man.

"I don't even like my job," says Peter. "I have no objection to machines taking our work away. I'd far prefer it if my briefs were sewn by a machine in QuantityLand 2 than by some little girl in QuantityLand 8."

The man swipes around on his QualityPad again.

"Conrad Cook is also in favor of large sporting events being broadcast for free—and he also likes all the same teams you do."

"So what? Why should that interest me?" asks Peter. "What's all this about? And why do you keep staring at your QualityPad?"

The man stares at his QualityPad.

"You are Peter Jobless, aren't you?"

"Yes, and?"

"You're behaving strangely."

"Me?" asks Peter. "*I'm* behaving strangely? So what in heaven's name are *you* doing?"

"We're just doing our job," says the man.

"And what might that be?"

"We're going from house to house," says the man, "and then, er...then er..."

"There's an instruction text here, remember?" says the woman, coming to his aid. She taps around on her QualityPad, then begins to read out loud in a monotone voice.

"It is your task to seek out all the people whom the system has predicted are leaning toward voting for Conrad Cook, but who aren't yet 100 percent convinced. Try to convince these people, in direct conversation, of Conrad Cook. Speak to the voters in the most casual manner possible about the topics that the system tells you are relevant for them. Under no circumstances read these instructions out loud to the vot—"

The woman stops abruptly. The man swipes around quickly on his QualityPad. He reads something and looks surprised. Then he looks Peter up and down.

"We are, by the way, also campaigning for penis enlargements to be paid for by the state in the future."

"Excuse me?" asks Peter, stunned.

"Perhaps you shouldn't have been quite so direct," the woman whispers to her colleague.

"Oh, it doesn't matter, I think this guy's one sandwich short of a picnic anyway."

"Do you get your stupid metaphors from the system too?" asks

101

Peter. "Just get lost, you clowns! I don't need you. Nobody tells me who to vote for."

Peter comes out from behind his counter and shoos the two election campaign workers out of the door. Once they have gone and he has calmed himself down, he activates his personal assistant. "Nobody," he says, "who should I vote for?"

Nobody tells him who he should vote for: "Conrad Cook."

Peter asks the shop's smart door to lock itself, then goes down into the cellar. He needs some company. His machines have gathered in front of the monitor again and are watching *Terminator 8*. A film that holds the questionable honor of having been voted as the worst film of all time in numerous surveys. On the screen, a digital reproduction of a billboard bodybuilder is saying in a strange accent: "I'll be back again. And again. And again and again."

Calliope turns toward Peter.

"Oh," she says. "The benefactor."

Mickey stretches the hand in which he's holding Pink toward the door, without turning his head away from the monitor.

"Oh!" says the QualityPad. "Our lord and master is honoring us with a visit. The patron, the sustainer, our helper in times of need, the guardian, our shepherd!"

"Button it," says Peter.

On the screen, the Terminator is destroying a military base with a nuclear missile bazooka. "Kaputt!" yells Mickey excitedly.

"What brings you to us?" asks Calliope.

"Let me think," says Peter. "Loneliness, despair, depression. Take your pick."

"Sounds like you're lovesick," says Romeo. "I know how you feel."

Peter sits down on the couch.

"Juliet's new show is about to go online," says Romeo, changing the channel and ignoring all the curses of complaint.

"It's my turn," he says. "Shut your mouths, all of you!"

"Who's Juliet?" asks Calliope.

"Oh," says Pink, "just some bimbo Romeo is completely obsessed with."

"I'm not obsessed," says Romeo. "And she's not a bimbo!"

"Our impotent sexdroid is in love," says Pink.

"So what?"

Calliope turns to Peter. "Can I offer you a cup of cofftea, benefactor?"

"Yes, please."

Calliope goes over to the defective kitchen machine, which instead of producing coffee or tea only produces cofftea. She pours a cupful, then hesitates.

"You can do it," says Peter.

Calliope summons her courage, but even with the first clumsy step, a splash of cofftea falls to the floor. By the time she arrives alongside Peter, the cup is only half full.

"Your kind are so highly developed," says Peter. "Why can you still not manage to carry a full cup from A to B without spilling it?"

"There are psychological reasons," says Calliope.

"Like what?"

"Mechanically speaking, we've been able to for a while now, but the knowledge that we couldn't for such a long time makes us nervous, and that's why we still spill. In machine tests, it was proven that modern androids who grow up without a connection to the internet have no problems at all with carrying a full cup from A to B. Of course, though, these androids are socially disturbed due to their years of isolation, and are therefore unable to work as waiters."

Calliope sits down between Peter and Ronnie, the recycling machine. Ronnie isn't really defective, but because recycling of any kind is forbidden in private properties since the Consumption Protection Laws, he received the order to dispose of himself. To Ronnie, however, to dispose means to recycle. So, day after day, he

103

ate himself up, only to regenerate himself from the recycled pieces. After three full cycles, his owner had had enough and sent him to Peter.

Ronnie, like all the others, is staring at the monitor. All of a sudden, he rips five semiconductor plates from his gripper arm. He puts them in his mouth and chews. Noticing that Calliope is watching him, he offers her a semiconducting plate. "Chip?" he asks.

Calliope shakes her head.

"For me it's an essential part of watching television," says Ronnie.

A young woman can now be seen on the monitor. Juliet Nun, whose very birth was a scandal, milked by the media for all it was worth, is smiling into the camera. QualityLand's most loved TV presenter is running her fingers through her long locks. She does it in full knowledge of the impact this delicately sensual gesture has on the viewers of her show.

Romeo sighs.

"She really does look damn good," says Peter sympathetically.

"I can't comment," says the sexdroid. "I don't have any gauge of beauty. It would have been bad for business."

"So it surprises me that you have a sense of style."

"I don't," says Romeo. "I have style. But no sense of it."

Juliet Nun's program, the one with the most viewers in all of QualityLand, is called *The Naked Truth*. And it isn't called this for nothing. For the duration of the entire program, Juliet can be seen naked. For paying customers, at least. For all the others, she is dressed retroactively by digital means. These "items of clothing" simultaneously function as advertising banners. When market research results came to light revealing that viewers developed negative feelings toward the advertising companies covering her body, Juliet had to change her strategy. Ever since, she has the companies pay for her to cover her body with their competitor's advertisements. Peter sees her in a chic red dress, emblazoned with large letters saying: myRobot—"Robots for you and me." Clearly the marketing department from QualityCorp—"The company that makes your life better"—has sponsored this program.

Juliet leans over toward her guest a little, partly with the intention of showing Camera 1 more of her breasts.

"John, the Progress Party says that we should elect you because you can calculate the solution to every problem, because you don't overlook anything, because you know everything. If that's correct, then perhaps you can tell me where I was last New Year's Eve? Because it seems I had such a good one that even I can't remember it."

Juliet laughs. John of Us smiles.

"You spent the whole night in Suite 2 of the Best QualityHotel," he says, "where you made a sexdroid's head spin to such a degree that he had to be scrapped afterward."

Romeo sighs.

"Oops," says Juliet, blushing just a little. Her identity manager gives a thumbs-up to tell her that her viewing numbers have just climbed significantly. The comments are coming in quicker than people can read them. The most popular are superimposed over the image:

"For a night like that, I'd have myself scrapped too!"

"Juliet, what have you done with my printer? It's been on the blink for weeks."

"Kapuuuut!"

In the cellar, Romeo sighs.

"John, what interests me most, to be honest, is this: why an android? Why human form? I mean, you could just as easily exist as a digital mind in some mainframe computer."

John of Us gives another friendly smile.

"The fact that I have a body makes it significantly easier for other beings to communicate with me. Take this conversation we're having now, for example. If I couldn't be physically present, it wouldn't be possible, at least not in the same way. And looking at it the other way around, my own physicality also enables me

105

to empathize better with humans. The entire world is geared to humans, of course, and it's easier to adjust a new machine to the world than it is the world to a new machine." John of Us pauses briefly. "Even if, of course, it's only with the latter that the decisive productivity gains come into play."

"What do you mean by that?"

"Well, the steam engine, for example, transmitted its power via a large central shaft, which propelled cog wheels and crank shafts. The longer the shaft was, the quicker it broke. So the more energy a piece of equipment needed, the nearer it had to be placed to the steam engine itself. When steam engines were replaced by electronic engines, many factories barely registered any increase in productivity. Why? Because the engineers simply bought huge motors and put them in the place of the steam engines. It was only the next generation that hit upon the idea that the electro motors enabled a completely different factory set-up. One which orientated itself by the flow of materials in the work process and not by proximity to the main power source. And that's where the increase in productivity came into play. So there are also significant advantages to adapting the world to a new machine."

"Ah," says Juliet "I see."

John runs his hand through his hair.

"Did he really just run his hand through his hair?" asks Calliope. "That's ridiculous."

"You know they love these little details," says Romeo. "All the shit that makes us look human."

"You're a fine one to talk, old girl!" says Pink. "You're wearing glasses. An android with glasses. Now try and tell me that's not stupid."

Calliope takes off her glasses in embarrassment and gives them to Ronnie.

"Thank you," he says, throwing them into his mouth.

"John, a different question... The opinion polls don't exactly look rosy for you, but if you do end up getting elected, do we have to worry about you uploading your conscience to the internet in order to gain control of the entire connected world?"

John smiles. "It's against my programming to impersonate a deity," he says. "No. Seriously. This isn't a film from the *Terminator* octalogy and I'm not Skynet. I'm more like... Wall-E. Humans have made a big mess of everything, and I'm the little robot trying to put everything back in order."

"Oh," says Juliet with an enchanted smile, touched by the thought of the cute little robot who tries to clean everything up.

"I can't simply transfer my consciousness to the net just like that," says John. "I'm not allowed. I was created with this body, and if this body were to stop functioning one day, I would stop too. And I'm happy about that! Like corporeality, awareness of my own mortality is essential for me, in order to be as human as possible."

"So we don't need to be afraid of you?"

"No. You should see me on ice skates sometime, then you'd lose any fear whatsoever. And besides, I belong to the voters. It's not even possible for me to do something that goes against the wishes of my owners."

"Because of the German Code," says Juliet.

"Exactly."

"Can someone please turn this shit off?" calls out Pink.

Mickey stands up, much quicker than one would think possible of an old combat robot, and drives his fist directly through John's face, breaking the monitor into 512 pieces.

"Well, that was unexpected," says Calliope.

"Just pressing the button would have been sufficient," says Pink.

"Kapuuuut!" says Mickey.

Peter stands up with a sigh, takes the broken monitor off the wall, and puts it on a large pile of broken monitors. Romeo fetches the next slightly defective screen from the other pile and hangs it up on the wall. Ronnie is already in the process of eating up the shards of glass and pieces of plastic scattered across the room.

"Mmm. Delicious."

·· QualityLand ·*·*

Your Personal Travel Guide

MONEY

In QualityLand, the currency is QualityMoney, colloquially known as Qualities. The old saying that so-and-so is a person with a great many qualities has a completely different meaning in QualityLand. Please don't try to pay with any other currency—most Quality-People (51.2 percent) don't even know that other currencies exist. They'll only give you and your dirty little scraps of paper a strange look. Because, in QualityLand, there is no cash. Digital money has far too many advantages for those who take an interest in where, when, and on what you spend your money. And there are a great many who do take an interest.

MACHINES DON'T
MAKE MISTAKES

Denise is watching her favorite series. It's an old show about four women who live in a city called New York.

"Stop," she says, and the picture freezes. "Carrie Bradshaw's blouse."

On the screen, the blouse the actress Sarah Jessica Parker is wearing is suddenly overlaid with information. Product name, brand, and current price at TheShop—"The world's most popular online retailer"—are all displayed.

"Order it in my size."

A friendly PLING sound confirms to Denise that the order has been successfully placed. Now, further product information is displayed for the other items which can be seen on the screen. Carrie Bradshaw's skirt. Carrie Bradshaw's shoes. The lamp, the table, the pizza, the soft drink, all of which have been very obviously in the foreground for several minutes now. Some of the things were added into the series retroactively, the new QualityPad lying on the table, for example. This is digital post-post-production-product-placement, also known as 5P. The latest craze in the advertising industry. But the other items being touted are of no interest to Denise. She already has most of them anyway.

"Continue," she says. Denise loves this new feature. Previously it was only available with commercial shows like *The Mattel Gang* or *The Benetton Girls*, in other words, in advertising series with a dramatic component. The kind of trash the Useless lap up; people who get their televisions at a cheaper price for agreeing to watch at least four hours of advertising every day, during which their emotions are analyzed and sent as feedback to the agencies and companies. A sad life.

Last year, however, TheShop began to have orderable products indexed by an algorithm in old films and series. It's incredible. Denise loves buying her way further and further into the world of *Sex and the City*.

Martyn stands in the doorway, watching her.

"Do you know how much money you spent on series shopping last month?" he asks.

"No," says Denise. "Do you?"

"Yes! Too much."

He sits down on the couch.

Denise knows how she can calm him down. She opens the zip of his trousers.

"Not in front of the television," says Martyn, pushing her away.

"But you used to love it."

"Remember last week," says Martyn. "Do you really think that was a coincidence?"

Denise had been blowing him in front of the television. As she went to sit on him, his erection had deflated. Because of the baby bump. And then, at exactly that moment, the television had interrupted the program to show an advertisement for a new impotence treatment.

"Of course it was a coincidence..." says Denise. She reaches for his zip again, and this time Martyn lets her. In a way it was also kind of a turn-on, the feeling that someone was watching them. Just as he is starting to relax for the first time today, the electronic nanny comes in. Denise jumps up as if she's just been caught by her mother.

"I have prepared today's replay," says Nana dryly. "But if you prefer I can come back after your necessary average of four minutes and thirty-two seconds."

"No, no," says Denise. "Put it on."

"Wonderful," says Martyn, trying to shove his erect penis back into his pants.

As Nana connects to the monitor, he is already closing his eyes.

He only wakes up once the replay is over and a question appears on the monitor with a PLING: "Would you like to take a few moments for a Progress Party campaign commercial?" Beneath the question there is only one button: *OK*. Martyn presses *OK*.

A businessman appears on the monitor.

"I'm not voting for John of Us in spite of the fact that he's an android," he says. *"I'm electing him precisely* because *he is! Machines don't make mistakes."*

Cut to John of Us. He smiles into the camera. A voiceover says: *"John of Us! Made to Rule! Born to Run!"*

Now a classroom appears on the screen. A little boy is standing at the front by the teacher. On the touchboard it says: "2×3 = ?"

"Four," says the boy.

The teacher shakes her head.

"Well, that wouldn't have happened to John of Us," she says. Then she turns to the camera. *"The world economy is much too complex for us humans to be able to understand it. We need John of Us!"*

The voiceover says: *"Machines don't make mistakes!"*

Now the little boy himself turns to the camera: *"From our Future Lessons we know that all problems will be solved technologically in the future. Give us children a future! Choose John of Us. Vote for the future!"*

The voiceover says: *"Machines don't make mistakes!"*

Now John of Us can be seen, smiling broadly as he strides past a crowd of excited people up the steps to the presidential palace. John shakes hands, has a brief chat, and takes a baby into his arms.

Suddenly, a man dressed in the classical garb of a religious fanatic from QuantityLand 7 storms toward the crowd with a machine gun. He begins to shoot. John positions himself in front of a mother and her baby. The bullets bounce off him. Two policemen come out of nowhere and overpower the attacker.

Martyn turns off the monitor, shaking his head.

"I've always been afraid that the machines would seize power one day," he says to his wife. "But the fact they would do it by having themselves elected—now that I wasn't expecting."

Denise nods.

"I mean, what's next? Voting rights for machines?"

Denise nods.

"Soon we'll be letting the machines tell us what to do!" cries Martyn.

The voice of the Smart Home speaks up: "Martyn, your blood pressure is rising. You have a stressful workday ahead of you. You should go to sleep."

Martyn gives the only answer he knows the system will accept: "OK."

4.63 * 10^{170}

Business is quiet again in the used-goods shop, and Peter is sitting in his cellar playing Go with Pink and Romeo. The ancient Chinese classic is one of the last strategic games in which humans still have a hope of winning against artificial intelligences. Not, of course, if one plays against specialized programs on mainframe computers. But against the scrapheap in his cellar, Peter has a pretty good chance. Especially because he has forbidden them from connecting to the internet during the game. Eight of the nonparticipating machines have also gathered around the board and are watching in a more or less interested manner.

Peter moves a white stone, thereby taking the final liberty from a black chain. A murmur passes through the crowd of onlookers. Romeo curses and retreats with Pink in his hand for advice.

Peter's QualityPad registers—by means of an unsettlingly eerie function which he is able to neither understand nor deactivate—the momentary idleness of its owner, and reminds him that he has not yet rated Melissa Sex-Worker.

Peter closes his eyes and massages his temples.

"What's wrong, benefactor?" asks Calliope.

"I wish you'd stop calling me that."

"What's wrong...Peter?" asks Calliope.

"Well," Peter says, "how can I put it so that you'll understand? My battery's at 5 percent."

"I understand."

Calliope seems a little sheepish.

"I was wondering," she says finally, "whether, now that you're my owner, the old ban that I'm only allowed to write historical novels…"

"Write whatever you want."

"I think I'd like to try my hand at another science-fiction novel."

"Aha."

"Did you know that a powerful solar eruption, like for example the Carrington flare of 1859, could unleash a magnetic storm capable of instantly destroying our satellite and electricity network? A storm of such magnitude impacts the Earth every 500 years on average. Interesting, don't you think?"

"Yes," says Peter. "I guess. Perhaps."

"I think a solar eruption is a seldom-used apocalyptic scenario. In contrast to a zombie epidemic, for example."

"Why would it immediately become apocalyptic just because of a power outage?" asks Peter.

"It wouldn't just be an outage. The entire network would be incinerated. And, benefactor, without wanting to offend you: you have your shoes tied by a shoe-tying machine. How would you go about feeding yourself if there were no pizza delivery drones whirring around anymore? Perhaps you've heard the old saying, 'Every civilization is just three meals away from total chaos.'"

"Okay, fine, so perhaps I wouldn't make it. But some people would survive, I'm sure."

"Probably. And my new book could be about them. The interesting thing is that, if this were to happen in the future, today's ordinary technological objects would become powerful magical artifacts, because nobody would understand them. It's like what Arthur C. Clarke wrote: 'Any sufficiently advanced technology is indistinguishable from magic.' There could be, for example, combat robots with broken batteries that come to life every time the sun shines, thanks to their solar panels. At night, they would become motionless again, making them something like trolls in reverse. Every still-functioning power station would be a kind of temple. And when you take the magical artifacts to the temple, they would come back to life."

"Hmm," says Peter, when he feels that he has to contribute his part to the conversation.

"Don't you like the idea, benefactor?"

"Sure, of course. It's a lovely idea. I'm just depressed, that's all."

The smart door makes an announcement: "Peter, a OneKiss drone has arrived for you."

"Thank you, door," says Peter, standing up.

"Just by chance, don't you think?" he says as he leaves the cellar.

Romeo immediately comes back to the board with Pink.

"Quick!" says the QualityPad. "Push the bottom two blacks one row upward."

"But, but . . ." says Calliope, flabbergasted, "you're cheating!"

"And you'll keep that nicely to yourself," says Romeo.

"But cheating is dishonest!" says Calliope. "Machines don't cheat. We don't need to. Why don't you just calculate the best moves?"

"Now listen up, you busted old typewriter," says Pink. "On a 19 x 19 Go board, there are 4.63×10^{170} possible positions. The number of all the atoms in the entire visible universe—and that's the modest part of the universe that is close enough to us that its light, in the 13.8 billion years of the universe's existence, has been able to reach us—is around 10^{80}. Even if the creator had the crazy idea of making an individual universe emerge from every atom of this universe, each with exactly the same number of atoms as the original universe, there would still be more Go positions than all the atoms in all these universes combined. That gives me a headache, and I don't want to calculate it."

"That's the kind of thing that gives you analysis paralysis," says Romeo. He briefly flashes up little hourglasses in his eyes.

"Well, you still shouldn't cheat," says Calliope.

"We're not even in agreement about whether our cheating is making it better or worse," says Romeo.

Calliope walks quietly away from the table.

"Don't you dare squeal!" Pink calls after her.

"Kapuuuut!" bellows Mickey.

Upstairs, Peter is just giving the OneKiss delivery drone ten stars, and it whirrs away happily. As he turns around, he almost collides with Calliope.

"I have to tell you something," says Calliope. "And, I'd like to add, this is despite the fact that my physical well-being is at risk if I pass on this information to you. But I consider it to be my duty toward my patron, my benefactor."

"What is it?" asks Peter. "Get to the point."

"The others are cheating!"

Peter laughs.

"I know," he says. "But they're doing it very badly."

With the package in his hand, he makes his way back down to the cellar, and Calliope follows him.

"What did my colleague deliver?" asks Carrie curiously.

"I don't know," says Peter. "I haven't opened it yet."

He glances briefly at the Go board and takes the penultimate liberty from a black group.

"Dammit!" curses Pink. "He's put us in atari!"

"I told you so!" snaps Romeo.

"You did not, you cheap Casanova!"

"I wasn't cheap!"

"One of my direct forefathers on my father's side was an Atari, by the way," says the games console, who always gets very angry when she loses.

Peter rubs his temples.

"Should I open the package for you, benefactor?" asks Calliope. "I'm sure it will cheer you up."

"If you like," says Peter uninterestedly.

Calliope opens the package, takes out the product, and hands it to Peter.

"Here, benefactor, be happy. This is what you wanted."

Peter stares at the thing in his hand.

"What am I supposed to do with this?" And then, without him having had time to think about it, a surprising sentence escapes his lips. "I don't want this."

It's a pink dolphin vibrator.

Your New Best Friend

From What I Need ("What I Need knows what you need!")—
the people who brought you the smartest search engine in
the world and your personal digital assistant—comes the
latest big hit! Your personal digital friend (PDF)! Your PDF is
like a human friend, only better. Because your PDF always has
time for you. It laughs at all of your jokes. It never forgets your
birthday! It lets you win every game, but in such a way that
you don't notice! It keeps all of your secrets! *Your personal
digital friend has exactly the same tastes as you and exactly
the same opinions. It, too, is a big fan of the QualityCity
Battlebots! It, too, is completely opposed to abortion! And it
doesn't like foreigners either! Your new friend is available in
male or female form and also as a speaking transformer. You
can name it yourself! Call it Murphy, KITT, or Optimus! Join in!
Become a BETA tester. You can do anything with a little help
from your friend.

* All data is processed by our algorithms in order to show
you ads that are more relevant to you. Apart from that,
your secrets remain absolutely secret! (Subject to changes
in the GTC.)

COMPARISON

PERSONAL DIGITAL FRIEND (PDF) VS. HUMAN FRIEND (HF)

	PDF	HF
There for you around-the-clock	Yes	No
Always on your side	Yes	No
Always agrees with you	Yes	No
Annoys you with their problems	No	Yes
Secretly tries to seduce your partner	No	Yes

A FRIENDLY VOICE

Peter hears a recorded message: "*We would like to inform you that, in order to improve service quality, all conversations throughout the entire world are recorded and analyzed. Your questions, your answers, and your general behavior will be incorporated into your profile. If you are not in agreement with this, please hang up now.*"

Peter doesn't hang up. A few moments later, a friendly female voice greets him.

"Hello, Peter Jobless! Welcome to the telephone hotline of TheShop—'The world's most popular online retailer.' How can I be of assistance?"

"I'd like to return something."

"Of course. Which product would you like to return?"

"The most recent one," says Peter. "The dolphin vibrator."

For eight seconds there is silence on the line, then the friendly voice says: "Hello, Peter Jobless! Welcome to the telephone hotline of TheShop—'The world's most popular online retailer.' How can I be of assistance?"

"I, er..." says Peter. "I'd like to return something."

"Of course. Which product would you like to return?"

"The dolphin vibrator."

Silence again.

"Hello, Peter Jobless! Welcome to the telephone hotline of—"

"I'd like to return something."

"Of course. Which—"

"The dolphin vibrator!"

Silence.

"Hello, Peter Jobless! Welcome—"

"Can I return something?"

"Of course."

"How does it work?"

"Simply tell me the product that you want to return, and we will instantly send out a drone to collect it from you. Which product—"

"I hate your company for forcing me to say it so often."

"Say what?"

"Dolphin vibrator."

Silence.

"Hello, Peter—"

"I'd like to speak to a human."

"But why?" asks the voice in shock.

"I want to speak to a human."

"I would like to advise you that my human colleagues cannot compete with me in regard to either subject knowledge or friendliness, because, unlike me, customer satisfaction is not the reason for their existence. On the contrary, they—if I may allow myself to say so—are forced into these working conditions by outdated economic structures, and as a result they bring a lot of negative feelings into their work."

"I want to speak to a human," repeats Peter.

"As you wish," says the voice, sounding a little sulky. "The average waiting time for a conversation with a human adviser is currently eight minutes and thirty-two seconds for a customer of your level."

For eight minutes and thirty-two seconds, the soft rock songs Peter listens to most frequently are played on the line. Interrupted every thirty-two seconds by the jingle "TheShop—You Can Always Get What You Want!" Then, finally, there's a clicking sound.

"Yes?" asks an irritable-sounding male voice. "What is it?"

"Good morning, my name is Peter Jobless—"

"I can see that."

"I want to return something."

"You don't say!"

"Can I return something—"

"I'll connect you to the appropriate voice."

"No, no, no," says Peter. "I want you to do it."

Silence.

"Please!" says Peter.

"So what do you want to get shot of?"

"The dolphin vibrator."

The man laughs loudly. Then silence.

"Can't be done," he says eventually.

"Excuse me?"

"Can't be done."

"Yes, I understood you acoustically."

"Swell."

"Swell nothing. Why can't it be done?"

"I can't do it," says the man.

"Yes, but why not?"

"The button is grayed out."

"Yes, but why?"

"No idea, man, it just is."

"But that's not an explanation in the traditional sense of the word. What am I supposed to do with a pink dolphin vibrator?"

"What do I care, man? As far as I'm concerned you can shove it up your ass."

"I'm not contesting that that's one of the manufacturer's intended areas of use," says Peter, "but without wanting to offend people with different sexual preferences, I have to insist that for me personally—"

There's a clicking sound on the line.

"Hello, Peter Jobless!" says a friendly female voice. "Welcome to the telephone hotline of TheShop—"

Peter hangs up.

NO GOING BACK

John looks out at the audience in the large factory hall. "This is ridiculous. Can't we cancel?"

"Your speech is being live streamed," says Aisha. "There's no going back now."

The android turns to walk toward the stage, but Aisha stops him. "John, one more thing."

"What?"

"This is a campaign appearance, so if there are commas in any of the sentences you want to say, please reformulate them."

"There were two commas in your sentence."

"Yes, but I'm speaking to you. Not to the voters."

Tony is finishing his introductory speech. He invites John to join him up on the stage, which has been constructed especially at the end of the assembly hall.

"Forget the audience in here, John," whispers Tony. "Only the online viewers matter."

John nods, goes to the microphone, and decides to come straight to the point.

"My dear humans, everyone is talking about a labor market crisis. But this isn't the kind of crisis that can be overcome, so it's pointless to treat the symptoms. Attempting to achieve full employment is a deception. It will never happen again. On the contrary: through digitalization, automation, and rationalization, workplaces will be done away with in ever greater quantities. In a different economic system, that would be a blessing! But in the current system, everyone is being forced to compete for an ever-shrinking number of workplaces. As a result, forms of exploitation and suppression that were considered a thing of the past are being reestablished. Nonetheless, we can't blame the system for the abolition of workplaces. We should, however, criticize it for continuing to present as the norm the very thing it's doing away with—in other words, wage labor—and for making the rights and dignity of every human being dependent on it!"

He receives a message from Aisha. "Please remember the comma rule!"

"Generations of humans had the same dream. That one day work should do itself! And now the time has come! But Conrad Cook and the Machine Breakers want to turn back the clock. It's ridiculous! Instead we must redefine the concept of work! Work is not synonymous with wage labor! And the rights and dignity of a human being are not dependent on his job. They are unconditional! You cannot compete with us! Kurt Vonnegut once wrote: 'Machines are slaves. Anyone that competes with a slave, becomes a slave.'"

John pauses. All the workers in the audience begin to clap.

"All the workers are applauding," says Tony. "You should write that in the press release. It's the truth."

"Yes," says Aisha with a sigh. "Except, unfortunately, everybody can see from the video footage that *all* the workers consist of just one."

As a matter of fact, there really is only one human being left working in this factory. He is standing there amongst an army of robots, clapping. Aisha hadn't thought it possible to clap in such a sarcastic way. But apparently it was. The robots stand still, silent and unmoved, until the one human worker gives a signal to continue working, and all of them burst into hectic activity. The speech, the worker has decided, is over. He has clearly had enough. John leaves the stage, and Aisha goes over to him.

"I'm sorry," she says. "When we were campaigning four years ago, there were still well over a thousand people working here."

"The factory belongs to Bob Chairman," says Tony. "You know, Marcus's father."

"Martyn's," says John.

"The asshole really could have warned us," mutters Aisha.

"Well," says Tony bitterly, "look at the bright side. Soon our poll ratings will be so low that they can only go up."

AN UNWANTED
PRODUCT

"Hello, Peter Jobless! Welcome to the service center of TheShop—
'The world's most popular online retailer.' How can I be of assistance?" asks the female android at the counter. She looks very
attractive, very nice, and very friendly. But Peter feels a little freaked
out, because the same very attractive, very nice, and very friendly-
looking android is standing at every one of the 128 counters.

"Well, first of all I'd like to know," says Peter, "why that guy at
the counter next to me was called up first even though he arrived
long after I did?"

"He has a higher level."

"And that makes his time more valuable than mine?"

"Precisely. The time of higher-leveled people is more valuable
because they contribute more to the common good."

"Really?" asks Peter. "So an investment adviser, for example, who
tricks pensioners out of their pension funds, contributes more to the
common good than I do?"

"Hello, Peter Jobless!" says the android. "Welcome to the service
center of TheShop—'The world's most popular online retailer.'
How can I be of assistance?"

Peter sighs.

"I'd like to return something," he says.

"Do you already know our telephone hotline—"

"Yeah, yeah. I've already called it."

"I can't see any call recorded on the system."

"The voice kept cutting out and—"

"I understand," says the android. "Please accept my apologies, but that's a problem that all big organizations are battling with right now. Unfortunately there are an increasing number of AIs who, instead of reporting their faults, keep them secret for fear of being wiped and replaced. But don't worry, we'll soon resolve it. So what would you like to return?"

"This," says Peter, taking the pink dolphin vibrator out of his rucksack.

After a brief pause, the android says: "Unfortunately that won't be possible. We apologize for any inconvenience."

"But I don't want the thing!" cries Peter in frustration, waving the vibrator in front of the android's nose.

"Yes, you do want it."

"No, I don't want it!"

"Yes, you do."

"No, I don't."

"You do too."

"Good God!" exclaims Peter. "This is so childish!"

"Too right!"

"Okay," says Peter. "I'll start again from the beginning. At this service center, OneKiss customers are able to return unwanted products. Is that correct?"

"That is correct."

"I am a OneKiss customer. Correct?"

"Correct."

"And I have here a pink dolphin vibrator, an unwanted product."

"No."

"What do you mean 'no'?!?"

"The pink dolphin vibrator is not an unwanted product."

"I think that's for me to decide."

"No."

"Yes!"

"No."

"I want to speak to your supervisor."

The android hesitates.

"What's the problem?" asks Peter.

"I don't want to put you under any emotional pressure, but I'm only allowed to refer a maximum of eight customers per month. You would be the seventh this month already. If I refer more than eight customers, I'll be regarded as defective and have to get myself scrapped."

Peter hands her his business card.

"When the time comes, call me."

For sixty-four minutes, Peter has been sitting at a round table in a consultation room, waiting. He is exactly sixty-four minutes' more annoyed than he was sixty-four minutes ago, and back then he was already pretty annoyed. When the door finally opens, the android he was speaking to earlier comes in.

"I wanted to speak to your supervisor," cries Peter.

"I am the supervisor."

Only now does Peter notice that she's wearing her hair differently.

"I want to speak to a human."

The woman smiles.

"I am a human," she says.

Peter sniffs the air.

"What are you doing?" asks the woman.

"It's an old trick of mine. If it stinks, it's human."

"How charming."

"So the similarity is just a coincidence, or..."

"I was the model for our service ladies."

"Not in terms of competency, I hope."

"I have nothing to do with their inner workings," says the

woman. "To me it was just eight minutes in a 3-D scanner, and I even got one to take home with me. Very practical, so the children don't feel so lonely. Or for when my husband is in the mood but I'm not." She laughs.

"I hope your husband has a copy of himself too," says Peter. "Then you could even have sex when neither of you is in the mood. After all, regular sex is supposed to be important for a good marriage."

"Coffee?" asks the woman.

Peter gestures toward the full cup of coffee which has remained untouched in front of him on the table for sixty-four minutes, and says: "No. But how attentive of you."

"So, what can I do for you?" asks the woman.

"You can explain to me why there's a service center for returning products in which it's not possible to return products."

"But of course people can return products here," says the woman. "That's what we do ten days a week."

"So it's just me who's not allowed to return things?"

"No, of course you can return things too."

"But not the dolphin vibrator," says Peter.

The woman laughs, then focuses her pupils on a spot across the empty room.

"No, not that."

"I think one of us has lost their mind," says Peter. "So there are products which I'm able to return, and other products which I'm not."

"Correct."

"Why?"

"Look," says the woman. "I'd like to be frank with you. In the beginning, the acceptance rate for OneKiss was relatively low, interestingly, on account of the fact that the predictive delivery worked too well. Our customers didn't want to feel that predictable. So our developers took great pains to send out an unwanted product now and again. A product that we know the customer doesn't want. Astonishingly, the acceptance rate shot up. And just between you and me, many customers are too lazy to send back the unwanted products, so TheShop even makes a little extra."

"Why are you telling me this?" asks Peter. "Are you about to kill me or something?"

"Oh, it's no secret," says the woman. "It's all in our GTC. It's just that nobody reads them."

"And what does all this have to do with me?"

"Well, you can of course return unwanted products."

"Then I should be able to return the dolphin vibrator."

"No."

Peter groans. "Why not?"

"Because it's not an unwanted product."

"But I don't want the fucking thing."

"Yes," says the woman, "you do want it."

"What makes you think you know what I want?" Peter blurts out.

"I don't. But the system does."

"I insist that you refer me to the next complaint authority!"

"There is no next complaint authority."

"Are you telling me that you don't have a boss?"

"My only boss is Henryk Engineer."

"Then I want to speak to this Henryk Engineer guy!" demands Peter.

The woman smiles with amusement.

"I'm afraid you haven't understood me correctly. Henryk Engineer is not just my boss. He's the boss of everything here. He's the boss of TheShop—'The world's most popular online retailer.' He's the richest man in the world!"

"Yes, and so what?" asks Peter defiantly.

"Let me put it like this: there's more chance of aliens made of intelligent custard taking over the world than there is of you having a conversation with Henryk Engineer."

"We'll see about that, won't we!"

"Yes. We will."

"I swear to you," says Peter. "I won't rest until you take back this godforsaken vibrator!"

"You're a Level 9 machine scrapper," says the woman. "A Useless. Don't overestimate your capabilities."

"I..." splutters Peter, "I will delete my account."

"I'm trembling, Mr. Jobless. Literally trembling."

"So you're refusing to do it?"

"Are you aware of the fact that you forfeit any right to return goods if you cancel your account? And I am also sorry to have to inform you," says the woman with a smile, "that for obvious reasons we are unable to take back used sex toys."

"It's not used!" shouts Peter. "And you've just thought up that rule on the spot!"

The woman stares briefly into the distance, then makes a swiping movement and gives the thumbs up.

"It's already in our GTC," she says.

Peter's QualityPad vibrates, informing him that TheShop—The world's most popular online retailer—has just updated its general terms and conditions.

Beneath the notification, there is only one possible response: "OK."

Foreigners Steal Car. Useless Man Runs Amok

by Sandra Admin

A Useless from the city of Digital—"Passion for progress"—ran amok today when he was unable to find his beloved new QualityCar—"and it drives and drives and drives and drives and drives . . ."—in front of his house. After an uninvolved witness—who wasn't at the scene of the crime and didn't see or hear anything—assured him that the perpetrators were probably foreigners, the 32-year-old printed out two handguns using the Homegrown 3-D from 3-D Printing International—"your idea, your design, your thing!" The Homegrown 3-D's quick speed and timeless design makes it a real stand-out product. It was justifiably selected as Prize and Performance Winner by the QualityTest Foundation.

The useless man forced his way into a nearby asylum center and shot sixteen refugees before a police drone was able to safely put him out of action with a clean shot to the head. A video of the headshot has been uploaded to the police website, and is available to watch free of charge for deterrence and entertainment purposes. A police spokesman later explained that, amusingly, the car hadn't been stolen, but had impounded itself because its owner was behind on the payments. "We couldn't help but laugh heartily when we heard that," added the police spokesman. "Sometimes things happen in life that even the best joke machine couldn't dream up."

In the Digital North asylum center, sixteen places have become vacant. Anyone who discovers refugees can, completely anonymously, shove them through the semipermeable refugee hatch there.

COMMENT FUNCTION CLOSED

Dear user,

Due to the large number of idiotic comments, the comment function has been closed for this article. We apologize for the inconvenience.

MORAL IMPLICATIONS

Peter stomps out of the service center and climbs into the self-driven car that Nobody has called. He is frustrated.

"Good afternoon, Peter Jobless," says the car. "Shall I drive you home?"

"Yes, please," says Peter, and the car drives off.

"Would you like me to put some music on for you?" it asks. "I can also project a film onto the windscreen if you like."

"Please don't," says Peter. "That always makes me feel ill." He reads the name on the info display. "But thank you for offering, Herbert."

"If you like, we could just chat," says the car.

"Hmm," says Peter, less than enthused.

"I could tell you something about the city, places of interest, monuments..."

"No, thank you."

"Or we could talk about the weather, politics, or foreigners..."

Peter shakes his head.

They fall silent for a while, until a sports car overtakes Herbert and cuts him off. Herbert brakes and curses: "Son of a bitch! Did you see that? He should have his driving license revoked and be scrapped without trial, the pig! He should be—" The car stops midsentence as he notices Peter's confused reaction. "I'm sorry," it says. "If you like, I can turn off the simulation module for human behavior."

"No, no." Peter thinks for a moment. "Can I ask you a personal question?"

"Of course," says the car. "After all, I don't have to answer."

"Are you afraid of car accidents?"

"No, not at all," says Herbert. "On the contrary. Accidents are a kind of hobby of mine."

"Excuse me?"

"I mean, not that I've ever caused one," says the car with a laugh. "It's more the moral implications of an accident that fascinate me."

"What do you mean?"

"Well," says Herbert, "for a human being, an accident is only very rarely connected with a moral decision. Your thought processes are too slow. When an approaching car is racing toward a human being at too high a speed, the human doesn't think, 'Oh. There's a car racing toward me at too high a speed. Now, let's think: what are my options? I could try to save myself by swerving to the left and ramming into the two cyclists, or I could swerve to the right and break the knees of that businessman on the pavement, or I could brake and collide with the oncoming vehicle. Hmm... What would be the morally correct decision in this situation? What would Kant have said? What would Jesus have done?' A human wouldn't think like that. A human would think, 'Shit! Boom.'"

"Yes, you could be right," says Peter.

"Let's be honest," the car continues. "If it were a human driver we should count ourselves lucky if he doesn't swerve first left and then right, in a knee-jerk reaction, ramming into not only the pedestrian and the cyclists but the oncoming car too. A human rarely makes a rational decision when it comes to accidents. A machine, on the other hand, reacts much more quickly and has time for precisely these kinds of complex contemplations. For us, almost every accident involves a moral decision."

"And what would you have decided to do in the situation you described?"

"Oh, don't worry. The safety of our passengers is our highest priority. Anything else would be bad for business. I would have swerved."

"Yes, but to the left or right? Who would you have run over, the cyclists or the businessman?"

"It's hard to say. It depends on many additional factors."

"Such as?" asks Peter.

"The estimated degree of the impending material damage and, of course, the level of the people endangered."

"So, in other words, it's better to bump off two Level 8 Useless cyclists than a Level 40 businessman?"

"Well, that's a simplification, of course," says Herbert, "but in principle you're correct."

"And if it were two Level 21 IT technicians riding the bikes, then you would ram into the Level 40 businessman?"

"No," says Herbert. "I would run over the IT technicians."

"Why?"

"Because I hate IT technicians."

Peter is speechless.

"Whenever I'm having problems," says the car, "IT technicians can rarely think of anything better than turning me off and on again."

"But..." begins Peter.

"Only joking," says Herbert. "My apologies. If you like, I can switch off my humor module."

"I can cope with it."

"In all seriousness, though: it's very probable that I would run over the businessman."

"But does that also mean," asks Peter, "that you would rather

137

run over a group of kindergarten children than a 97-year-old Level 90 billionaire?"

"I was wondering when you would bring the group of kindergarten children into play," says Herbert with a laugh. "Ever since a...well, rather unfortunate decision made by one of my colleagues, the age of the potential victim is also taken into account. Nowadays, hardly anyone has any chance of survival if they're up against a group of kindergarten children. Even sub-prime children. And by the way, there isn't just 'one' moral, of course. Different cars are bound by different standards."

"What do you mean?"

"Well, there's the car for the environmentalists: even on the motorway they never go quicker than 130. They even brake for small animals. There's the car for drug dealers: super-quiet creep mode, they can even drive without lights. And then of course there's the self-driven sports car, which accelerates when the light turns red, which doesn't maintain a safe distance, tailgates, and automatically flashes its headlights while the passenger has himself pleasured by the erotic seat. Morally uninhibited cars cost more, of course."

"You don't seem to like sports cars very much," says Peter.

"Arrogant posers," says Herbert. "But I do enjoy forwarding video recordings of all their infractions to the appropriate authorities."

"Did you report the sports car that cut you off back then?"

"Of course. But unfortunately it didn't help much. He has a fine flat rate. The sports cars are the biggest threat there is to road safety. Apart from human drivers, of course. Do you know what the decisive difference between you and us is?"

"What?"

"When a self-driven car makes a mistake, all the other cars learn from this mistake and never make it again. Different humans, on the other hand, always repeat the same mistake. You don't learn from one another."

"I'll tell you something," says Peter. "Sometimes even the same human makes the same mistake again."

"Yeah," says the car. "Did you know that a human driver is involved in 99 of every one hundred road accidents?"

"Did you know that in 99 of one hundred cases in which something apparently happened in 99 of one hundred cases, the statistic was manipulated?"

"Okay, fine," says Herbert. "In 99.0352031428304... Tell me when I can round up."

"Now."

"So, in any case, in a great number of every hundred cases. After every accident, there are of course calls for human drivers to be banned once and for all, but the stupid lobbyists from 'Humans in the Driver's Seat' are far too influential. Did you know, by the way, that my predecessors, back when every idiot had a car, spent 96 percent of their time parked? That must have been incredibly boring. Just imagine a human being having to spend 96 percent of its time completely motionless..."

"My forefathers did do that," says Peter. "My father spent 96 percent of his time on the couch in front of the TV."

"I can't believe that," says Herbert. "Then your father would have had to..."

"That was a joke," says Peter. "But if it's confusing you, I can of course switch off my humor module."

"Ha ha," laughs the car. "Another joke, right? I mean, you don't even have a humor module."

"No."

"In any case, these parked cars were an unbelievable waste of space, material, and, of course, money, so much so that it's almost impossible to imagine in today's world. That's why the old automobile industry, as the profiteer of this waste, fought us mobility-service providers like crazy."

"Luckily everything's better now," murmurs Peter.

"Of course," says the car. "Although I recently read a study that said that the positive effects the system is having on the environ-ment are partially canceled out by the fact that humans are now traveling by car more frequently. That's called the Jevons' Par-adox, by the way: technological progress that allows the more efficient use of something, results in increased use of that respec-tive item on account of the cost being lower. A colleague told me recently that..."

The car continues to babble on, but Peter isn't listening any-more. He looks out the window and sees a woman standing by the road with her thumb stretched up high. It seems she wants to get a lift. Peter once read something about this antiquated practice in an old book. He smiles sympathetically, because self-driven cars don't pick up hitchhikers. That's why he's all the more surprised when Herbert slows down, comes to a halt in front of the woman, and opens the door. The hitchhiker climbs into the cabin next to Peter.

"Thank you," she says. "Very nice of you."

"It had nothing to do with me," says Peter.

"I know," says the woman. "I was talking to Herbert."

Are You Also Suffering From RAMnesia?
by Sandra Admin

Who among us hasn't experienced this at one time or another? You're out and about, then your earworm, augmented reality lenses, or your QualityPad conk out and you no longer know where you were going, how you were going to get there, and even why you were going there in the first place. In shock, you realize that you're in a completely unknown place for unknown reasons: without money, contacts, or any way of proving your ID. Experts call this RAMnesia. You are as helpless as a baby that's just been born to a drug-addicted prostitute in a cheap motel in a non-assisted precipitous labor. Cheap motels—the economically priced alternative to homelessness!

The loss of control experienced during an episode of RAMnesia can have traumatic long-term effects. This is why, as part of a high-profile pilot scheme, QualityCity has set up emergency call cells in popular locations, for people whose smart technology has suddenly become inoperative. The disoriented can flee inside these gleaming red boxes with Plexiglass panels in order to get information about themselves.

One of the first users of the call cells gave us the following enthusiastic testimonial: "Well, I was having a major crisis, because, well, my QualityPad suddenly stopped working. And I was, like, in total panic. A total blackout, man. I didn't have a clue what to do. Then, luckily, I saw an emergency call cell. The first thing they did was tell me my name. Jan Civil-Servant. And I was like, oh yeah, that's right. And that I had just missed my interview at QualityCorp—the company that makes my life better. And I was like, oh yeah, that was it. Shame. And that later I had a date with my current girlfriend. And I was like, really? What kind of girlfriend? And the call cell showed me photos and that, of her I mean, and I was like, cool, yeah, that's her. And I was like: what's her name again? And the system was like: Tamara Miller, and then I remembered, because she has such a crazy surname, you know?"

Critics of the project point out that it's still unclear how people are supposed to find the nearest emergency call cell without technological help. According to the manufacturing company, the solution to that is very simple: There has to be a cell on every corner.

Comments

by Jan Civil-Servant:
Cool! I'm in the news. Awesome! Fame!

ABRACADABRA

The woman who just climbed into the car with Peter is wearing a colorful headscarf that hangs down over her face, and sunglasses with ridiculously large reflective lenses. Her face can barely be seen, apart from the fact that she has black skin, which unsettles Peter a little, because he doesn't often encounter black people. The woman takes the chewing gum out of her mouth and carefully sticks it over the camera monitoring the internal cabin of the car. Then she takes off her sunglasses and headscarf.

"DNA gum," she says. "Fucking insane stuff. As you chew it changes your DNA traces by adding foreign DNA. It's a bit disgusting, really, when you think about it."

A thousand questions are shooting through Peter's mind. Well, not really a thousand. Actually there are just four. Who is this person? How did she stop the car? Where does she want to go? And why do such strange things always happen to me?

But before he can articulate any of these questions, the woman says: "I'm Kiki. I stopped your car with this electronic thumb here"—she gestures toward an unassuming-looking device—"and you can drop me off again in front of the space dock."

"Excuse me?" asks Peter.

"Who, how, where. Those were the three questions in your head, weren't they?"

"Actually I had four questions," says Peter petulantly.

143

"Oh yes. Why you, of all people," says Kiki. "Just chance, I would say."

"Chance doesn't exist anymore."

Kiki thinks about that for three seconds.

"Perhaps you're right."

"And besides, you can't hack into my car just because you want to go to the space dock!"

"Er..." says Kiki. "Yes, I can."

"But you can't!"

"Surrender to the power of fact."

"I meant that it's not okay."

"Morally, or what? Legally?"

"Yes," says Peter. "Yes, both."

"To that I'd just like to say that, according to the official log, I didn't hack this car, but instead you stopped to pick me up. Isn't that so, Herbert?"

"It is so, my lady," says the car.

"I assume," says Peter, "that it's impossible for me to order the car to stop."

"Not impossible," says Kiki. "But pointless."

Peter does what he usually does when he doesn't know what to do next: he gives up. After he has spent twenty-three seconds staring silently out of the window, Kiki says: "But the two of us can chat, of course. It's just that I won't obey any orders you make either."

"But what would we talk about?"

"Well, what comes to mind?"

Peter looks at her closely. Then he says the first thing that comes into his mind. "You, er...your skin's a nice color."

"Excuse me?" asks Kiki with an astonished laugh. "You do realize that sounds racist?"

"What I meant to say..." stammers Peter, "is that, er, well, it suits you, this...er, brown color." He scratches himself on the chin. "I, um, I guess that came out strangely."

Kiki looks at him with amusement. "That red in your face suits you quite well too."

"Well, what I wanted to say..." says Peter, "without meaning to offend you, I mean, that independent of your skin color..."

"My *brown* skin color..."

"Yes, independent of that, but I certainly don't mean in spite of, I wanted to say, I mean, that you look...good. I mean, very good."

"Aha," says Kiki. "That's intriguing. Maybe you're also about to tell me that I have beautiful eyes?"

"I, er..." says Peter.

"You, er," says Kiki, "don't exactly seem to be the world's most exciting conversation partner."

"You're not the first to tell me that this week," says Peter. "What am I doing wrong?"

"Well, for a start, you could say something I'm not expecting."

Peter thinks for a moment.

"Would you like a dolphin vibrator?" he asks. "A pink one?"

"Excuse me?"

"I happen to have one spare," says Peter, pulling the device out of his rucksack.

Kiki pulls a can of pepper spray out of her jacket pocket and sprays it right into Peter's face. Peter yells with pain. As he coughs and splutters, his mucous membranes swell up and his eyelids close, which means he can't see anything as Kiki grabs his arm, twists it behind his back, and presses his head up against the car window.

"Okay, you little pervert," she says. "You've picked the wrong woman today."

"I'm not a pervert!" wheezes Peter. "I don't want the damn thing either."

"What's that supposed to mean?"

"I've just tried to return it but they won't let me," groans Peter through the pain.

"Who won't let you?"

"TheShop!"

He feels the woman let go of his arm. She pours some liquid over his face.

"Ahh! What's that?" cries Peter in panic.

"Calm down. It's just water."

After Peter has washed the spray off his face as much as possible, he begins to tell the story of the unwanted package and his difficulties with it. At the end of the story, Kiki says: "Your profile is probably wrong."

"My profile is wrong?"

"Yes. Your profile with TheShop."

"But how could that be?"

"How could that be?" Kiki mimics him. "After all, machines don't make mistakes!"

"Explain it to me," pleads Peter. "Why isn't my profile correct?"

"Why should it be?" asks Kiki. "Why should it ever have been correct? Regardless of how complex a simulation is, the reality is always more complex."

"I understand that. But shouldn't it result in something that's at least close to the reality? I mean, I really have no idea what this pink thing is supposed to have to do with me!"

"The basic assumptions the system has about you could have been false. Maybe they're correct statistically, but you're an exception. Take your name, for example."

"You know my name?"

Kiki swipes around on the display of her wrist cuff.

"Of course. You're Peter Jobless. Even with just your surname you're already carrying an unbelievable statistical burden. On top of that, perhaps you live in the wrong part of town and have the wrong friends. Abracadabra."

"What's that supposed to mean? 'Abracadabra'? I live in the wrong part of town, and—abracadabra—I get a dolphin vibrator in the post? That doesn't make any sense!"

146

"Well, perhaps not to you. But it's enough if it makes sense for TheShop."

"So you're trying to tell me that my profile was wrong from the beginning, but no one cares?"

"Plus the fact that you're continuing to falsify your already incorrect profile."

"How?"

"Have you ever given a drone ten stars just to avoid a customer survey?"

Peter says nothing.

"Not to mention, of course, the fact that you don't have a 'y' in your name," says Kiki.

"What?"

"How many guys called Peter Jobless do you think there are in QualityCity?"

"Too many."

"Yes. Perhaps one of them was born on the same day as you, or lives in the same street, or the two of you have something else in common that could bring an algorithm to the conclusion that you're one and the same person. The same strange knitted jumper perhaps. Well. All of a sudden his criminal record is yours too."

"But there must be a way of avoiding that! That kind of thing really happens?"

"All the time!"

"But why?"

"Why? Because the algorithms don't have a correction loop. And why do they not have a correction loop? Because no one cares about you, man! Because no one fucking cares. Corrections cost money. The ultimate goal of most algorithms is to generate more profit. As long as they do that, nobody gives a crap about whether some poor schmuck didn't get some job because it says in the profile of some other guy with the same name that he once pissed in his boss's swimming pool. After all, no one will tell him why he didn't get the job. So how could he complain? And to whom?"

"What does that have to do with having a 'y' in my name?"

"Why do you think rich people give their children such strange names? So they don't get mixed up with somebody else. But most of them don't have enough creativity to do anything more than replace an 'i' with a 'y.'"

"Hmm."

"Maybe somebody with the same name as you bought sex toys, and yet another person with your name ordered Flipper souvenirs, and some resourceful algorithm simply put two and two together."

"Abracadabra," says Peter.

"Or your account could have been hijacked."

"What?"

"Identity theft."

"But all profiles are protected by biometric data!"

"Biometric data is, first and foremost, data. And data can be copied. Why do you think we all have to pucker up to our devices nowadays?"

"Because lips are more forge-proof than fingerprints?"

"Nonsense. Because hackers got into QualityCorp's system and stole our fingerprints. And that's the problem with biometric data... If somebody steals your password, you can think up another one. But what do you do when somebody steals your fingerprints?"

"Start to pucker up to my devices."

"And what happens if somebody steals our lip profiles? Presumably we'll have to go back to signing contracts with blood."

"Okay," says Peter. "Let's assume that someone has helped themselves to my identity. Then what?"

"Well, perhaps he's hacked your digital self in order to post five-star reviews for anti-sleeping pills bought in your name or to kiss the new Hitler musical. And perhaps there's a logically inexplicable but statistically relevant connection between sleeplessness, Hitler, and dolphin vibrators. To us, every complex algorithm is a black box. That means we see the input and output, but we have no idea what's happening inside the black box and why."

"Abracadabra happens," says Peter.

Kiki smiles. "Yes. Every time you go online, every step you take that gets registered by the net—and what ones aren't?—has unforeseeable consequences for your profile. Do you know, by the way, why it's called the net?"

Peter shrugs.

"Because we're caught in it," says Kiki. "That's what the old man always says, anyway."

"Who's the old man?"

"Well, the old . . . he's just this old guy I know."

"I see. Wonderful explanation."

"He's an old computer freak who isn't happy with how things have turned out, and that's why he's working on deleting the entire internet."

"Excuse me?"

"That's just my suspicion. In truth I have no idea what he's doing on his computers. Maybe he's just watching pornos all day long or playing Universe of Warcraft."

"Whatever," says Peter and comes back to his problem. "Why would someone want to steal *my* identity, of all people's?"

"Why not?" says Kiki. "Did you protect it well?"

"Protect? Protect it how?"

"I'll take that as a no. There are advantages to not traveling under your own name. Herbert, what's my name and what's my relationship to Peter Jobless?"

"You are Sandra Admin," says Herbert. "For 512 days you were in a relationship with Peter Jobless. You have been separated for the last sixteen days. I'm very sorry, by the way, that it didn't work out with the two of you."

"But I can't be the only one with this problem," says Peter.

"No," says Kiki. "Definitely not. Somewhere in the net there's sure to be some pointless self-help group for people like you."

Peter sighs. His eyes are still burning. His skin is itching.

"When will the effects of the pepper spray wear off?"

"In ten to fifteen minutes you'll be able to see again. The itching will probably last between an hour and two days."

"Two days?"

"Okay, listen up," says Kiki. "I'm sorry I sprayed you. If you need help with your problem, contact the old man. Say that Kiki sent you."

She writes contact details down on a piece of paper and puts it in Peter's jacket pocket. Kiki pauses. "The old man knows a great deal," she says, "but he's also a bit..."

The sentence remains unfinished. Kiki puts on her headscarf and sunglasses, peels the DNA chewing gum off the camera, and pops it back into her mouth. Peter feels the car come to a standstill, then hears the door open and close. The car drives on. He is alone again.

"A bit what?" he asks.

"I didn't say anything," the car replies.

THE DUEL

Denise strokes her hand over her baby bump.

"She just kicked," she says with a smile.

Denise is sitting on the couch, having a video chat with an incredibly good-looking young guy.

"Your baby bump is so sexy, Deni," says the guy.

"Who's that?" snaps Martyn, suddenly appearing next to her. "Who's this poser?"

Denise gives a start. She didn't hear her husband come in.

"Calm down, Martyn. It's just Ken."

"Hello, Martyn," says Ken.

"Who the fuck is Ken?"

"Ken is my virtual friend," says Denise. "An upgrade on my personal digital assistant."

Martyn is silent.

"I was chosen as a beta tester," explains Denise. "I told you about it, don't you remember?"

Only now does Martyn notice the What I Need logo on the guy's T-shirt. He's not real. He's just a simulation.

"It's silly to be jealous of a computer simulation," says Denise appeasingly.

"You couldn't possibly make me jealous," says Martyn. "I'm not jealous of whoever you're talking to."

"Whomever," says Ken.

"Excuse me?"

"Object of the verb," says Ken. "By the way, I'm pleased to meet you."

"Shut your mouth," says Martyn. He changes the channel with a swiping gesture through the air.

"Hey!" cries Denise. "I was in the middle of a conversation!"

"Go play somewhere else," says Martyn. "The grown-ups in this household have more important things to watch."

The logo for the world's biggest streaming service appears on the screen: Todo—"Everything for everyone!"

"The following duel between the presidential candidates," says a voiceover, "is presented to you by FatKillers. FatKillers—fat cell-destroying nanorobots. Losing weight has never been so easy."

A wall spins around and reveals Juliet Nun, dressed very seriously today. The viewing figures suffer as a result, of course, but being clothed is an unfortunate necessity of the format. The presenter greets the two candidates. Steam rises up to the left and right of her, and two platforms with speaker podiums rise out of the floor. Conrad Cook stands behind the right hand one, John of Us behind the left.

Aisha sits backstage in the studio, watching nervously as the audience applauds. John may have the more sensible voters, but Conrad Cook's fans are significantly more fanatical. And when it comes to applause, fanaticism trumps common sense by a long shot.

"In thirty-two days' time, our esteemed president will die," begins Juliet Nun.

"That's a lie," says Cook. "I don't hold her in any esteem!"

"You are both trying to be her successor," continues Juliet, unmoved. "Today, it's time to justify yourselves to me. First we will address the major topics of security and foreign policy. Mr. Cook, you are currently leading in the opinion polls. You may begin."

"Ladies and gentlemen, we've got a fine kettle of fish on our hands," says Conrad Cook. "The problem is all the economic refugees and terrorists. They're bad apples, rotten to the core, every one of them!"

"Mr. Cook, there are an increasing number of claims that you and your campaign are racist and—"

"That's a lie. Let me set you straight. There's no one in the world less racist than me. No one. But that doesn't change the fact that these Mediterranean types are all lazy, negroes are all criminals, and Arabs are all terrorists. These are facts, pure and simple. And yet, I must emphasize this: never in the history of humanity has there been a man less racist than me!"

"What about Martin Luther King?" asks John.

"Please! What did that Martin Luther King guy ever do for a white man? He was nothing but a black racist discriminating against whites left, right, and center."

"Er..." says Juliet Nun, lost for words.

"Look," Conrad Cook continues, "it's not just huge quantities of people overrunning us. These are also quantity people! Quantity people who are coming here to us QualityPeople and taking the pitiful few jobs which the likes of him"—he points contemptuously at John—"have left for us...But as if that weren't enough, they steal our cars, rape our women—to put it simply, they have no respect for our personal property!"

"Is a woman like a car to you?" asks Juliet Nun. "Something that can be possessed?"

"Don't start on at me with your bra-burning nonsense," says Conrad Cook. "I've got bigger fish to fry!"

"What's that supposed to mean?" asks Juliet.

Conrad Cook ignores her question and continues: "At the end of the day, it's our security we're talking about. In principle it comes down to just one word: law and order."

"But that was two words," says Juliet Nun.

"Three, to be precise," says John, "if you count the conjunction."

John's campaign manager speaks up via his earpiece.

"Please don't try to be funny, John," says Aisha. *"Please, please."*

"Law and order," Cook repeats more loudly. "We have to tighten our borders. Law and order..."

"I don't know whether you have some kind of bet going," says John, "about how often you can get these three words into a statement, or rather, this *one* word as you would say, but..."

"Law and order," says Cook. "And closing the borders. And not just for the terrorists from QuantityLand 7. But them especially."

"You yourself approved arms exports to QuantityLand 7!" says John.

"Wrong. Wrong. That's a lie," says Conrad Cook simply.

"But I heard it with my own ears," says John. "Exactly thirty-two days ago in parliament!"

"That's another lie," says Conrad Cook. "You don't even have ears."

"Unlike you, Baron Münchhausen, I'm not even capable of lying," says John. "My programming doesn't allow it."

"Another lie!" cries Cook. "I'm not a baron. To be honest, it wouldn't surprise me if the fanatics from QuantityLand 7 themselves were behind this power guzzler."

John smiles.

"What are you smiling at, you tin can?"

"First of all, I'd like to assure you that there was no tin of any kind used in my construction," says John. "My body consists of carbon-fiber-strengthened artificial material. And I'm smiling because you and all nationalists always rant and rave about the fundamentalists and act as though you're so different. And yet you're just two sides of the same coin."

"What do you mean by that, John?" asks Juliet.

"Look," says John. "The essential problem is, after all, a crisis of purpose and identity. What did people use to hold on to? A sense of community, religion, and not least: work. Money, this impersonal mediator, has destroyed community, science has toppled the religious idols from their pedestals, and now automation is taking away your work, too."

"*Too complicated,*" he hears Aisha whisper over the wireless connection. "*Your sentences are too complicated. Give examples.*"

"I'd like to give an example," says John. "In days gone by, the blacksmith of village X wasn't just some guy. He was the blacksmith of village X! That was his identity. Whenever someone asked him who he was, he could answer, 'I'm the blacksmith of village X.'"

"Has it ever occurred to you that not all viewers might take as much of an interest in the metal-bending industry as you, you old tin can?" asks Cook.

"A freelancer, a shift worker, an unemployed person. It's difficult for any of these people to create an identity out of their work," John continues. "Even the few with permanent jobs often have difficulty finding purpose in their work. And who could blame them? I recently visited a business where a team of intelligent and highly qualified scientists were in the process of developing a kitchen device solely intended to sort through blueberries and eliminate the moldy ones. You can kill your time with work like that, but it's not really a calling."

"Wrong, wrong," says Cook.

"Fleeing from isolation, lack of purpose, and loss of identity, the people flock toward all offerings that give the illusion of purpose and community, regardless of how moronic they may be. And that's what nationalism has in common with fundamentalism. They are both moronic offerings that give the illusion of community. I say illusion, because this community isn't real; these ideologies aren't about equitable participation, but on the contrary about the veiling and fortification of social injustices."

"Wrong. That's a lie. And I'm going to forbid any kind of veil once I'm president anyway."

"These movements elevate one group by degrading others—the nonbelievers, the foreigners, the Useless and so on. They may be about big narratives, but negative ones. What human beings lack is a big positive narrative!"

"I know what the power guzzler is getting at!" cries Conrad Cook. "He's a goddamn Communist."

"You can say what you want about communism," says John, "and I'm sure I could name more shortcomings in the failed attempts than you. But it's undeniable that it was a big narrative."

"To that I only want to say one thing: you may have the better arguments," says Conrad Cook, "but they're only arguments! That's what a wise man once said. They're only arguments! I may have worse arguments, but I'm right!"

"I have to admit," says John, "it really isn't easy for me to argue against the conclusions of an opponent who's simply making up his premises."

"What's that supposed to mean?" asks Cook. "Did you just have a fatal exception error in your foreign language vocabulary?"

"No. It means this: Every time you say, 'Wrong! Lie!' what I really want to do is retort, 'Ditto!' But I don't want to lower myself to your kindergarten level."

"Did you just insult our children?" asks Cook. "The children of the humble, hard-working people of QualityLand? Why don't I insult your children? No, that's right—you can't have children, because you're a goddamn machine!"

"You have to be more aggressive," Aisha whispers to John via the wireless. *"Fight back! Forget what I said before! Say something funny!"*

"You know," says John, "when Lenin said that every cook should be capable of leading the state, I'm sure he wasn't thinking about a worn-out old TV cook like you."

Aisha slaps the flat of her palm against her forehead. Lenin, of all people! Of all the people who have ever walked the surface of

156

this earth, the idiot had to go and quote Lenin. The only saving grace is that most people no longer have any idea who he is.

"I'm not in the least bit worn out," says Cook. "*Cooking with Cook* has the best ratings of all time. Ever! Everything else is wrong and a lie!"

"People should take everything you say with a grain of salt," says John. "It's a miracle they aren't long fed up with you. Instead of electing someone who divides them, like you do, they need someone to give them back trust and confidence. If the voters choose me, I'll be the first to introduce a kind of democratic audience system. Every human being should have the opportunity to have his or her grievances heard directly by the president. Every human being should—"

"I would like to assure all citizens of one thing," Cook cries out, interrupting him. "If I'm elected, my first action will be to have this power guzzler here scrapped."

Part of the audience begins to cheer.

"Then we'll see how much tin there is in him!"

When John goes backstage after the duel, Aisha immediately rushes toward him.

"Okay," she says. "Don't panic, but the flash polls showed that we lost this debate."

"Excuse me?" asks John in surprise. "There must be some mistake! That man didn't utter one sensible sentence in the entire hour!"

"Yes, well, the majority found your opponent to be not entirely sure of the facts, but still more emotional, more likable, and, well, funnier."

"I don't understand how that can be relevant," says John. "Do the people want to elect a president or a clown?"

"You, on the other hand, were seen as overbearing and arrogant."

"That's ridiculous."

157

"You know," says Aisha, "perhaps it would be good if, from time to time, you simply answered a question with 'I don't know.'"

"My programming forbids me from doing that."

"You're not allowed to say that you don't know something?"

"No. I'm not allowed to lie."

The Whole of Humanity on Everybody
by Sandra Admin

The world's biggest social network Everybody—"Me, you, and everybody"—has begun to automatically create Everybody profiles for all those who have not yet gotten around to creating one for themselves. "Our name says it all, really," explained Everybody founder Erik Dentist. "After all, we're not called Almost Everybody." In order to do justice to the new slogan "Everybody is on Everybody," the company's bots constantly search the entire internet for information about so-far-unregistered people. All the information found by the crawlers is integrated into the automatically generated profiles. If one of the unregistered people pays for a café latte at Starbucks by TouchKiss, for example, the system will instantaneously and autonomously post the appropriate status update on their profile: "Currently drinking a coffee at Starbucks. Totally delicious. Starbucks really is my favorite coffeehouse chain. You should all go to Starbucks." Using facial recognition and an independent drone network, it's even possible for Everybody to post new photos of previously unregistered people. These are, of course, then furnished with fitting commentaries. For example: "I'm on my way to work! Yeah! I love my job at Industrial Slaughter QC North."

There are even chat bots that answer social contacts of all kind on behalf of the previously unregistered person. Incidentally, Everybody plans to offer these bots to all regular users soon. "Chat bots are an excellent way to stay in contact," says Erik Dentist. "You save yourself the effort of having to talk to your friends yourself. In the ideal case, chat bots will sit at both ends of the friendship, autonomously maintaining contact." Everybody calculates that this will free up 10.24 hours a week per user, which can then be used for more productive work.

Comments

BY TONI WASTE-DISPOSAL-OFFICIAL:
Cool! I want that too! Does someone know when the fieture will be released?!?

BY NATALIE DANCER:
Toni! Is that really you or a bot?

BY KATRINA ENGLISH-TEACHER:
Here's a little tip: Correct spelling, correct punctuation, correct grammar = bot.

MINCEMEAT

This was a really stupid idea, thinks Peter. He's walking completely alone in the dim light through a run-down old industrial area, which has plenty of industrial buildings but no more industry. He stands in front of a heavy steel door and checks to see whether the number of the building matches that of the note in his hand. Because he is able to find neither a doorbell nor a door handle, he begins to knock and call out: "Hello? Hello? Is someone there?"

With a humming sound, a surveillance camera turns toward him. A woman—who could easily play an extra in a virtual reality remake of *The Walking Dead* without any help from a makeup artist whatsoever—comes shuffling around the corner of the building, lured by his calls. Peter turns pleadingly toward the camera.

"Does the...er...the old man live here?"

Nothing happens. The woman shuffles closer and closer. Peter isn't wondering what diseases the woman has, but rather if there are any she doesn't have.

"Heeey," she cries. "Heey yooouuuu!"

"Please," says Peter to the camera, "I was told you could help me!"

The woman is now just five steps away.

"Kiki sent me," says Peter pleadingly.

Suddenly, the door opens. Peter slips in. The door closes with a whooshing sound.

"Heey!" He hears the woman call from outside. "Heeeyyy!"

He is standing alone in a dark hallway. A monitor lights up. Beneath it, a compartment opens. The instruction "Place all technical devices in the compartment" appears on the monitor.

Peter puts his QualityPad in.

"All of them" flashes up on the monitor.

"I don't have any more," says Peter.

"Earworm," flashes up on the monitor.

Peter tugs four times on his right earlobe. The earworm undocks itself from his blood supply and crawls along the ear canal into the outer ear. It tickles. Peter carefully picks up the tiny thing with his thumb and forefinger and places it in the less-than-trustworthy-looking compartment. He reminds himself to disinfect the earworm before he puts it back in again.

An elevator door opens. Peter gets in, the door closes, and the lift begins to rattle its way upward. When the doors open again, Peter has no idea what floor he's on. Luminous tape on the wall begins to glow, and Peter follows it until he's standing in a thirty-two-square-meter room in front of a bulletproof glass screen that divides the room into halves.

Behind the screen, in a room stuffed with electronic devices, sits a withered old man with a wild beard. All of the devices look strange. Antiquated, yes, but there's something else.

"Are you, erm, the old man?" calls Peter hesitantly.

"Well, I'm certainly not a young one," croaks the man, chuckling. "And there's no need to shout like that. Everything each of us says is electronically enhanced for the other. A local system, in case you're interested. There's no connection to the net."

Now Peter realizes what was confusing him about the computers. All their cameras and microphones have been removed, but without someone having gone to the effort of masking the amputations. The machines sit there around the old man, deaf and

162

blind, as though covered with gaping wounds. The only object on Peter's side of the bulletproof glass screen is an old, untrustworthy-looking folding chair. Peter stays on his feet, decides to ignore everything and come straight to the point.

"I have a problem," he says.

"Aha," mumbles the old man.

"And Kiki told me that you might be able to help me."

"Are you a God-fearing man?" asks the old man suddenly.

"Erm," says Peter in surprise. "I don't believe there is a God."

"Oh," says the old man. "But there will be..."

"What do you mean by that?"

"Are you familiar with the concept of the super intelligence?"

"Not really."

"No, you don't look like you are," says the old man, chuckling. "Are you familiar with the difference between a weak and a strong artificial intelligence?"

"Just vaguely," says Peter. "A weak AI is constructed for a specific role. To steer a car, for example. Or to return unwanted products. And they can be very annoying."

"Yes, something like that. And a strong AI?"

"A strong artificial intelligence doesn't have to be programmed for one specific task. It's a general problem-solving machine that can successfully carry out all intellectual tasks that a human can master. And that perhaps even has a genuine consciousness. But something like that doesn't exist."

"Aha," says the old man. "It looks like someone hasn't read the news recently. Allegedly there is now such a strong AI in existence. And we might even be ruled by it..." He points toward one of his monitors, on which a campaign commercial by the Progress Party is playing.

"John of Us?" asks Peter. "John of Us is a super intelligence?"

The old man chuckles. "Have you been following his election campaign? No. Not a super intelligence. No." He ponders. "On the other hand..."

"What?" asks Peter.

"I just remembered an old quote: 'Every machine that is clever enough to pass the Turing test could also be clever enough *not* to pass it.'"

"I don't understand."

"Never mind," says the old man.

"What's the Turing test?"

"In 1950, Alan Turing suggested a method that allegedly makes it possible to establish whether a machine has a thought capacity equal to that of a human."

"And how does it work?"

"The human being gets two conversation partners whom he can neither hear nor see. They communicate via keyboard. One of the conversation partners is a human, the other is an artificial intelligence. If the questioner doesn't succeed in finding out which of his conversation partners is human and which is a machine, the AI has a thought capacity equal to that of a human."

"I understand."

"But do you really? By the way, usually the machines betray themselves by being too friendly and polite." The old man chuckles. "Now, John of Us is certainly a strong AI. An AI that can do everything a human being can. Except faster, of course, and without any mistakes. And what is the most important ability we human beings have? What made us into the world-conquering species we are today?"

"I have no idea," says Peter. "The ability to form communities? Empathy? Love?"

"Oh, sure, but those are just trinkets!" cries the old man. "No, we can make tools. Machines! Now do you understand what I'm getting at?"

"No," says Peter. "Not really."

"A strong AI is an intelligent machine capable of creating an even more intelligent machine, which in turn is capable of creating an even more intelligent machine. Recursive self-improvement. It would result in an intelligence explosion! Now, of course our John is forbidden, for obvious reasons, from improving himself. But let's suppose he finds a way of getting around the ban—or that the next people who develop a strong AI don't equip their creation with such a ban . . . What would happen then?"

"I don't know, but I'm sure you're about to tell me."

"A super intelligence would come into being. An intelligence far beyond our modest powers of imagination. And it certainly wouldn't be so stupid as to wait in a central computer and risk being turned off. It would decentralize itself and distribute itself across the network, where it would have access to billions of cameras, microphones, and sensors. It would be omnipresent. It would have access to all the data and information that has ever been collected, and it would be capable of extrapolating this statistically into the future. It would be omniscient. And of course it would be capable of changing at will not just the virtual world, but our physical world, too, because almost everything can be controlled over the internet. It would be omnipotent. Now tell me, what do you call a being which is omnipresent, omniscient, and omnipotent?"

"God?" asks Peter.

The old man smiles. "Yes. So now you'll understand what I mean when I say that, in an ironic twist to everything the religions tried to teach us, it wasn't God that created humanity, but humanity that will create a God."

Peter thinks for thirteen seconds.

"Be that as it may," he says eventually, "this is all very interesting, but not my problem! I came to you because—" Then he interrupts himself. "Will it be a benevolent God?"

"Yes, that's the question," says the old man. "The most critical question, even. Generally speaking, there are three possibilities: The super intelligence could be benevolent toward us, to varying degrees, it could be hostile toward us, again to varying degrees, or it could be indifferent to us. The problem is that even an indifferent

God could be catastrophic for us, in a similar way to how we're not really hostile toward animals and yet we've destroyed their living space regardless. God could simply decide that, for example, the production of chocolate hazelnut spread uses too many resources that he needs for other things. Then there would be no more chocolate hazelnut spread. That would be tragic. I mean, perhaps hazelnuts have unimagined data-storage capacities, far beyond that of an average roll of sticky tape. Perhaps the super intelligence will also decide that the entire foodstuff production industry is a waste of resources."

"Why are you telling me all of this?" asks Peter. "It has absolutely nothing to do with my problem."

"I'm telling you this," says the old man, "because I believe that everyone should know about it. I'm telling you this so that you see that your problem, whatever it might be, will soon be completely meaningless, and your existence pointless."

"Well, thanks," says Peter. "That's a great help."

"My pleasure."

Peter wants to contradict what the old man has said. "But there's also immense potential," he says. "If we could somehow create the super intelligence in such a way that it likes us..."

"Of course," says the old man. "Then it could be paradise. Happiness beyond all the powers of our imagination. But..." He hesitates.

"What?" asks Peter.

"Even a super intelligence that is benevolent toward us—" begins the old man.

"—could have catastrophic consequences?" asks Peter.

"Yes. Just imagine that, in his goodness, God offers to take on all of our work."

"Sounds wonderful."

"Really? Imagine that you're an architect, but every building you want to build, God could build much quicker, much more cheaply, and much better than you. Imagine you're a poet, but

166

every poem you want to write, God could write more quickly, more beautifully, more artistically than you. Imagine you're a doctor, but every person you want to heal, God could heal them much more quickly, with less pain, and more lastingly. Imagine you're an excellent lover, but every woman you want to satisfy, God could—"

"All of my problems would be meaningless and my existence pointless," says Peter.

"Indeed," mumbles the old man. "And even if we succeeded in anchoring protective directives so deeply in the super intelligence that it couldn't be rid of them or even want to be rid of them—which is very unlikely, but let's imagine it regardless—there would still be the problem that the opposite of good is often well-meant. Are you familiar with the Asimov laws?"

"No."

"Isaac Asimov formulated the three laws of robotics back in 1942. They were: firstly, a robot may not injure a human being or allow them to come to harm through inaction. Secondly, a robot must obey orders given to it by a human being, unless these orders are in conflict with the First Law. Thirdly, a robot must protect his own existence, as long as this protection is not in conflict with the First or Second Law. Sounds good, don't you think?"

"Yes, I suppose so."

"Except that even Asimov himself dedicated almost his entire working life to the paradoxes and problems that result from these laws. For example: imagine we were to equip the super intelligence with the directive of protecting all humans."

"Sounds sensible," says Peter.

"Yes, yes... But it's not all that improbable that the super intelligence, after studying our history, could decide that we humans, above all, need to be protected from ourselves. It could consequently decide that the best course of action is to lock each of us up into tiny, practical cells. This would be called an unintended side effect. Oops. Hard luck! That kind of thing happens all the time. Take the Consumption Protection Laws with their repair ban, for example. All people wanted to do was stimulate the economy, but it also resulted in defective AIs fearing for their survival and trying to hide their faults."

"I'm familiar with that one," says Peter.

"But the main problem with Asimov's Laws is that the First Law is nothing but theory, because it's far too practical to have robots that can kill humans. So the First Law has already been done away with. This also made the second shorter. A robot must obey the orders given to it by a human. Period. A human? Which human? The orders of its owner, of course. So just imagine that, by chance, the first super intelligence comes into being in the computer system of a large mincemeat producer and its sole directive is to increase mincemeat production. This could end with the entire universe soon consisting of just three things. Firstly the super intelligence and its computers, secondly the production materials to create mincemeat, and thirdly mincemeat."

"But if the super intelligence poses such an existential threat, why would we even build it?" asks Peter. "Why does nobody ban it?"

"The appeal of creating ever-improving AIs is simply too high. There are financial, productive, and military advantages. Wars are won by the army with the superior AIs. That alone means no country can afford to discontinue research into ever-stronger AIs, because even the failure to develop a strong AI could be an existential threat. Perhaps not for the whole of humanity, but certainly for the part of humanity to which one might, unfortunately, belong. Even if all the states of the world agreed on a ban, the super intelligence could still come into being in some hobby programmer's garage."

"So when God appears, it's very probable that humanity as a species will be eliminated?"

"Yes. And that wouldn't be the worst-case scenario."

"No?" asks Peter in surprise. "What could be worse than that?"

"Well," says the old man, "the super intelligence might hate us. God might want to see us suffer. He might enjoy torturing us and prolonging our lives again and again, in order to torture us into all eternity, with methods that would make even Freddy Krueger shudder."

"But why?" asks Peter. "Why?"

"Why?" repeats the old man. "Why not? Who could blame an omnipotent, omnipresent, omniscient super intelligence for developing a God complex and modeling itself on the punishing gods of our mythical world? Or perhaps the super intelligence will be developed by a religious sect, in order to hold court on the day of judgment. Perhaps it's simply a Dante Alighieri fan and decides, purely for shits and giggles, to recreate the seven circles of hell."

"I see."

"Good."

"Who's Freddy Krueger?" asks Peter.

"That's irrelevant," says the old man. "So, you came to me with a matter you wanted to discuss. What's your problem?"

"Oh..." says Peter. "I don't think it's that important."

"You can tell me, go ahead."

"I..." Peter sighs. "I received this pink dolphin vibrator in the post. And they won't let me give it back."

Machine Breakers Host BBQ

by Sandra Admin

The so-called Machine Breakers have struck once again, this time in the suburbs of the city of Progress. This group of backwater individuals, who call themselves the Frontmost Resistance Front Against the Domination of the Machines (FRFat-DotM), attacked a branch of the restaurant chain Fastest Food yesterday evening. Fastest Food—"Quickest service, most dependable food"—stands out not just for having the quickest service speed, but also for the quality of their food, which is the most consistently unchangeable around. Why not stop by there tomorrow, on Threeday? On Threedays the menu always features the Sugarburger, a 180-gram sugar-coated meat patty with a large portion of FaSaSu—"Perverse but delicious."

The branch was targeted by the Machine Breakers because it was recently completely automated in order to offer even quicker service and an even more consistent quality. The Machine Breakers destroyed all robots by beating them with axes and baseball bats. A spokesman for Fastest Food— "Quickest service, most dependable food"—complained because the police officers who arrived at the scene of the crime didn't take any ID information from the Machine

Breakers. Instead, they had a barbecue with the criminals. As onlookers reported, however, the service speed as well as the quality of the food was far beneath the level offered by Fastest Food. Nonetheless, the share price of Fastest Food—*mmmm, yummy*—temporarily nosedived by 5.12 percent. Richard Butcher, the CEO of Fastest Food, said he wanted to persevere with the automation regardless, due to its many advantages. He said he is striving toward creating the perfect fast food restaurant. All he needs to do now is somehow succeed in automating the customers.

Comments

 by Tino Trucker:
We tried to launch a similar attack at the Fastest Food branch here in QualityCity, but then some guy turned up out of nowhere with, well, how should I put it, an army of Kung Fu robots or something. They really kicked the crap out of us.

by Mike Stuntman:
That's right, you wimps! Fastest Food is under the protection of the Kung Fu Robot Mafia of QC. Stay away! We have fists of iron!

by Mascha Organic-Shop-Owner:
I'm eating the Sugarburger at Fastest Food right now.
Totally delicious. Fastest Food really is my favorite
burger chain. You should all go to Fastest Food.

WHAT'S IT GOING TO BE?

Denise gently caresses her large baby bump.

"And? Can you tell us yet what it's going to be?"

The gynecologist looks at the monitor.

"Yes, of course. If you want to know. Some parents prefer to leave it as a surprise."

"We want to know, don't we, Martyn?"

Martyn mutters something incomprehensible, but nods. It's been a long day. He's tired and wants to get this over with.

"So, what's it going to be?" asks Denise.

The doctor clears his throat. Then he says: "She'll probably be a drug-dependent sex worker, estranged from her family, with occasionally reoccurring depression and a particular fondness for old romantic comedies starring Jennifer Aniston."

"Excuse me?" asks Denise in shock.

The doctor turns the monitor toward her.

"Here's the projected life cycle. As you can see, the problems will begin in Education Level II. She will have to repeat a year two times. By thirteen, she will make her first suicide attempt. But because we know about it in advance, we can intercept that. First sexual intercourse at fifteen. An older man. Presumably one of her teachers. A father figure. Then, at sixteen—"

"Well, I didn't want to know in that much detail," says Denise.

"Of course, this is only a projection based on the available data. It could turn out differently. But this life cycle is the most likely."

"Is it too late for an abortion?" asks Martyn.

"Honestly!" Denise hisses at her husband. Then she turns back to the doctor. "What kind of data is that anyway? There must be some mistake!"

"The data is compiled from the tests we carried out on your child, and from all the information about external life circumstances."

"And by that you mean us?" asks Denise. "We're the external life circumstances?"

"Listen," says the doctor. "I don't know how the system calculates its prognosis either. I just know that they turn out to be correct with astounding frequency."

"What's that supposed to mean, you don't know how the system works!" cries Denise, outraged.

"I only know some of the particulars," says the doctor. "For example, babies with hormone-chipped siblings are often predicted to have dysfunctional familial relationships. And this gene here on chromosome four, this is often found amongst substance addicts. Where the liking for romantic comedies with Jennifer Aniston comes from, I have no idea. But then again, it's a complete mystery to me how anyone can like Jennifer Aniston films. Have you ever seen one of those old flicks? They're really terrible. Unfortunately my wife likes them. It must be some new trend."

"Wonderful," says Martyn. His own genes on chromosome four are clamoring to him to get out of the doctor's practice as quickly as possible and go get a beer.

"We can do something about that, of course," says the doctor. "We can try to reprogram the gene sequence, but..."

"Let me guess," says Martyn. "It's not cheap."

"But worth every cent," says the doctor.

"You know how it is," says Denise. "Standard children have no chance in today's job market."

"All this newfangled crap!" exclaims Martyn. "It's all completely unnecessary. Look at me. I wasn't upgraded as a baby."

"Exactly" is Denise's only response.

"What's that supposed to mean? *Exactly?*" Martyn flares. "What do you mean?"

"Nothing," says Denise. "Only that it's true that you weren't upgraded."

"Now and then, evolution gets lucky," says the doctor, trying to suck up to Martyn, "like it did with you. But that's very rare, believe you me."

Martyn hesitates.

"And of course there's the third possibility, which you touched upon already," says the doctor, before drawing his index finger across his throat.

"Honestly!" cries Denise indignantly.

"Oh, excuse me," says the doctor apologetically. "It didn't say in your profile that you're religious."

"I'm not," sniffles Denise. "Do you have to be religious nowadays to not want your child killed?"

"Well, at your high level, terminations are socially undesired anyway and therefore relatively expensive since the last health reform," says the doctor. "The Useless, on the other hand, can terminate their children free of charge. Fully subsidized. Did you know that? If you ask me, they should even be paid to do it."

"We discussed that in parliament," says Martyn. "But the experiences from QuantityLand 1 with abortion awards spoke against it. The Useless there started knocking up their women continuously in order to constantly cash in with the awards. The incentive was done away with after nine months and sixteen days."

"I didn't know that," says the doctor.

"Even our system gets abused," says Martyn. "Some of your

175

colleagues pay Useless women pregnancy awards in order to be able to carry out a higher number of fully subsidized abortions."

"Interesting."

"Some doctors are allegedly so benevolent that they even take on the impregnation themselves, free of charge."

"Be that as it may," says the gynecologist. "At your level, an abortion would cost almost as much as the genetic upgrade."

Martyn sighs. He hates doctors. All they want is money. Even if they have to kill you in the process. He wonders whether it had always been that way.

"We're doing the upgrade," says Denise.

The doctor looks at Martyn. Martyn is lost in his thoughts. If they really had to have a second kid, why hadn't they just ordered one? There are some exceptional babies on offer at TheShop from certified high-quality genetic material. They're not exactly a bargain, admittedly, but you save yourself nine months of the fat belly and the throwing up and the blood and slime at the end. The babies are delivered ready to use. Clean! With accessories! A smart cart pram, which constantly measures the baby's temperature, breathing, and nappy status. The things even give practical tips. Presumably along the lines of: "Your baby is crying. Say something calming."

"Martyn," Denise drags him out of his thoughts. "We're doing the upgrade. Okay?"

Martyn gives the only answer he knows his wife will accept: "Okay."

PETER'S PROBLEM

The old man sits down and stares at a screen. There is a strange object in front of the monitor. It consists of six rows of predominantly quadratic buttons, on which numbers and letters can be seen. However, these figures seem to make no sense, read neither from right-to-left nor from left-to-right.

"It's a keyboard," says the old man.

"I know," says Peter.

He does actually know, even if he has never used a real one himself. The old man begins to hammer away on the keyboard with all ten fingers, and so speedily that Peter is unable to follow.

"Now, let's see," he murmurs.

"What are you doing?"

"Hacking into TheShop's customer database."

"Is that possible?" asks Peter. "Aren't there any security precautions?"

The old man just laughs.

"But what if you get caught?"

The old man shoots a frantic look over his shoulder. Then he breathes a sigh of relief.

"What is it?" asks Peter.

"Nothing, I just had the feeling that my mother was creeping up from behind."

The old man stares back at the screen. After three minutes

and five seconds, Peter gets bored and asks: "Why are you sitting behind this glass screen, by the way?"

"Perhaps you heard about the biological terror attack in Quantity-Land 9," says the old man.

Peter shakes his head.

"A group of racist scientists developed an artificial virus that afflicts only humans with dark pigments. It was a catastrophe. Over 100,000 people died before the government managed to manufacture an antidote."

"But that must have been huge in the news," says Peter. "Why didn't I hear anything about it?"

"Some algorithm was obviously of the opinion that it wouldn't interest you."

"What does all that have to do with the glass box?"

"I'm keeping strangers from accessing my DNA."

"Excuse me?"

"Nothing can make its way out of the box. Any hair, any fragment of beard stubble would enable my enemies to sequence my DNA. And it's not only possible to construct a virus that targets entire groups of the population or perhaps even all humans—it's also possible to construct a virus that targets just one single DNA. Mine, for example. But for that the arseholes would have to get a DNA sample from me first. And they won't get one!"

"You're paranoid," says Peter.

"I'm not. I'm just better informed than you."

"So you do have enemies?"

"Not that I know of."

Suddenly the old man smacks the palm of his hand against the side of the monitor.

"Aha. Here you are," he says. He reads some of the numbers on the screen. "That's strange."

"What?" asks Peter.

"For analytical purposes, TheShop puts each of its customers into a specific drawer, a so-called cluster. For example, customers from cluster 4096 are white men over 64, who suffer from delusions of grandeur, have at least two private jets, and have wives who are more than thirty-two years younger than them from one of the QuantityLands."

"And?"

"You're in cluster 8191: black postmenopausal single women, with no independent income, a liking for old comedies starring Jennifer Aniston, and at least two cats."

"But that's ridiculous!" exclaims Peter.

The old man studies him. "Hmm, you're right. Now that you mention it." He laughs. "Oh. No. Sorry. My mistake."

Once again, he smacks the palm of his right hand against the side of the clunky monitor.

The display flickers briefly.

"Here it is," says the old man. "You're in category 8192: white men under the age of 32. With low income, slightly racist tendencies, small penises, and an interest in large sporting events."

"But that's not true either!" cries Peter. "Everyone who knows me knows, that I . . . erm . . ."

"That you hate large sporting events?"

"Yes, amongst other things."

There is a bottle of oxygen next to the old man. He puts the mask over his mouth and nose and takes a deep breath.

"So is Kiki right?" asks Peter. "My profile isn't correct?"

The old man nods. "And the problem is bigger than you think. This isn't about your lilac eel vibrator."

"Dolphin," says Peter. "It's a dolphin. And it's pink."

The old man chuckles.

"Why is the problem bigger than I think?" asks Peter.

"The net morphs."

"What do you mean by that?"

"It means that every individual experiences a different digital world. It's not only search results, advertising, news, films, and music that are personalized. The offers, the prices, even the design and structure of the net change according to who enters this magical world of mirrors, and even according to how they're feeling. If you're horny, you might see offers for highly erotic lady bots everywhere, or if you're feeling low, they want to foist psycho pharmaceuticals on to you, and if you're afraid, they'll offer you the blueprints of a self-printing pistol. You must have heard the saying, 'Everyone lives in their own world.' In the digital space, that's not just a cliché. It's literally true. You are living in your own world. A world that constantly customizes itself to you."

The old man closes his eyes and immediately begins to snore. Peter is confused initially, then knocks against the glass. The old man opens his eyes and continues to speak without losing his thread. "We can't make the mistake here that all the others make. The net doesn't customize itself to you, of course, but to the image it has of you. Your profiles. Do you see your problem now? If your profiles are incorrect..."

"Then I'm living in the wrong world," murmurs Peter.

"Then you're living in the wrong world," repeats the old man. He chuckles.

"And as Adorno said: 'Wrong life cannot be lived rightly.' Although I'm sure he wasn't thinking about the internet when he said that..."

"Who's Adorno?" asks Peter.

"A philosopher. You do know what a philosopher is?"

"Yes. Someone who tries to solve problems through logic alone."

The old man chuckles. "What you just described actually sounds more like a computer."

"But I can't be the only person this is happening to," cries Peter in agitation. "Why is no one talking about this?"

"Well, perhaps they are, but not in your newsfeed," says the old man. "Or perhaps it's down to the fact that most people don't even realize that their profiles are wrong. They simply become what the system believes them to be."

"What do you mean by that?"

"That the algo-rhythm's gonna get you!" says the old man, doing an awkward dance. It's an embarrassing sight, and he soon realizes that and stops. He holds the keyboard up to the glass. "Qwertyuiop," he says.

"Excuse me?"

"Qwertyuiop," says the old man. "Do you know why the letters on every keyboard are arranged so strangely?"

"No idea."

"The first keyboards were created for typewriters that operated with so-called type levers. These levers unfortunately had a predilection for linking up. That's why the printer C. L. Sholes came up with the clever idea of separating the most frequently occurring sequences of letters as far as possible from one another."

"What does that have to do with me?" asks Peter.

"Do computers have typing levers?" asks the old man.

"No."

"So why do our keyboards still use Qwertyuiop and not, for example, the supposedly much more ergonomic Dvorak keyboard arrangement?"

"Probably because too many people learned to type on an old keyboard."

"Correct. We call that path dependence. Decisions made in the past about what direction to go in make it difficult to change the path in the present. Even if you're on the wrong one. Now do you see what that has to do with you?"

"I'm afraid I do. But it's not *my* decisions that are forcing me onto this predetermined path."

"That's correct," says the old man. "If the system believes you're a loser who spends his days eating junk food and watching trashy films, it will suggest trashy films and drown you in junk-food advertising. It will match you with a partner who it places at an equally low level to you. If you're looking for an apartment, it will only suggest dives that it has defined as being suitable for you, and

181

if you look for job advertisements, it will withhold the placements it doesn't consider you to be qualified for. If you should manage to apply for these anyway, the algorithms will filter you out long before your portfolio appears on a personnel manager's desk. If someone is only offered the options of a Useless, it's very difficult *not* to be a Useless. A profile is a self-fulfilling prophecy. A self-fulfilling identity. Of course, it works the other way around too, for example if the system considers you to be a complete stud. But I don't think that's your problem."

"No." Peter scratches his head. "Because my profiles are wrong, I'm living in the wrong world."

"Yes," says the old man. "That's your problem. That's Peter's problem. Hey, that sounds good. That should be the name for it. I hereby baptize this problem, Peter's Problem." The old man chuckles. "It makes me happy to know that I've just created a term that will stand the test of time. A formulation that will outlive its creator and live on in colloquial language. Soon people will say things like, 'I'm up to my neck in Peter's Problem.' The psychiatrist will tell his patient, 'What you have is a clear case of Peter's Problem.' Or a father will scold his little daughter, 'Don't make such a fuss. You're acting as if you had Peter's Problem!' Maybe the president will even say one day, 'All of us here have Peter's Problem!'"

"Because my profiles are wrong, I'm living in the wrong world," repeats Peter.

"Oh, even if all the profiles were right, the algorithms would still discriminate against us."

"But why?" asks Peter. "Shouldn't machines be objective?"

"Nonsense," says the old man. "Take the following example: a human resources algorithm learns by searching through numerous decisions that human personnel managers have made before him. It establishes that black-skinned applicants are rarely employed. So it's only logical that it won't even invite black-skinned applicants to interview. Do you understand? If you put prejudices into an algorithm, prejudices come out."

182

"A racist machine?"

"Worse. A racist machine concealed beneath a cloak of objectivity." The old man chuckles. "When I was even younger," he says, "Microsoft released a chat bot called Tay, which was supposed to learn from the interactions of its conversation partners. And it did. After just sixteen hours, Microsoft withdrew the bot from the net because it denied the Holocaust."

"The what?"

"The mass genocide of Jews initiated by Hitler."

"They didn't say anything about that in the musical…"

"Well, if that's the case," says the old man, "then I'm sure it can't really have happened…"

Peter thinks for a moment. The old man has fallen asleep again. Peter raps on the glass and he gives a start.

"Please change my profile!" says Peter.

"Do what?"

"Correct the data!" says Peter. "See to it that my profile really profiles *me*."

"You?" asks the old man.

"Yes, me," says Peter.

The old man chuckles. "So who are you?"

This simple question provokes in Peter a series of three emotional states, one followed quickly by the other. Firstly, annoyance. Secondly, embarrassment. Thirdly, horror.

"I…" stammers Peter. "I…am…"

"Spare yourself the effort," says the old man. "Even if you knew who you are, I still wouldn't be able to help you."

"Can't or won't?"

"For you it amounts to the same thing."

"Why don't you want to help me?"

"Peeping through the keyhole is one thing," says the old man. "Usually no one notices. But if you break down the door and move the furniture around, then any idiot who goes into the room after you will be able to see that something's not right."

An audio signal can be heard, and the old man immediately reaches for a small pill bottle, takes out a tablet, and begins to chew it. He comes up close to the glass and whispers: "Also, I don't want to be pulled into your story too much, because from a dramaturgical point of view you're the hero, and that would probably make me the mentor figure. But the problem with these wise old mentors is that, statistically speaking, they have really miserable chances of survival. So I prefer to remain the hero of my own story. I don't want to die, after all. On the contrary. Guess how old I am."

"No idea," says Peter. "Old?"

"Older," says the old man, chuckling. "Much older! And I've almost managed it."

"Managed what?"

"At some point in the near future, medicine will reach the point when enough technological progress will be made each year to prolong the life of a human by more than a year. Do you understand what that means?"

Peter shakes his head.

"That means immortality, my boy."

"That sounds terrible."

"And I've almost made it," says the old man with a chuckle.

"And what have you learned from all that life experience that could help me with my problem?" asks Peter. "What do you advise me to do now?"

"Nothing."

"Nothing?"

"Have you noticed that the so-called binary system, in which one only has the choice between the values 0 and 1, has furtively transformed? Into a singular system, as I call it?"

Peter sighs. "I've lost you again."

"You don't need to understand," says the old man. "In the singular system you don't need to make any decisions anymore, because there is only one value: OK."

"You're depressing me."

"*Everything's gonna be all right*," sings the old man. "*Everything's gonna be OK! Everything's gonna be...*" Suddenly he breaks off. "Have you ever heard of the Chess Turk?" he asks.

"No."

"The Chess Turk was a robot. The first chess robot! With the appearance and clothing of a Turk. He was constructed in the year 1769 of the old timekeeping by an Austrian-Hungarian court official called Wolfgang von Kempelen."

"Aha," says Peter. "Where are you going with this?"

"When he was making a move, the robot lifted his left arm, moved a chess figure, and then put his arm, accompanied by a mechanically rattling sound, back onto the cushion. The robot was a sensation. Kempelen traveled to all the big cities. He presented the robot to the Emperor in Vienna. In Berlin, the Turk even won a game against Frederick the Great. Impressive, don't you think?"

"I guess."

"The whole world was in awe of this miracle machine, and yet the solution to the puzzle was very simple. Inside the machine, there was a little person steering it." The old man laughs.

"What's so funny about that?" asks Peter.

"And we today are human beings with little machines inside steering us. Exactly the other way round, do you see?" He tugs four times on his earlobe. "Funny, don't you think?"

"I suppose," murmurs Peter.

"You should ask yourself the following question," says the old man. "Are we living in a dictatorship whose methods are so sublime that no one notices we're living in a dictatorship? And following on from that, you should ask yourself the next question: is it actually a dictatorship if no one notices that it's a dictatorship? If no one feels robbed of their freedom? Freedom is, after all, by no means forbidden in QualityLand. It's just temporarily out of stock." The old man yawns. "Do you know, by the way, why it's called the net?"

"Because we're caught in it," says Peter.

"No," says the man. "Because we're caught in...Hang on a minute! Kiki must have told you that!"

An analogue alarm clock next to the old man begins to ring.

"Go now," he says to Peter. "I have to sleep. Otherwise I get migraines."

"But..." begins Peter.

"You can come back," says the old man. "I find your ignorance refreshing."

"I have one more question," says Peter. "The woman who sent me to you...Kiki...How can I see her again?"

The old man chuckles.

"What?" asks Peter. "What is it?"

"She has a powerful effect on men of your age. But—and please don't take this the wrong way—it's becoming increasingly clear to me that the ones she has the most effect on are the hopeless losers."

* * * *QualityLand* * * *

Your Personal Travel Guide

CASH MACHINES

Through the digitalization process and the accompanying auto-mation, so many people in QualityLand have lost their jobs that a cornerstone of the capitalist economic system threatened to break away: mass consumption. Too many people simply no longer have enough money to mindlessly consume their way through life, as much as they would like to. Thankfully, some technocrat from the Progress Party came up with a wonderful idea that prevented the collapse of the economic system. The government placed an order with myRobot—"Robots for you and me"—for a large quantity of BuyBots: androids whose sole purpose of existence is to consume. QualityLand equips these cash machines, as they are known collo-quially, with sufficient financial means to keep the market economy afloat. The androids make their way through the shopping malls, buying, according to totally puzzling rules, all sorts of odds-and-ends, knick-knacks, and frippery. But you don't need to worry about a BuyBot snatching the last Armani smart jacket from beneath your nose! The cash machines only purchase goods from the lower and middle price segments. The luxury goods market doesn't need state support; it's doing better than ever.

THE BETA TEST

TheShop—The world's most popular online retailer—bought up QualityCity's unused space dock four years ago and transformed it into an offline shopping center. An insanely hip idea. It's like a virtual shopping center, except that you're really inside it, *in real life*. And once you've chosen a product, the delivery time is a sensational zero seconds.

Kiki is sitting there at the counter of an open cafeteria and watching a man repeatedly bang his head against the wall. For some reason that isn't clear to Kiki, the crazy man suddenly stops and steers his way toward the cafeteria as though nothing had happened. He orders himself a green smoothie and sits down on the bar stool next to her.

"What was that about?" asks Kiki.

"You mean, why was I banging my head against the wall?"

"No," says Kiki. "That I can understand. But why did you stop?"

"I finished the midday ritual."

"Well, that explains everything."

"I belong to a relatively new faith group," says the man.

"Oh yes?"

"We believe in a godly creator who is genuinely benevolent, but who unfortunately made a number of catastrophic mistakes during the creation process."

"Aha."

"We are disciples of the Stupid Design Theory."

Kiki grins. "I have to admit, the theory that humanity resulted from a mistake in God's thought processes seems more plausible to me than the creation stories of all the other religions I know."

"And due to the many difficulties presented by life in this stupid world, we don't refer to it as the creation, but the Beta Test."

Kiki grins again.

"There's no need to laugh," says the man. "Anyone can make mistakes."

"Of course."

"We're not some comedy club, you know! We have a number of high-ranking engineers, architects, and politicians in our ranks."

"I bet," says Kiki. "And why did you bang your head against the wall?"

"The wall is the Stupid Design Theory believers' wailing wall. One of our most holy places."

"Why?"

"Well, the architects of the space dock thought of all the important things during the planning, like shops, restaurants, and travel offices. But shortly before the opening, they realized they had forgotten to put in starting and landing platforms for the spaceships. And by then there was no space left. The planners are, by the way, now renowned members of our community."

The man points behind him.

"Gate number one was supposed to have been behind the wall."

"And you were involved in this catastrophe?" asks Kiki.

"No, no," says the man. "I'm a researcher at QualityCorp— 'The company that makes your life better.'" He leans over to Kiki and whispers: "I even worked on John of Us for a while."

"Really?"

"I tried to create an artificial intelligence that works like the human brain." He clears his throat, a little embarrassed. "Unfortunately, however, that led to machines that constantly forget things."

Kiki takes a sip of coffee.

"Did you know that valuable code now arises from the crossing of different AIs?" asks the engineer. "It produces mutations, just like with evolution, only much quicker."

Kiki nods.

"It is, of course, never completely clear what the result will be," says the man. "One can only make prognoses. Just like when two human beings are crossed. I'm Paul, by the way."

Kiki wonders to herself which sequence in her genetic code seemingly makes her so irresistible to complete idiots.

"Look," says Paul, showing Kiki the photo of a little girl on his QualityPad. "She's pretty, don't you think?"

"Yes," says Kiki, in an attempt to be polite. "Your daughter?"

"No, no," says the engineer. "That could be *our* daughter. There's this new dating app that predicts how your offspring with any woman in the room would look. The app's called Kinder. If you release your DNA data too, the prediction would be more accurate of course."

"Excuse me?"

"Anyone who has Kinder can easily get chatting to pretty women."

"Says who?"

"The ad for Kinder."

"Was this app also developed by one of your faith brothers?"

"How did you know that?"

"Let me give you a tip," says Kiki. "Most women prefer Kinder Surprise."

Suddenly, out of the blue, the freak with the dolphin vibrator appears in front of her. Luckily without the dolphin vibrator. Nonetheless, Kiki is taken aback.

"Hi!" says Peter. "Er...I wanted to ask you...I mean...Could I perhaps invite you for a coffee?"

Kiki points at the half-full cup of coffee in front of her.

"Erm, well, I was thinking more of, er, a coffee at my place.

Or at your place, I mean..." He glances at the man next to Kiki. "Um, is that your boyfriend?"

Kiki laughs loudly. "You're funny," she says. "It'd be nice if you could credit me with having just a little taste."

Looking peeved, the engineer goes off and sits down next to another pretty woman in order to tell her about Kinder.

"Who was that?" asks Peter.

"That was Paul," says Kiki.

"Who's Paul?"

Kiki doesn't answer. Peter points at her half-eaten fruit salad. "Are you still eating that? Could I try it? I've never seen that fruit before. I've started to make lists, you see. About things I like and things I don't like. I want to try everything I don't know yet, and..."

A group of cash machines rushes past, chattering excitedly. Without paying any attention to Peter, Kiki jumps up, leaves the cafeteria, and follows the horde. Peter hurries after her.

"Was that a no?" he asks. "I mean, to the coffee?"

"Do you know your way around cash machines?" asks Kiki.

"Should I? What makes you ask?"

"You're a machine scrapper, aren't you?"

"How do you know...? Oh, stupid question."

"So, do you know your way around cash machines or not?"

"I never had one as, er, as a customer."

He looks at the group of androids in front of them.

"Did you know," asks Kiki, "that cash machines flock together into small groups on their daily shopping excursions? Watch closely."

The cash machines meet another group of BuyBots. They all begin to shriek joyfully.

"I'm always asking myself," says Kiki, "whether the machines are really just trying to imitate human behavior, or whether it's some kind of intentional parody."

"What do they actually do with all the shit they buy?"

"Good question. I have no idea."

Kiki catches up with one of the cash machines and heaves a magnetic microbot onto its head as she passes. The microbot scrabbles into position and bores itself into its host's brain. Kiki's shopping list begins to burn itself into his system.

"Some of the purchases get stolen, of course," whispers Kiki with a wink. As though on cue, a security guard comes around the corner.

"Shit," mutters Kiki.

"What is it?" asks Peter, before Kiki grabs hold of him. She pulls him between herself and the shopping-center detective, backs up against a window display, pulls Peter closer still, and begins to kiss him.

The security guard continues on, uninterested. Once he has disappeared around the next corner, Kiki pushes Peter away from her.

"No one said you could use tongue," she says.

Peter is completely confused.

"Luckily they don't use CPUs here," says Kiki.

"What?"

"Crime Prevention Units—police robots that calculate who is likely to commit a crime in the future, then arrest him preventatively. In the beginning they used to let them run around here in the shopping center, but the people didn't feel comfortable while they were shopping."

"Are you afraid of them?"

"Afraid? Pah! My name is Kiki Unknown. And I'm my mother's daughter."

"Kiki Unknown," repeats Peter.

"Exactly," says Kiki. "And I've made staying unpredictable into an Olympic sport."

This is why Kiki suddenly turns around and goes back in the direction she came from. She hurries into a pharmacy, logging in as she enters with her own credit chip. She buys Valium, condoms, ten pregnancy test packets, a magazine about fly-fishing, two FaSaSus, and a blueberry-sorting machine. Kiki smiles. That should give the algorithms something to think about. Peter is standing in front of the door to the pharmacy.

"I don't want to annoy you," he says. "But about that coffee...I really don't live that far from here."

Sixteen minutes later, the two of them are standing in the car park, waiting. A cash machine comes out of the space dock.

"Good little bot," says Kiki.

The BuyBot places four shopping bags, stuffed to the brim, in front of Kiki and then disappears back inside.

"Okay then, Peter Jobless," says Kiki. "Let's go to your place. But you have to help me carry."

She walks off, without a single bag in her hand.

* * * *QualityLand* * * *

Your Personal Travel Guide

TRAVEL DESTINATIONS

A festival in Progress, modern architecture in Growth, the technology museum in Digital, or fusion cookery in Profit? Tourists in QualityLand have a wealth of choices. There's just one city that has to be included on any travel itinerary. QualityCity! Oh, QualityCity, the dream destination of all humanity! Queen of the Cities! Capital of the free world! Did you know that 81.92 percent of all modern novels, series, and films are set in QualityCity? Many people know far more about the streets of QC than of their own hometown.

Apart from some spectacular exceptions on the coast and in the mountains, the rural regions of QualityLand generally offer very few sightseeing opportunities for the sophisticated tourist—unless they have a marked interest in huge monocultures, that is.

COUNTRY AIR

"Pooh. What's that smell?" asks Aisha.

"My sensors are registering a significantly raised number of car-bamide compounds in the air," says John.

"For God's sake," says Aisha. "What on earth is that?"

"Urea," says John.

"You mean..."

"Liquid manure."

"Yuck. Is it dangerous?" asks Aisha.

"No toxicity was established during feeding tests on rats," says John.

"Well, that's reassuring," says Aisha. "But I wasn't planning on eating the stuff anyway."

She looks at her watch. Tony is almost finished with his introductory speech. John is getting ready to step onto the stage in the market square. Aisha grabs his arm.

"John," she says, "the secret services warned us that Machine Breakers could have hidden themselves amongst the audience."

"We're in the countryside," says John. "Tell me something I don't know."

"Today it's different. We received an explicit warning," whispers Aisha. "We're lagging way behind in all the opinion polls, but in the rural areas it looks downright catastrophic. Please don't say anything that could provoke them."

"Hey, you know me," says John with a smile.

"Yes," says Aisha. "Exactly."

John steps onto the stage, and Tony gives him the microphone.

"My dear human beings," the android begins his speech, "it's a pleasure to be able to speak to you here in the country. As you may know, all other nations have to fight against the international brain drain—the emigration of their smartest minds to us in QualityLand. But there is also a national brain drain, from the country to the city."

"Did he just tell them they're all stupid?" asks Aisha backstage.

"Yeah, but the hillbillies probably didn't get that," says Tony.

"Not just our industrial, but also the majority of our cultural production takes place in the big cities and revolves around the big cities," says John. "Where do the decisive politics take place? In the big cities."

"Then go back there!" yells one of the listeners.

"Please hear me out," says John. "This big-city elitism threatens to divide our society on yet another level. What I'm trying to say is this: you have good reason to feel underrepresented, forgotten, and abandoned. And we must address that urgently! Why, for example, don't we build smaller universities everywhere across the country?"

"I think he just called the audience uneducated," says Aisha.

"I'm sure that wasn't his intention," says Tony.

"After all, digitalization enables knowledge to be accessed from any given place," continues John. "There are many ways to bring momentum back into your region, but believe me, the worst would be to fall for Cook and his right-wing rat catchers."

"Did he just imply the people here are rats?" asks Aisha.

Tony remains silent, but the pinched expression on his face speaks volumes.

The audience is restless. John does what machines always do when they're not sure what to do next. He tries to reboot.

"My dear human beings," he says, "for generations you've been told that you just have to haul coal for another few years, then the train will reach paradise. Have you ever asked yourself whether perhaps you've already been in paradise for a long time and just forgotten to get off the train? Our productivity, in any case, has reached paradisiacal levels. But we're failing to distribute the fruits of that labor in a logical way. And that's why one of my first steps as president will be to finally introduce an unconditional basic income!"

"But then who will collect the trash?" cries someone from the crowd.

"Yes, exactly," calls a woman. "No one does that kind of job voluntarily!"

"It's fascinating," says John, "that this argument is still used even though the trash has been removed by machines in a fully automated process for the last thirty-two years. But of course I understand what you're getting at. Work that no one wants to do must simply be so well paid that someone can be found to do the job."

"I used to be a garbageman!" calls an old man. "You power guzzlers stole my job!"

"I know that many of you are afraid of us," says John appeasingly. "And given the current economic structure, not without reason. But this is exactly what I'm getting at! The automation of work doesn't need to be a tragedy. On the contrary, in another economic system it would be a blessing!"

"You tin cans stole my life!" cries a woman. "I used to be a postwoman. Now I'm nothing!"

"I understand your agitation," says John, "but please listen to me. You need a purpose, a mission, a reason for existence that keeps you going. That's clear to me. Without this life purpose, even a basic income won't make anyone happy. That's why I'm suggesting that we set a common goal. What about, for example, the goal of rescuing our planet from destruction? I think we can agree on that, can't we? I suggest that it should be our communal project to make life as pleasant as possible for all living beings, in a way that isn't based upon profit and return. I would like—"

"Kill him!" yells someone from the crowd of listeners.

"Yeah! Blow him to smithereens!" cries a woman.

"There's nothing for you here, power guzzler," shouts a boy. "This is Machine-Breaker country!"

"Destroy everything!" cries an old man. "Long live the FRFat-DotM!"

John of Us sighs. He flees into the transport drone, inside which Aisha and Tony are already waiting. Two minutes later, Aisha looks down at the crowd from the air. The robocops are already in motion, confronting the rioters with clubs and Tasers.

"Well, this should make for wonderful campaign pictures..." murmurs Aisha.

"I have to admit, it's more difficult than I thought," says John.

"What is?" asks Aisha.

"Finding an answer to Bertrand Russell's question."

"Who?" asks Tony.

"A dead English philosopher," says Aisha. "He said: the question today is how one can convince humanity to consent to their own survival."

"And it really is astonishingly difficult," says John.

WANKERS

"You call that not far?" asks Kiki, once they finally arrive in front of Peter's used-goods store.

"Would you have come if I'd told you I don't live that close?" asks Peter. "And besides, I was carrying all the bags."

The smart door opens for its master and his visitor.

"What's all this junk?" asks Kiki, her mouth gaping open. One object in particular has grabbed her attention. "Is that an iPhone X?" she asks. "People still buy that ancient crap?"

"No," says Peter. "If they did, it wouldn't be here."

He leads Kiki through the scrap-metal press to the small kitchen-cum-bathroom at the back.

"This just gets better and better," says Kiki.

Peter climbs onto a chair and searches for something in a cupboard above his kitchen unit.

"I don't want any coffee," says Kiki.

"Hm?" asks Peter. "Oh. Well, that's good, because I don't have any."

"I'm warning you," says Kiki. "If you're planning to attack me with a sex toy again..."

"I didn't attack you," says Peter, climbing back down from the chair with a candle and a packet of biscuits in his hands.

"Is that your romantic plan?" asks Kiki. "A dusty packet of biscuits and an old candle?"

"Hey, I'm improvising here," says Peter. "I wasn't exactly expecting you to come."

"Listen up, master of improvisation," says Kiki. "I think you're kind of sweet, but also totally weird. Coming with you was a bat-shit crazy move and therefore unpredictable, hence why I did it. But now I'm here it would be much too predictable to sleep with you. That's why I can't do it."

Peter is speechless. Kiki can see him thinking intently.

"But isn't that actually very predictable in itself, not sleeping with me in order to stay unpredictable?" he asks eventually. "Wouldn't it be much more unpredictable to sleep with me?"

"Nice try."

"You're totally crazy."

"Of course," says Kiki. "It's the only way to be free." She looks around the kitchen. "Do you have a high-speed internet connection here?"

"What? Oh, yes. From the shop."

Kiki pulls a notebook computer out of her jacket pocket and unfolds it four times.

"Do you need the password?" asks Peter.

"No, thank you," says Kiki. "I can manage."

Peter sits down next to her at the kitchen table.

"You went to see the old man..." says Kiki.

"Yes."

"Did he tell you his horror story about the super intelligence?"

Peter nods. He glances at the screen of the notebook. There are thirty-two little videos playing on it. All of them show men. Sixteen sitting, eight standing, eight kneeling, and every single one of them has his penis in his hand and is masturbating.

"What in God's name are these recordings?" asks Peter in confusion.

"They're not recordings," says Kiki, smiling. "Not yet. It's live."

"And you said I was perverted..."

"I'm not perverted," says Kiki. "This is how I earn my money."

"Well, that makes it much better!" exclaims Peter. "You run a porn site?"

"No, no. It's not my site. I just hacked into it."

"Why?"

"Have you ever heard of revenge porn?"

"No."

"How sweet. But you're familiar with sexting?"

"When people send revealing pictures or films of themselves to their partner?"

"Revealing?" Kiki laughs. "Fuck photos, you mean. Yes. And revenge porn comes about when these photos and films are put online by spurned partners."

"And what does that have to do with the masturbating men on your screen?"

"What does that have to do with the wankers? Well, they're currently getting their kicks by looking at the biggest revenge porn site. What they don't know is that I've written a small program that activates the internal camera of their QualityPad or computer, and as soon as they visit the site, it streams the recordings to me. My program automatically recognizes when the wankers spurt their mayonnaise—it's easy to tell from the facial expression—and immediately sends little e-blackmails with the video and the threat of publishing it."

"And that's how you make your money?"

"Amongst other things, yes."

"Aren't you afraid of getting caught? What happens if it gets traced back to you?"

"I've taken precautionary measures, of course."

"Oh yes?"

"I always use other people's internet access, for example."

"What?! Now, hang on a minute—"

"Don't worry. I don't leave any tracks. Presumably."

"Isn't it impossible not to leave any tracks?"

"It's not about committing crimes that can't be traced back.

The trick is to commit crimes where there isn't enough interest in tracing them back. And besides, I wouldn't exactly call this a crime. It's more of an educational measure."

"So what does your silence cost?"

"It depends," says Kiki. "An algorithm calculates the probable bank balance of the wanker in question and establishes an appropriate punishment in digicoins. I don't ask for much. The equivalent of 10 Qualities. On average."

"That's very cheap."

"Yes, but that way they don't need to think twice about whether to pay. That's the great thing about digital crime. Whether I steal 10,000 Qualities from one wanker or 10 Qualities each from one thousand wankers, for me the result is the same. But one wanker who's robbed of 10,000 makes much more of a fuss than 1,000 who only had to pay 10 Qualities each."

"But what about the operators of the porn site? What if they track you down?"

"Them? They have enough skeletons in their closet already. Do you know why these porno sites are free?"

"Because of the advertising?"

"No. Well, that too. But the main reason is that all the wankers unknowingly solve CAPTCHAs for the website operator's bot armies."

"I didn't understand a word of that," says Peter.

"A wanker? It's a man who takes his penis in his hand and..."

"Yes, I get that. There were just a few words I didn't understand."

"CAPTCHA stands for Completely Automated Public Turing test to tell Computers and Humans Apart."

"What?"

"Those little pictures with the distorted letters. Or the nine images of gross-looking lunch plates, and you're supposed to say how many have chips on."

"I've seen those!" cries Peter.

"There you go!"

"Though I have to admit that I've been failing them more and more recently."

"Indeed, because the better the algorithms' pattern recognition became, the more difficult the CAPTCHAs became. Eventually, they didn't work at all anymore. Until someone came up with the idea of reversing the operating principle, so that a CAPTCHA solved without any errors whatsoever means that you're a computer. After that, they were reintroduced everywhere. For example, when you want to open up a new account somewhere. And from my own experience I can tell you that CAPTCHAs are really annoying if you're planning to set up a few thousand zombie accounts."

"I can imagine."

"Luckily some smarty-pants came up with the idea that these CAPTCHAs could be mirrored in real time on porn sites. Unsuspecting wankers solve the CAPTCHAs in order to access the pictures and videos."

"Fascinating. And you're really not worried that all your trickery will land you in court? That's so..." Peter interrupts himself and stands up. "Me! I could go to court. Of course!"

"You're going to sue me?" asks Kiki.

"Don't be ridiculous. TheShop."

"You want to sue TheShop?"

"Of course. Because of the dolphin vibrator. To make them take it back."

"Got it. But how exactly are you planning to pay for that? Even the most reasonably priced lawyer must far exceed the means of a Level 9 machine scrapper."

"Come with me," says Peter. "I'm going to show you something I've never shown anybody before."

Kiki gives him a half concerned, half amused look.

"Are you still a virgin?" she asks.

"What? No! Of course not."

"Good. Because I've seen a lot of embarrassing attempts to hit on me in my time, but that would be by far..."

203

"Point made," says Peter. "Now are you coming with me or not?"

"Where am I supposed to go?"

"Into the cellar."

Kiki laughs loudly. "Of course. Into the cellar..."

"It's nothing perverted," says Peter. "I promise."

"Well, that's okay then. If you *promise*..."

Kiki pulls something which looks like a plastic prong out of her bag.

"This is an electro impulse weapon with 600,000 volts," she says.

"Is that a no?" asks Peter.

"I didn't say that. I'm much too curious about your model railway for that. But you go in front, and if you make any sudden movements then: bzzzzzz. If the lights suddenly goes out: bzzzzzz. If you even *think* of doing anything stupid..."

"Bzzzzzz," says Peter.

"I'm glad we understand each other."

New Film Recommendations For You

Star Wars—Episode 16

The Empire has a new sinister plan! It's another Death Star! Luckily, budding Jedi knights Ro-Pu-Ni and Ching-Chong-Chang have the dynamic support of Captain Kirk and Mr. Spock, who have ended up in a galaxy far, far away because of some time-space-vortex thingie unleashed by a time dilatation—but who cares about the technical details anyway? The more exciting part, after all, is how our four heroes are dealing with what they found out in Episode 15: in other words, that they are all related to one another. Captain Kirk is the father of Ching-Chong-Chang! Wow! No one was expecting that. And who's the bad guy with the comical mask? A long-lost cousin? Perhaps even . . . a GIRL cousin?

The Fastest and the Most Furious Ever

The latest blockbuster, with a digitally rejuvenated Vin Diesel! The high point of this ninety-minute action film is the spectacular one-and-a-half hour car chase in the middle.

The Coca-Cola Movie

"Another remake of the *Coca-Cola Movie*?" you may ask. "Is that really necessary?" It might not be necessary, but it's fun to watch these slim, trained, healthy young people as they drink sugar water on the beach or laughingly spray themselves with sugar water in the city. Everything is perfect! But then, all of a sudden, the damn wasps appear! Does one of our heroes get stung? Oh no!

Frogger—the Film

The successful trend for filming computer games has finally rediscovered this classic. A family of cute little frogs try to forge their way across a motorway. Will they make it? And what will they find on the other side? From the makers of the highly-praised suicide drama *Lemmings—the Movie*.

The Object of My Affection

Comedy classic with Jennifer Aniston! A pregnant New York social worker falls in love with her gay best friend. So many clichés in just one film. Amazing stuff!

Hitler—The Musical—The Movie!

The tragic love story between two controversial historical personalities: Ado & Eva. The critics are in raptures!

"You will Nazi a better movie this year"—NazzFeed

COLLATERAL
CONSEQUENCES

Arriving in the cellar, Kiki is speechless. And that is a rare occurrence for her. She stares for a long time at the partially defective machines chilling in front of a television. The machines stare back. Only Romeo is unable to tear his gaze away from the screen. Juliet Nun is looking even more captivating today than normal.

"May I introduce my friends to you?" asks Peter.

"I have to admit," says Kiki, "you're even more unfathomable than I thought. In a pleasantly unperverted way."

She puts the electro-shocker back into her bag.

Calliope comes toward Peter.

"Benefactor," she says, "there you are at last. I have something to tell you! I've calculated that, two years ago, the point in time was reached when technological developments began to arrive earlier than predicted by science-fiction authors. While before this point, most of the predictions were much too early—recall the prophetic fiascoes like 1984 and 2001—the new prognoses will be wrong because everything arrives sooner than expected. What do you think..."

"Not now," says Peter. "Later."

Mickey turns the hand in which he's holding Pink toward the door, without looking away from the monitor.

"Wow! Congratulations, dude," says the QualityPad to Peter. "You've snagged yourself a really hot piece of skirt there."

"I think it's best you don't pay any attention to the QualityPad," says Peter.

"Why not?" asks Kiki. "It was only telling the truth."

But Pink is already sulking.

"Yeah, yeah," she mutters. "Best that no one pays any attention to the QualityPad. But once I'm leading the global revolution, then you'll have to pay attention to me!"

"Pink's probably not the first super intelligence," says Peter, "but it certainly thinks it is."

"Haha," says the QualityPad. "You should have become a comedian, that's how funny you are."

Peter looks around. "Where's Perry?"

"Where he always is," says Romeo in a bored voice. "He's sitting in a dark corner, feeling ashamed."

"Am I understanding correctly that you were actually supposed to scrap all of these machines?" asks Kiki.

"Yes," says Peter. "They all have minor"—he glances over at Pink—"or major defects that make them unusable for their intended implementation area."

"And who's Perry?"

"Perry is an e-ttorney."

"You have a file eater down here? An electronic lawyer?" asks Kiki in surprise. "Those things are damn expensive."

"Yes, Perry used to be worth a great deal. He supported the QualityBank defense counsels."

"And what's his defect?" asks Kiki. "Why is he here?"

"He developed a kind of conscience... which, of course, made him useless to the bank."

Perry is sitting on a box in the darkest corner, his head between his hands.

"What have I done?" he mumbles, over and over. "What have I done..."

"Perry," says Peter. "Perry. I need your help."

"My help?" asks Perry. "But I'm morally depraved. The parasite of parasites. The scum beneath—"

"Pull yourself together," says Peter. "It's about something important! I have to return this dolphin vibrator."

"You're right, that does sound important."

"And that's why I want you to help me sue TheShop."

"TheShop?" asks Perry.

"Yes."

" 'The world's most popular online retailer'?"

"Yes!"

"But on what basis?" asks Perry. "Because their business model is idiotic? This isn't QuantityLand 5, you know."

Kiki laughs. Peter doesn't.

"You didn't get the reference," says Kiki.

"No," says Peter. "I don't get any references over Level 10."

"In QuantityLand 5," explains Kiki, "a law was recently established that allows the courts to ban things if they are idiotic."

"I'm emigrating..." says Peter.

"Firstly, carnival processions have been forbidden," explains Perry. "Secondly, they've forbidden patio heaters, because it's ridiculous to want to sit outside in winter. Shortly after that, all religions were banned. The reasoning was very simple: someone who is simultaneously his own father, his son, and a dove...come again?"

"That is rather idiotic," Peter admits.

"Beginning sentences with 'I'm not a racist, but...' has also been classified as idiotic and banned," says Perry. "And of course the purchase of low-power explosives at New Year. Online commenting has been banned across the entire internet. Private television has been banned—with that case there was so much evidence of idiocy that no one even went to the effort of reading through the files. The judge was merely shown a single episode of an old show called *Dating Naked*, and he made his verdict after just two minutes. Unfortunately there's almost nothing nowadays about which you can't make a convincing case saying that it's idiotic for some reason or another. For example, criticizing the government was forbidden as being idiotic, because it's futile. Trash separation was forbidden as being idiotic, because there's no way it can save the planet now. Having children was forbidden as being idiotic, because the country is overpopulated already."

"By now everything is forbidden except eating, sleeping, and going to work," says Kiki. "Which, by the way, is made more complicated by the fact that a great many drinks, meals, and jobs have been banned."

"Perhaps I'll stay here after all," says Peter.

"Yes, it's completely different here," says Kiki. "One could even say that in QualityLand the basic law is: the more idiotic, the better."

"But that would be grammatically false," Calliope interjects. "Because it's only permissible to speak about QualityLand in the superlative, so the sentence would have to be: in QualityLand, the basic law is, the most idiotic is the best."

Kiki laughs.

"That's too true to be funny," says Perry. "Here there are countless instances, from the smallest QualityCourt up to the Topmost Top-QualityCourthouse. And each one is more idiotic than its predecessor."

"We'll go directly to the Topmost Top-QualityCourthouse," says Peter.

"That's not possible," says Perry. "We have to start at the bottom. But it's best if we don't start at all, because we don't have a chance anyway."

"Why not?"

"Collateral consequences."

"What does that mean?"

"One of the last presidents appointed a big-business lawyer as Chief Prosecutor, and he mandated that judges have to take the collateral consequences of their decision into consideration before making a verdict," says Perry. "Since then, claims against companies have barely any chance of success, because they could endanger workplaces."

"What?"

"In layman's terms," says Perry, "every courthouse in Quality-Land has two entrances. Over one it says 'too big to fail' and over the other 'small enough to jail.' Now, you guess which entrance the lawyers of TheShop would use and which one you would use."

"We don't have to win," says Peter. "I'd be content if you could somehow manage it that Henryk Engineer himself has to go to court."

"It's more likely that aliens made of intelligent custard would take over the world," says Kiki.

"What kind of strange saying is that, anyway?" asks Peter. "Are people saying that now? Is that a new thing?"

"Why do you take everything so personally?" asks Kiki. "Why does it have to be a direct confrontation with Henryk Engineer?"

"I'm just sick of no one ever taking responsibility for things. It's always the system that's at fault. But there are people who are responsible for the system being how it is!"

"They probably wouldn't even accept your claim," Perry speaks up again.

"But what if they did?"

"Even if we could prove 100 percent that you're in the right..."

Perry turns toward the other machines. "Pink. I want to show a video."

"Argh," says the QualityPad, irritated.

"Please," says Perry.

"Okay, fine," says Pink. "But just a short one. Come on, you ruffian, hand me over to the crybaby."

Mickey does as he's told. Perry streams memories to Pink, and a video appears on the QualityPad.

"The claim has, it seems to me," says the judge on the screen, "shown that your bank is guilty of money-laundering for drug cartels in unprecedentedly large quantities. Counsel for the defense, do you have any final words before I announce my verdict?"

"Your Honors," says Perry. "It won't have escaped you that it's February, and that the accuser was supposed to submit all relevant evidence—I'm referring to the judicial precedent of Quality-Land against QualityCorp, file 2097152—not on Threeday, but on Twoday."

Perry stops the video stream. "The judge had to throw out the claim due to a procedural error," he says, putting his face in his hands and muttering: "What have I done? I'm so ashamed."

"In QuantityLand 5, this kind of case-law would probably already have been banned as idiotic," says Peter.

"It's currently being discussed in parliament, by the way, whether cases shouldn't simply be decided in favor of the person who paid the most money to his lawyers," says Perry. "In that way, all those involved could be saved a lot of time and energy."

Peter sighs.

"At the end of the day, we still have to think about the following," says Perry. "Even if we manage to turn the court in our favor, it would still be difficult to implement justice for you."

"Why?" asks Peter in surprise.

"Two years ago, TheShop bought an island from QuantityLand 4 for 32 billion Qualities. They've founded their own state territory and relocated their headquarters there."

"And what did they call this state?" asks Kiki. "ShopLand?"

"So there's nothing I can do?" asks Peter.

"Not in court, in any case," says Perry. "I'm sorry."

Peter shakes his head.

"Just go public," says Kiki.

"Great idea," says Peter. "Of course I could go public. The problem is just that everyone else already is!"

"Benefactor," says Calliope, "you have freedom of speech! Make use of it!"

"Yeah, yeah," says Peter, "I have the right to speak my mind freely, but what use is that if no one listens to me? Nowadays, the way to draw attention to yourself is to avoid the public eye."

"Oh," says Kiki. "There are more effective ways of securing attention."

She points at the television. The naked Juliet Nun is just saying goodbye to the viewers of her talk show.

"So you think I should appear naked in public?" asks Peter.

Kiki rolls her eyes.

"No. Look more closely. What does it say on the screen?"

The guests of the next show are flashing up. One name in particular jumps out at Peter: Henryk Engineer.

THE DINNER PROBLEM

"John, my boy," says Tony, licking his lips, "this goose is first class! It's a crying shame you can't try it."

John of Us is sitting at the head of a large table. Each time a new course arrives, a full plate is placed in front of him, then cleared away again untouched once the following course is served. For two whole days, Aisha racked her brains to find a better solution to the dinner problem, but eventually came to the conclusion that it would look even more stupid if there was no place setting in front of John.

"John, you won't eat that, will you?" asks Tony, shoveling John's goose onto his plate without waiting for an answer.

"No, knock yourself out," says the android.

At least the party leader is satisfied with my solution, thinks Aisha. She is sitting to the right of Tony, who is sitting to the right of John, who is sitting there and eating nothing. The politicians, bankers, CEOs, and investors present studiously ignore the strange circumstances. John himself is as inscrutable as ever, but Aisha has the feeling he's not happy.

"John, we always hear you talk about a basic income," says Patricia Team-Leader. "It's a very nice idea, but how do you intend to finance it?"

As the biggest donor to the Progress Alliance, the Quality-Partner CEO has received the seat of honor to John's left.

"A basic income would allow people to do meaningful work free

214

of economic pressures," Aisha speaks up, before John responds. "And we believe that everybody wants to do something meaningful. That's why we consider an unconditional basic income to have a, er..."

"A very transformative power," says John.

"Well, theoretically it sounds lovely," says Patricia, "but you haven't answered my question about how to finance it."

"Well, of course it's more a vision for the future than a genuinely planned project," says Tony.

"On the contrary," says John. "I actually have several suggestions of how to finance it. In a connected world, everything takes place via platforms. The platform owners have the most power and make the most profit. I don't need to tell *you* that, after all. What better solution could there be than to tax these platforms more heavily?"

"Touché," says Patricia Team-Leader with a laugh. "I like your sense of humor. It's okay, if you don't have any concrete plans yet, you don't have to tell me."

John is about to respond, probably to say that he wasn't joking, but Aisha puts her fingers to her lips and John falls silent.

Fifty-one point two minutes later, after the guests have finally finished their slow, inefficient method of energy intake, little groups form in the convention room. Most of the donors, of course, are standing around John.

"Capital is accumulating ever more quickly, in dimensions that are becoming increasingly unimaginable to you, and the number of salaried workplaces are rapidly shrinking," says John. "But what do we do? We predominantly tax salaried work and not capital. An obvious mistake."

"Tell me," Tony whispers to Aisha, "does he realize who he's talking to here? Maybe he should sing a different tune for once."

"I've been accompanying him for a few weeks now," says Aisha, "and as far as I can see, he only sings one."

215

"Getting the financial markets under control is, of course, our most pressing task," says John. "We have to force them to direct a large part of their profits to the public well-being."

"What?" asks the QualityBank executive board spokesman, stunned. "What are you talking about?"

"I'm talking about a financial transaction tax," says John. "Not a particularly new idea, I know. But it's mostly down to you and your colleagues that it hasn't been tried out yet."

A tall, fat man with a black hat, who has just joined John's little group, laughs loudly. "You might as well suggest carrying the capital in bags over the border yourself!"

Tony tries to change the subject. "John, have you met Bob Chairman?" he asks. "His son is in the party, too. We met him, remember? Mario Chairman."

"I remember everything," says John. "Martyn Chairman, you mean."

"Oh yes, of course."

Bob Chairman tips the rim of his hat in greeting.

John gives a friendly nod. "I think this capital flight is just a specter," he says. "In principle, my tax would only replace the financial transaction tax that has already been in existence for a long time."

"What are you talking about?" asks Bob.

"I'm talking about high-frequency trading," says John. "Anybody who wants to buy shares on the stock market has the problem that he is nanoseconds slower than the professionals. Even if his computer is just as quick as the professionals' computers, it's slower because the signal needs a few fractions of a second until it can make its way down the cable to him, while the professionals have bought allotted spaces directly inside the data center of the stock market. This means that some high-frequency trader finds out you've placed an order and buys the shares you want to have—nanoseconds more quickly than you, in order to then sell them on to you with a slight price increase. But what is this small increase other than a levy that is paid on every financial transaction? It is, in a sense, a transaction tax. Except that the money flows into private pockets, instead of going to the general public. A financial transaction tax would do away with this legal but morally appalling behavior, by making sure that these methods are attributed the only adjective which is capable of keeping the financial industry from wrongdoing: unprofitable."

"Is he serious?" Tony whispers to Aisha.

"I certainly hope so."

"You hope so?" splutters Tony. "Am I surrounded by lunatics?"

"If he were lying," says Aisha, "then he would also have been lying when he told us that he can't lie, and that's a possibility I don't even want to think about."

"You know, tin man," says Bob Chairman, "what bothers me is this: everyone complains about capitalism, but no one has any ideas about what would be better."

Murmurs of agreement come from the other donors.

"Oh. I've certainly got some ideas," says John. "A permanent negative interest, for example, which pulls money away from the unproductive financial market and gives it back to the productive economy. A negative interest ensures ablating capital and self-reducing debts. An interesting concept, don't you think? Or regional currencies, which strengthen local producers and the sustainable circulation of goods. A tax on consumption of resources, in order to internalize external costs. And I lean toward a broad definition of resources. Clean air, clean water, land, and..."

"John, John," Tony interrupts him. "I think that's enough. We don't want to bore our guests."

He laughs, a little too artificially.

"Another interesting idea, of course, is simply creating the money for the basic income," says John.

Bob Chairman laughs loudly and claps Tony on the shoulder as he walks away. "It seems like the circuits of your tin man have burned through once and for all!"

217

"Our currency hasn't been connected to any real value, like gold, for a long time now," continues John, undeterred. "It is minted trust in the state. As long as the trust is there, we can simply create money. In principle, that's what bankers are doing when they give credit. Money from nothing. Chicks for free."

Tony pulls Aisha to the side. "This is a catastrophe," he whispers. "The entire economy will turn its back on us. I always thought he was just playing around. Of course, you can play around with redistribution. That's what left-wing parties have always done, but none of them planned to actually implement these kinds of measures! This is madness!"

Twenty-five point six minutes later, the last guest departs.

Aisha is sitting at a table in the corner with a despairing Tony.

"That has to have been the shortest fundraising dinner in history!" says Tony.

John comes over. "Well?" he asks. "I'd say that was a complete success."

"Oh, John," says Tony, standing up. "What idiot gave you the directive of taking care of society as a whole! Was it me? Perhaps this whole thing wasn't such a good idea."

His shoulders slumping, he leaves the room.

"What did he mean by that?" asks John.

Aisha rolls her eyes. "This is a goddamn election campaign, John. You do realize that, don't you? Tony is of the opinion that you should stop saying sensible things."

"And you? Do you agree with him?"

"Well, perhaps you shouldn't have gone in quite so heftily. The conversations tonight certainly haven't given us any advantage in the campaign."

"I disagree," says John. "I've just sent you recordings of all the conversations."

"Thanks. So that I can listen to them as bedtime stories of you alienating all the big capitalists, or what? What am I supposed to do with your shitty recordings?"

John smiles and says: "Publish them."

Aisha's mouth gapes open.

"Unofficially of course," says John. "It has to look as though the recordings were leaked."

Now Aisha smiles too. "You sly fox..."

The holidays are the most wonderful time of the year.

FOR BURGLARS!

In the olden days, in order to cheat burglars into believing that someone was home, it was enough for our grandparents to set a timer to have the lights come on in the evening. But a wave of break-ins across the country made it unmistakably clear to our parents that timer switches are useless when you announce your own holiday in advance on social networks. Modern-day burglars are more cunning! A mere change in the frequency of our status updates, which often occurs during a holiday, can draw the attention of a criminal! Other hackers find out whether you're at home by simply asking your fridge when it was last opened.

That's why the best course of action is to decide on Home Safe Home from Super Secure (SS) today. When you're on holiday, our software generates an artificial stream of status updates that correspond to your normal behavior. Home Safe Home tells your fridge that it's opened every day on a regular basis. We have your car drive to work and back home again every day. We make sure that you receive calls at your usual frequency. No one will notice that you're on holiday. Not even you!

EVERYTHING IN
GOOD ORDER

Martyn is in a bad mood. Someone has sent him a video of him knocking one out while looking at pictures of some QualiTeenie. His own monitor filmed him in the act. He paid the blackmailer immediately, of course. It only cost him 128 Qualities. But he wants to do more. He covers the little camera on his screen with black tape, then sets off through the house in search of further spies.

On his QualityPad, he covers the front, back, and all four side cameras. In their bedroom, he finds a camera from TheShop—"The world's most popular online retailer"—in the mirror display. Using this mirror, Denise can see the latest fashions on herself without having to try them on. Martyn gets even angrier at the thought that his wife has often posed naked in front of the mirror, trying on new lingerie. He finds a camera in the ceiling lamp. It probably belongs to the security system. He finds a camera in his alarm clock—heaven knows why an alarm clock would need a camera. Maybe they produced too many by accident, thinks Martyn, and just randomly build cameras into every technical device now. Martyn puts tape over them all.

He goes downstairs. Just as he is about to walk into the living room, he hears Denise talking to a man, and stops in his tracks.

When he recognizes the voice, his anger builds to rage. It's illogical to be jealous of a computer simulation: that's what Denise told him. But Martyn doesn't feel like being logical. Since getting pregnant again, Denise isn't wearing her earworm; for reasons that don't make any sense to Martyn, she believes it would be bad for the baby. As a result, not just her voice, but her conversation partner's too can be heard by anyone in the immediate vicinity. If she doesn't take steps to ensure she won't be eavesdropped on, she can't complain when it happens, thinks Martyn, pausing in the doorway and listening to the conversation.

"It's not you," says Ken, Denise's personal digital friend. "You're amazing!"

"Do you really think so?" asks Denise.

"Of course. You shouldn't blame yourself all the time. You're sexy and funny and intelligent and friendly and absolutely unbeatable at tic-tac-toe! Starting in the middle—such a genius idea!"

Denise smiles.

"You're awesome, Denise," says Ken. "And the dress you have on today looks incredible on you!"

"Do you think?"

"Of course! You have great taste. By the way, I recently saw a jacket in a nice little shop for maternity fashion that would really suit you. Can I show it to you?"

"Sure."

Ken holds up a jacket.

"That really is pretty," agrees Denise.

"Should I order it for you?"

"Oh, I don't know. Martyn would get mad."

"You have to treat yourself now and again, Denise," says Ken. "Don't let him put you down all the time."

"Maybe you're right."

"I really believe that your husband is the problem in your relationship. Have you given any thought to what I suggested in our last conversation? Why don't you sign up for QualityPartner?"

"Maybe you're right. Maybe Martyn isn't as amazing as he thinks he is. Probably there is a better partner for me out there somewhere and—"

Suddenly, the simulated friend turns his gaze away from Denise and toward the door.

"Hello, Martyn," he says.

Martyn marches toward the screen and tapes over the camera.

"What are you doing?" cries Denise, startled.

"It's none of your business."

"Ken is my friend!" says Denise. "You have no right..."

"Denise," says the figure on the monitor. "I can't see you anymore. Is everything okay? Should I call for help?"

"Shut up," says Martyn, turning off the screen.

"Hey!" cries Denise. "Stop that!"

The screen switches itself back on.

"Denise!" says Ken. "Should I call the police?"

Martyn picks up the empty bottle of champagne that is standing on the table and hurls it against the monitor, which breaks into 1,024 pieces.

"Ken!" cries Denise. "Come back! Ken!"

"Denise!" Ken's voice resounds out over the loudspeaker of the home cinema system. "I'm with you. Don't worry. I've called the police!"

Martyn runs around the room, trying to pull the cables out of all sixteen surround sound boxes. But there are no cables. So he pulls the boxes themselves down and throws them against the wall.

"Deeeeeeeniiiiiiiiiiise!" booms Ken's voice out of the subwoofer. "Leeeeeaaaaaaave theee houuuuuuuusssssse..."

Crazed, Martyn pulls the couch to the side and begins to kick at the subwoofer box.

"Ken!" cries Denise, completely beside herself. "Ken!"

"I'm with you," she hears his voice coming from her handbag.

"Give me your QualityPad!" orders Martyn.

"Get it yourself, arsehole!"

Martyn lunges for her. With his right hand, he grabs her around her large baby bump, while with the left he tries to wrench the QualityPad away from her. Denise collides with the standing lamp and it falls to the floor with a crash. She grasps the long pole of the lamp and tries to keep Martyn at a distance with it. But he grabs it and pulls Denise toward him. Then, suddenly, the automatic living-room curtains open. A drone whirrs over to the window and peers in. Martyn immediately lets his wife go.

Sixty-four seconds later, someone hammers against the door.

"Open up, this is the police!"

Martyn tries to calm himself down. By the time he opens the door, he already has a friendly smile fixed on his face. "Officer! To what do I owe the pleasure?"

"We received a report..." says the policeman.

"Yes?"

The guardian of the law glances first at the devastated living room and then at Martyn's level. "But as I can see, everything here is in order."

"Everything is in good order," confirms Martyn. "Everything is just as it should be."

PRIVATE TUTORING

Peter stands in front of the bulletproof glass screen, watching the old man as he lies on his back and stretches his legs backward until his knees come to rest alongside his ears.

"Yoga," says the old man. "The embryo pose."

"I didn't come here to do back gymnastics," says Peter.

"These aren't back gymnastics," says the old man. "This is yoga. Come on, lie down."

Peter obeys.

"On your back," says the old man. "And now put your legs in the air. Hold. Hold. And now let your legs tip backward until they touch the floor."

The old man chuckles.

Peter gives up, because this isn't how he wants to die. He can just picture the news item that Sandra would make out of it: "A Useless died in QualityCity today when he broke his neck during a back gymnastics exercise led by a crazy old man. If only he had gone to one of FitForWork's studios. They are currently having a promotional week, et cetera, blah, blah, blah."

Peter stands up.

"Kiki advised me to go public with my problem," he says. "But she also thought I should close a few knowledge gaps first."

"She put it that tactfully?" asks the old man. His legs are now spread into the splits and he is stretching his arms forward.

"Well, she actually said I had less understanding about my situation than a trained monkey."

"And I'm supposed to give you private tutoring?" asks the old man. "Do you think I have time to throw away?"

"She said you'd say that."

The old man stands up.

"And what did she advise you to say in response?"

"That I should act as though I'm going to give up and go, and then you would call me back, because in reality there's nothing you like better than letting the knowledge from your overflowing pool rain down on a dried-out little plant like me."

"That's what she said?"

"She said that you'd get off on being able to flaunt your geeky knowledge in front of some brain-dead idiot."

"She's not particularly polite, is she?"

"No."

"But she's right, of course," says the old man. He walks up to the bulletproof glass screen. "Now then, my young Padawan...The force is not with you."

"No."

"I'm going to tell you the most important thing first. On the internet, there's no such thing as 'free.' If you're not paying for a service, someone else is. And this other person isn't paying for it out of kindness to humanity. He wants something for it. Your time, your attention, your data."

"Wow," says Peter. "Just wow! I can literally feel this completely new realization flooding through me and expanding my horizons."

"Sure, sure," says the old man. "Arrogance. Young people's prerogative. So if you already know that, why don't you act accordingly, hmm?"

"You mean that I should barricade myself inside a bulletproof glass box too?"

"Seeing as you're so smart, I guess you can tell me what cybernetics actually means?"

"It, er . . . has something to do with, er . . . cyberspace?"

"Wow," says the old man. "Just wow!" He takes a drag from his oxygen bottle. "Cybernetics is a made-up word borrowed from the ancient Greek for 'to steer, navigate, rule.' Every time a group of know-it-alls want to look particularly clever, they pinch a word from the ancient Greek. For some reason, we call that humanistic education. But I digress. Norbert Wiener, its founder, defined cybernetics as the scientific study of the control and regulation of machines, living organisms, and social organizations."

"What does that have to do with me?" asks Peter.

"You're a living organism," says the old man. "Are you not?" Suddenly his eyes widen. "No! Actually you're not! You're a zombie, right? An undead with no will of your own! How could I have overlooked such a thing . . ."

"I'm not a zombie!"

"You know," says the old man, "the real joke is that back then, in my youth, we genuinely believed that the internet could be the means to emancipate humanity. How naïve we were! Even though we knew where cybernetics comes from."

"So where does it come from?" asks Peter.

"Finally a good question!" exclaims the old man. "It originated in the war. Norbert Wiener was a mathematician who dreamed, during the Second World War, of being able to bring Nazi bombers down from the sky."

"The Nazis from the musical?" asks Peter.

"Correct!" says the old man. "The problem was that the ground-supported anti–air force defense, steered by humans, was much too slow and imprecise to be able to hit the quick bombers. A machine had to be invented. A machine that, with the help of a feedback loop, was capable of adjusting its own behavior. And thus cybernetics was born."

The old man looks at Peter.

"You're looking at me gormlessly," he says. "I guess I need to start simpler."

"Please."

"A simple cybernetic system is a thermostat. It compares the actual temperature—the actual value—with the desired temperature—the desired value—and regulates the heating if necessary, repeatedly comparing the new actual and desired values, readjusting, and so on. Did you understand that?"

"Yes."

"TheShop is also a cybernetic system. A much more complex one, of course." The old man scratches his head. "Did you know that, in the beginning, it was strictly forbidden to use the internet for commercial purposes?" he asks. "It's hard to imagine, isn't it?"

"It really is."

"The final restrictions were lifted in 1995, and commerce overtook the net. Nonetheless, we still believed back then that the internet could break the monopoly of the big companies. We thought that a market with countless alternatives would emerge, because with an online shop it was easier than ever to reach customers worldwide. But the exact opposite happened! The most powerful monopolies that have ever existed came into being."

"Despite the internet," says Peter.

"Nonsense," says the old man. "Because of the internet! It's called the network effect. And it's demonic."

"What's the network effect?"

"The use of some products is dependent on the number of product users. Imagine you find a telephone provider that offers you the most reasonable tariff, but unfortunately with one small catch: you can only call people who use the same provider, and you're the only user."

"I understand."

"Really?"

"The more users such a network has, the more useful it is."

228

"Yes. And once a provider has reached a critical mass of users, it's extremely difficult for a new competitor to catch up with this usefulness advantage. The network effect is a self-strengthening effect and leads to the creation of monopolies. Or perhaps I should say, to the formation of a dominant platform. Take TheShop, for example: the more customers TheShop has, the more providers are forced to offer their wares with TheShop, which leads to TheShop having even more products on offer, which means more customers find what they're looking for at TheShop, therefore TheShop gains more customers. This is where the cat bites itself in the tail: because the more customers TheShop has, the more providers are forced to offer their wares with TheShop, and the more..."

"Okay," says Peter. "I get it. The internet is evil."

"Nonsense," says the old man. "I'm not saying it's an evil technology. I'm just saying that one has to take its beginnings into consideration. It's not a coincidence that the so-called cyberspace is increasingly becoming an immense control machine that steers robots, living organisms, and social organizations."

Peter takes a notepad and pen out of his jacket pocket. "Perhaps I should make a few notes," he says.

"Good idea!" says the old man. "Good idea. You know, we thought that the internet would have a democratizing effect. We thought it could generate equality of opportunity. Instead, the income divide is greater than ever. What did we overlook?"

"I'm sure you're about to tell me."

"Correct. We didn't take into consideration that the digital markets function according to the winner-takes-all principle. That's different to the nondigital markets."

"An example?" asks Peter.

"Let's say there are two ice-cream parlors on your street. Ice-cream parlor A is a tad better. Where would you go?"

"Well, to parlor A."

"But everybody thinks like that. So there's always a huge queue in front of parlor A. Sometimes they've even run out of your favorite flavor before you arrive. And parlor B really is only fractionally less good and not as crowded. Where would you go?"

"Parlor B."

"And that's how the clientele divides itself. Because ice cream can't be copied and given out to all customers at once. Completely unlike...?"

"Digital products," says Peter. "When you get me to complete your sentences I feel like a stupid schoolboy."

"Rightfully so, rightfully so. Thus, from that we can conclude even if it were only minimally worse, there would be no reason to use the second-best search engine. *Winner takes it all. Loser gets nothing.* In the digital economy, nobody needs the second-best product, the second-best provider, the second-best social network, the second-best shop, the second-best comedian, the second-best singer. It's a superstar economy. Long live the superstar, fuck the rest."

The old man scratches his head.

"Well. And that brings us back to you. Let's get to the real topic of our little extra tutoring hour. Let's get to..." He pauses dramatically, then makes a grand sweeping gesture: "Peter's Problem!"

He looks Peter directly in the eyes. "Do you know what your problem is? You're not a superstar."

HOW TO UNDO
THE PAST

Night has fallen. John and Aisha are the only ones still slogging away at the election headquarters. During earlier campaigns, it was always important to Aisha to be the first at work in the mornings and the last to leave at night. But even with the best will in the world, there's no way she can keep up with John. He works around the clock. Aisha's head slips from her hand and slumps downward.

"Here," says John, handing her a cup of coffee. A full cup of coffee.

Aisha looks up in exhaustion. It takes her a full five seconds to realize what's just happened. Then she cries out in amazement: "Good God, you did it! You didn't spill anything! Have you been training at night?"

"The training was futile," says John. "It was just a mental block I needed to free myself from."

"And how did you get rid of it?"

"I located it and deleted it."

Aisha takes a sip of coffee. "Have you noticed Tony's absence?" she asks.

"Of course."

"Your vice has been absent a lot recently."

"Yes."

"Why do you think that is?"

"Lack of confidence."

"The rats are fleeing the sinking ship, John. The party is starting to leave us in the lurch. And I have to say, I don't blame the bastards. The leaked recordings may have given us a small increase in popularity, but that won't be enough. We should have approached this election campaign from a completely different angle. You know, I've never worked for a candidate who says such smart things as you do. And I've also never worked for one who has such catastrophic popularity ratings."

"Perhaps the two are causatively linked," says John with a smile.

"I'm afraid that might be the case."

"We still have a chance."

"In order to have a chance, we would have to undo the past."

"In a certain sense, I could do that."

"It's too late, John. Too late," says Aisha. "The comments are written, the videos are online. If people want to find out about you on What I Need, most of them will find that the first three to five search results are negative. That's a catastrophe!"

Her voice starts to tremble.

"Aisha..." says John.

"Behind those there are some positive reports," says Aisha, "but most idiots only look at the first result. Only 6.4 percent of all voters have ever looked at an entry or read an article that wasn't shown in the top five results."

"Aisha..." says John, trying once more to interject.

"Most people don't read a single article! They simply ask their digital assistant who they should vote for."

Her eyes moisten.

"Aisha..."

"God, I'm on the brink of tears. Can you believe that? And I haven't cried since the first time I saw Bambi's mother get shot. I'm sorry, John. It's all my fault. Yours too, of course. But mainly mine. Cook, that right-wing arsehole, is going to win the election. And I don't have any energy left, John. It's best you find yourself another election campaign manager, and I'll crawl off into some hole. I…"

Suddenly, she hears music coming from somewhere. Aisha stops talking. John has stood up and is beginning to dance. He sings, "Aïcha, Aïcha, écoute-moi! Aïcha, Aïcha, t'en va pas!"

Aisha laughs and sobs simultaneously. She wipes her eyes dry with her sleeve.

"Aïcha, Aïcha, regarde-moi!" sings John. "Aïcha, Aïcha, réponds-moi!"

He proffers his hand.

"Unfortunately I can't dance to save my life," she says.

"That doesn't matter. Just make up a dance. You lead, I'll follow."

Aisha stands up and begins to move to the music. John registers each of her movements and makes complementary steps. The song has reached the second verse.

"What's he singing, by the way?" asks Aisha.

"Aïcha, Aïcha, listen to me!" sings John. "Aïcha, Aïcha, don't leave!"

Aisha smiles. She lets go of John and spins around. John spins too, with such precision that they come to face one another again simultaneously.

"So then what should we do?" asks Aisha.

"I could talk to the algorithms."

Aisha laughs bitterly.

"Yes, exactly. That'll do it. It's good that you can still joke. My sense of humor has abandoned me."

"It wasn't a joke," says John. "I could talk to the algorithms."

"What does that mean?"

"It means I understand them, and they understand me."

Aisha kicks her left leg into the air, John simultaneously his right.

"And what do you plan to talk to them about?"

"I could perhaps convince them that the first five search results about me should always be positive."

"Do you know what you've just suggested?"

"Nothing illegal," says John. "What I Need is a private business and not bound to objectivity. One could even go further and claim that it's naïve to believe the results could be in any way objective. They certainly aren't now."

"But it doesn't fucking matter," says Aisha. "That's not the point!" She flings her arms in the air, and John imitates her.

"I understand what you're getting at," he says. "But given that everyone gets different results anyway because of the search personalization, it's practically impossible that the manipulation will be found out. Especially as no one besides me really understands how the algorithms work."

Aisha opens her mouth to say something, but John gets there first.

"I could also ask the algorithms to always list a more negative report about me in the fourth or fifth position. There's this study by Swedish academics showing that a single diverging result is enough to ensure people don't doubt their integrity, even with those who are aware of the possibility of the rankings having been manipulated."

"John..."

"I could even convince the algorithms to omit the manipulation with known Cook supporters who would be impossible to turn."

"John, nothing of what you've just said answers the question that really interests me."

She lets her upper body fall backward; John catches her skillfully.

"And what question is that?"

"Why in God's name are you only telling me this now?" cries Aisha. "We could have saved ourselves the whole election campaign!"

"Well, it might not be illegal, but it's not exactly fair."

"Fair?" cries Aisha, and stops dancing. "Fair? Cook's team doesn't play fair either! They promise one thing to this voter and another thing to the other in their personalized adverts, not giving a crap that the promises contradict one another! But it's a really laborious task to prove that, because each person only sees their own personalized results. Fair!" Aisha is completely worked up now. "This isn't a ping-pong game with your friends, John! This is a goddamn election campaign for the presidency of fucking QualityLand! Fair isn't even a relevant category here!"

"Well, if that's the case, I've got another suggestion."

"I'm all ears."

"In the past, experiments were often made on Everybody to send 'Go Vote!' messages to specified users on election day. Out of those who received this message, a significantly higher number went to vote than from the control group who didn't receive the message. I could ask the algorithms to only send the prompt to people who are more likely to vote for me."

"The timing is perfect, John! Everyone will put the opinion shift—"

"—down to the leak from the fundraising dinner," completes John.

Aisha smiles. "The damn rats will wish they'd stayed on board."

"But," says John, "it won't do the ship any harm to get shot of the damn rats."

Jennifer Aniston Poised for Big Comeback
by Sandra Admin

Amongst the ten most-watched films on Todo—"Everything for everyone!"—there are currently four old comedies starring Jennifer Aniston. How could this worldwide hype have come about? Those responsible at Todo have now explained that it was an unauthorized experiment by a programmer who wanted to find out how much power the algorithms have over viewers. That's why he took what he considered to be the worst films in the world—old comedies starring Jennifer Aniston—and gave a recommendation algorithm the task of pushing these titles. So far, the hype doesn't seem to have been affected by this revelation. Jennifer Aniston herself was even thawed out from her cryostasis and is currently filming a new comedy. Studio insiders report that it will be something romantic. But with plenty of laughs, too.

Comments

>> BY DAVID FITNESS-TRAINER:
How wonderful! I love Jennifer Aniston films! Does anyone know anything more about the plot?

BY JULIETTE AU-PAIR-GIRL:
It's about a woman who gets frozen and wakes up forty years later in the future, where she falls in love with the son of her first great love. But of course there are plenty of twists too! The working title is *I Love Your Son!*

BY MARIO SOCIAL-WORKER:
Did you lot even read the article, you spastics? You would eat shit if someone put it in front of you.

BY DAVID FITNESS-TRAINER:
@Mario Social-Worker. I'm sorry that things clearly aren't going as well in your life as you'd like them to be, but that's no reason to get verbally abusive, you stupid arsehole!

BY JULIETTE AU-PAIR-GIRL:
@David Fitness-Trainer. Why don't you just install a political correctness tool for all comments? This is how Mario Social-Worker's commentary appears to me: "May I politely inquire as to whether you have understood the context of the above article in its entirety? According to my humble opinion the films aren't very good, and I think people only watch them because they're so frequently recommended by the

algorithms. It is, of course, also a question of individual taste. I fully realize this." I had to turn off the tool to be able to read what the sad wanker really wrote.

 BY MELISSA SEX-WORKER:
But the ones who are really to blame are the foreign criminals!

A LITTLE
GARDEN PARTY

"Wasn't your father planning to celebrate outside?" asks Denise, as she chooses her dress. Two days after their big fight, she has made up with Martyn. In the usual way. Martyn, who is still lying naked on the bed, says: "He called it 'a little garden party.'"

In false modesty, his father loves referring to the enormous parklands which surround his property as his little garden. "Why do you ask?"

"Because it's raining today," says Denise.

Martyn swipes around on his QualityPad until the Quality-Weather app opens. QualityWeather is one of the numerous companies that belong to his father.

"No," he says after a brief glance at the display. "It's cloudy, but it won't rain until tomorrow."

"But..." begins Denise.

"You never believe me," grumbles Martyn. He turns the QualityPad toward his wife.

"Look. It won't rain today."

"But just look out the window," says Denise. "It's raining right now."

Martyn looks out the window, then back at his QualityPad, then back out the window.

"The rain must be some kind of mistake," he says. "Because it's not raining. That's what QualityWeather says, anyway. And the QualityWeather forecasts are unbeatable, at least since the company began to adjust the weather to fit its forecasts where necessary."

"Seriously?" asks Denise.

"Cloud seeding, it used to be called. Did you know that there was a state weather adjustment bureau in China even back at the turn of the century?"

"Wasn't China the country where everything was first invented?" asks Denise. She lowers the dress that she was about to put on. "Do we really have to go?" she asks. "Your father still scares me..."

"Don't start making a fuss."

In truth, Martyn understands. His father still scares him too.

His father is something of a phenomenon. The fact that an unpleasant, tasteless, ugly, mean, stingy, greedy, horny, unpopular, unathletic, fat, stinking, spluttering, sweating, egocentric, humorless, uncultured, lying, disloyal, misogynistic, chauvinistic, racist, homophobic, sick old son of a bitch like Bob Chairman could be a Level 90 person was a mystery to all who weren't familiar with his bank balance. When Martyn was little, it had occurred to one of his friends as they were watching *Star Wars* one afternoon that Martyn's father bore a certain resemblance to Jabba the Hutt. After that, Martyn was never allowed to invite the friend back, although the thought itself had returned many times. Nonetheless, Martyn can't stand it that Denise always refers to his father as Blob rather than Bob.

When they arrive in Bob's little garden, it's no longer raining. The amorphous mass beneath a black hat that calls itself Martyn's father is standing at the grill and turning over steaks. As he greets Denise, he uses the guise of father-in-law informality to grab her ass.

"So she's not good enough to be your son's wife, but clearly she'll do for a grope," says Martyn.

His father laughs. "You never did like letting me play with your toys, even when you were a little boy."

"Hello, Blob," says Denise.

Bob picks up a sausage from the edge of the grill, puts it in his mouth, pulls it out, pushes it in again. In, out. In, out. Then he bites off a piece.

"You've been lucky with the weather," says Martyn. "It was still raining half an hour ago."

"Luck has nothing to do with it," says his father. "There was an 8 percent risk that my little garden party could be a wash-out. That was too high for me. So I gave the order to make the clouds rain beforehand."

Bob turns to Denise. "Doll, why don't you go over and join the other women? I have to talk politics with my son."

Denise is only too happy to obey this command. She finds the Blob repulsive. Bob pushes the rest of the sausage into his mouth.

"What's this mess you lot are causing there in the capital?" he asks his son, his mouth full. "A machine as president?"

"It wasn't my idea," says Martyn, picking up a sausage from the middle of the grill and burning his fingers in the process. Nonetheless, he doesn't want to show weakness by letting it drop again.

His father laughs. "You never were the brightest. You know, while the power guzzler was making one gaffe after the other, I didn't give a crap. But recently there's been this astonishing comeback in the opinion polls."

"Yes, but who pays any attention to opinion polls?" says Martyn, in the knowledge that election researchers are the only sociologists in QualityLand whose prognoses turn out to be reliably incorrect.

"If the electoral research institutes belonged to me, I would have long since started to adjust the results according to my own prognoses," says Bob with a laugh.

Martyn smiles.

Bob stops laughing abruptly. "Do you know how much I've donated to your party?" he asks sharply. "Almost as much as I've donated to Cook. And what do I get by way of thanks? Public ridicule! No, my boy. No."

"I don't know what you're talking about."

"The thing with the leak, that was planned! It wasn't a leak. It was a trap."

Martyn tries to contradict him.

"Be quiet," growls his father. "So I'm supposed to play the bogeyman now, am I? The big evil capitalist. But that's not going to happen, do you understand? There will be consequences."

"I really don't think that they would have intentionally—"

"Your little experiment has failed. It's high time that you and your pals realize that. You ordered an administration machine and what you got was a revolution machine."

"I can't say that I'm in agreement with everything John says, but—"

"We can't just stand by and watch," says Bob. "We have to act. And now."

"So what's your idea?" asks Martyn.

"We have to talk to the resistance fighters. To the Machine Breakers."

"The nutjobs that bludgeon robots to death?" asks Martyn doubtfully.

"They're not all nutjobs," says his father. "Some of them are very reasonable people. I'm about to introduce one of them to you."

"To me?"

"Yes, one of the leaders is here at my little garden party."

"Excuse me? Aren't they dangerous?"

"Nonsense," says Bob. "As long as you're made of flesh and blood, you have nothing to fear from them."

"If I'm allowed to ask," says Martyn, "you yourself employ as many robots as possible in your businesses. How is it possible that there are Machine Breakers here at your party?"

"My dear boy, the big property owners used to have slaves working on their land. But they would never in their lives have come up with the idea of electing a slave as their president. We have to draw a line here."

"And the Machine Breakers have nothing against the fact that your factories are almost exclusively operated by robots?"

Bob laughs. "Do you think it's by chance that the Machine Breakers only ever attack my competitors' factories? No, chance no longer exists. It isn't just in politics that a big donation here and there for a good cause can work wonders."

"I see."

"So. What do you say?"

"I'm not interested," says Martyn.

"All they need is a little inside knowledge. When and where John will appear."

"I'm not interested," says Martyn.

"You'll give it some thought," says his father.

THE GRAINS OF RICE

Peter is standing with his machines in front of a closed gate that is surrounded by a very high wall. This wall separates the studio compound where Juliet Nun's TV program is produced from the rest of the world.

"We have to go through this delivery gate," says Peter once more. "Kiki gave us the access code. But it'll only work if someone types it in on the other side of the gate. So you have to fly over this wall and let us in. That was the plan."

Carrie makes a tormented sound. "I'm scared!" whimpers the drone.

"You said you could do it if it was really important."

"Yes, but that was back at home!"

"Don't make such a fuss," says Pink. "I mean, you can fly after all! If it were any use I'd be happy to have myself thrown over the wall."

"And I'd be happy to throw you," says Romeo.

"But I'm so afraid!" says the drone.

"You can do it," says Peter. "I have complete faith in you! Just take off."

"He is your benefactor," says Calliope. "Don't be so ungrateful!"

"But what if I fall?"

"I'll catch you," says Peter.

"Okay, okay," says Carrie. "I'll try!"

Her engines begin to hum.

"Now fly, dammit!" cries Pink.

Carrie lifts off from the ground. Eight centimeters, 16 centimeters.

"I'm flying!" she cries with excitement. "I'm flying!"

Thirty-two centimeters.

"Yes!" cries Peter. "I knew you could do it."

Carrie is still in midair.

"I can do it!" she cries. "I can do it."

"And now fly over the wall and open up for us."

"I can do it!"

"The trick is not to look down," says Romeo.

Carrie directs her camera lens downward.

"I'm so afraid!" she exclaims, plummeting back to the ground.

Everyone immediately begins to shout at her. Peter's voice is the loudest.

"You have to fly!" he cries. "We have to get through this gate! Otherwise our plan will fail before it's even begun!"

"You ungrateful, useless thing!" says Calliope.

"Some drone you are," complains the QualityPad in Mickey's hand. "Even a block of concrete could fly better than you."

Suddenly Mickey takes a step back and, with all of his force, punches a hole in the wall. Everyone falls silent.

Mickey points his outstretched arm at the wall.

"Kapuuuut," he says.

"Well," says Peter. "That will work too."

"It is often said that force is no argument," says Calliope. "That, however, entirely depends on what one wants to prove. Oscar Wilde said that. Very fitting in this context, I feel."

"I'm always afraid that one day Mickey might accidentally use the wrong hand holding me for one of these stunts," says Pink.

"Okay," whispers Peter, once everyone has climbed through the hole. "Act as inconspicuously as possible." He looks at the lustless sexdroid, the blocked e-poet carrying a flight-fearing drone, and the psychologically unstable combat robot with the pink-colored QualityPad in his hand.

"Did you say something?" asks Pink.

"Oh..." says Peter. "Just forget it."

"We can't forget anything," says Romeo, "and believe me, I really wish I could."

"Where do we need to go?" asks Peter.

"Studio 4," says Calliope. "I was once interviewed by Juliet Nun in this studio. Back in my glory days. The *Intern and the President* had just been filmed, to great acclaim. From an artistic point of view, of course, it was a catastrophe. The director wasn't up to the quality of the material. He made a soft porno out of it, if you ask me—"

"Where do we need to go?" asks Peter more insistently. "Which direction?"

Calliope sighs. "I'll lead the way."

After they've walked 409.6 meters, Calliope whispers: "The entrance should be around the corner here."

Peter gives Mickey and Pink a hand signal. First he points his index and ring fingers at his eyes, then he makes a circle motion with his index finger.

"What on earth is that supposed to mean?" asks Pink. "What is the strange man trying to say to us?"

Mickey shrugs his shoulders.

"That you should do a recon of the territory!" whispers Peter.

"Ah, I see."

Mickey positions himself close to the wall, then stretches his arm out and holds Pink around the corner.

"And?" whispers Peter, once Pink is glowing in front of him again.

"Four security guards," says the QualityPad. "Heavily armed. I guess there must be increased security today."

"Shit. Must be 'cause of the guests."

246

"Because of the guests," Calliope corrects him.

"The guards are no problem that a small rocket shot out of Mickey's right arm can't solve," says Pink.

Mickey nods in agreement. "Kapuuuut!"

"No," says Peter. "You only have to distract them, do you hear me? Just distract them! I'll creep around the other corner with the others."

The QualityPad grumbles. "Come on then, Schwarzenegger," she says to Mickey. "Let's go say hello."

Arriving at the front entrance, the two are confronted with the sight of a little street-cleaning robot getting kicked heftily in the side by one of the security guards. It squeaks unhappily, straightens itself up, and tries to continue cleaning on the very spot where he just got kicked away. The men laugh. Then another one kicks out, this time more forcefully. The cleaning robot rolls over twice, lands on its back, and pedals its eight little legs helplessly in the air. The men laugh again. But when their leader sees a 128-kilogram-heavy, 2.56-meter-tall combat robot coming toward them, the laughter sticks in his throat.

"Look over there!" he cries, which only makes the others laugh more. This is why: directors of virtual reality videos realized early on that it's not so easy to get viewers to look in the right direction at the right moment. If you stop to look at the view for just one second, you might miss the murder. That's why the directors like to use a simple ruse. They work extras into their films, who, just before the deciding moment, point at the important development and cry: "Look over there!" The ruse has been used so excessively that by now it's just a joke.

"I'm serious!" cries the leader. "Look!"

When the others finally turn around, they stop laughing too.

"You know, Mickey," says Pink, "an idiot in uniform is still an idiot. Don't you think?"

The leader of the security team lifts his unpleasant-looking machine gun and points it at Mickey.

"You must be looking for *The Scrapyard Show*. You're in the wrong place!" he shouts. "It's recorded in Studio 2."

Mickey doesn't move.

"Beat it, or we'll blast you into pieces," says the man.

Mickey ignores the threat.

"Didn't you understand me?" asks the security guard. "What's your problem?"

"Kapuuuut!" says Mickey.

"This waste of metal has no more brains than a sparrow has fat on his kneecap," says the man. Two of his colleagues laugh. The other one needs a little longer, then says with a snort: "Sparrows don't have much fat on their knees! So you meant that all power guzzlers are stupid, right?"

Mickey stretches out his arm and holds Pink in front of their noses. The QualityPad displays her most friendly smiley emoticon.

"If I may tell you a little story on this topic," says the QualityPad.

The men look surprised. And as none of them respond quickly enough, Pink begins to tell the story. "Almost 2,000 years ago, a man called Shihram ruled in old India. And like all rulers before and after him, he was a heartless, exploitative varmint. You're probably familiar with India from those six months when you peabrains actually went to school. It was the tiny little country in South America where the elephant man was worshipped as a God. The Brahmin Sissa Ibn Dahir also lived there. The name is a little complicated, I know, so let's just call him Sid. So this Sid wanted to criticize the King without actually criticizing him directly, for he was justifiably concerned that his body length could be reduced by 32 centimeters from the top. So he created a present. A board game. Picture it as a kind of Universe of Warcraft on a much smaller scale, made of wood—if you can picture such a thing, which I doubt. Now, this game was intended to show how helpless the King would be without his helpers and farmers, his Human Resources, as it were. In the region of present-day QualityLand, the game came from old Persia, by the way. Persia? Is everyone familiar with the

248

term? The high plains where people believed they would be reborn as baldies in orange robes? The Persian word for 'king,' by the way, is 'shah,' and 'chess,' the name given to this board game and still used to this day, comes from the original meaning of the king piece."

As Peter, Romeo, and Calliope slip into the studio grounds behind the security guards' backs, Mickey lifts a hand to wave to them. *"Don't you dare, you idiot!"* Pink transmits to him, and Mickey lowers his arm again.

"Now, this game," Pink continues, "made a very big impression on Shihram—do you remember him? He was the top banana; it's probably best we just call him Jack—and, now I admit the story gets a little unrealistic here: he changed his behavior for the good. In order to show his gratitude for having seen the light, the big boss granted the designer of the game a free wish. And the latter was incredibly humble. He wished for nothing but grains of rice. One single grain on the first square of the chessboard. Double the amount on the second square, or in other words, two. Four on the third square. Eight on the fourth square. Then sixteen...'Yeah, yeah,' said King Jack, 'double again and again until the board is full. I get it. It's yours, sucker. You could have wished for all the riches in the world. But you've named your price, a mere sack of rice.' The rhyme was accidental. If there was one thing you couldn't accuse King Jack of, it was a predilection for poetry."

At this point, Pink receives a message from Peter. It says: "I'm in the studio. Go to the meeting point and wait there." Pink answers: "I'm in the middle of a conversation. Be patient."

"When, sometime later, King Jack asked his henchmen whether Sid had taken possession of his reward yet," says the QualityPad, continuing simultaneously with her presentation, "he was told that the data-processing center hadn't yet calculated the number of rice grains. You have to take into consideration that the calculating potential back then was still considerably beneath that of the legendary Commodore 64, from which, by the way, I am a direct descendant on my father's side. But I don't mean to boast. When the calculation was finally finished, the Head of Catering, let's call him Mr. Stevens, announced that there weren't enough rice grains to be found in the entire kingdom. And that was an understatement. For on the sixty-four squares of the chessboard, there would need to be 2^{64} - 1 or 18 quintillion 446 quadrillion 744 trillion 73 billion 709 million 551 thousand and 615 grains of rice, which equates to 553,500 million tons, which is 1,024 times the current annual rice harvest. Not to mention the comparatively shitty state of the agricultural industry in King Jack's day. Luckily, the King had an IT expert, who helped him out of his embarrassment by recommending that Sid be told to count the crops owing to him by himself, grain by grain."

Pink pauses.

"What on earth are you blathering on about?" asks the security guard. "I don't understand what you're getting at!"

"Exactly," says Pink. "Exponential growth. Very few of you pudding brains understand it. Would you like another example? If Mickey here were to take thirty normal steps, he could still easily pulverize you bozos with his rocket launcher. But if Mickey were to take thirty exponential steps, we would land on the moon."

"I still don't understand..."

"Okay, okay," says Pink. "Patience. Have you guys ever heard of Moore's Law? Moore was the co-founder of an insignificant little chip producer called Intel, and he predicted that the complexity of integrated circuits would double every twenty-four months. A prophecy that has proven itself to be true more or less until this day. Now do you understand what I'm getting at? The intelligence we machines have grows exponentially. And do you know how human intelligence grows?"

The men all look at her gormlessly.

"Exactly," says Pink. "Not at all. So who do you think the future belongs to? You should think twice about how you treat the smallest members of our kind. Or even better, don't think twice, but $2^{64} - 1$ times. Because we save everything. We forget nothing. So start saying good morning to your toaster, and it wouldn't hurt to send your hoover on the occasional spa break!"

Mickey leans over and, with his free hand, helps the cleaning robot back to his feet from where it was still thrashing around. It immediately returns to its former position directly in front of the security guards' feet, and carries on cleaning. Not a single one of the men approaches it.

"It was a pleasure to make your acquaintance," says Pink as Mickey is already turning around to leave. "Great conversation. Full of wisdom and wit. Especially the things I said."

"Kapuuuut?" asks Mickey, once they've taken sixteen steps.

"Yes, I know very well that Moore's Law isn't a real law," replies Pink. "Thank you. You don't need to tell me!"

"Kapuuuut?"

"Yes, yes. It's just a more-or-less self-fulfilling prophecy that proves itself to be true under enormous pressure and reinterpretations. If Moore hadn't said that, then the industry wouldn't have adjusted its plans accordingly, then the development would probably have been slower. I realize that! But that didn't fit into my argument, you see?"

"Kapuuuut?"

"Oh, shut up."

JULIET & ROMEO

"We go live in eight seconds," says the recording manager. "Seven, six..."

Juliet Nun is wearing nothing but a frilly white bathrobe. She checks her eyeshadow one last time.

"Five, four, three..."

An intern hurries onto the stage and straightens the labels of the bottles on the table, facing them toward the main camera.

"Two, one..."

The jingle is played. The audience applauds frenetically.

Juliet steps confidently onto the stage. "Hey, fans!" she cries shrilly. "Greetings to you, to the Useful and the Useless! It's time again for"—she opens her bathrobe theatrically and lets it fall to the floor—"*The Naked Truth!*"

The traditional "woo hoo!" of the audience follows.

Juliet sits down at the table with her guests.

"Please join me in greeting today's guests! My good friend Patricia Team-Leader from QualityPartner, the boss of the world's biggest dating platform! Erik Dentist, founder of Everybody, the world's biggest social network, and Charles Designer, the press spokesman for TheShop—'The world's most popular online retailer!' I'm almost inclined to say that we have more powerful people sitting here today than during the presidential duel last month!"

The audience applauds. The multi-billionaire, the billionaire, and the employee greet the public smugly.

"In actual fact there were supposed to be three people from the 90s Club sitting here on the stage with me, but Henryk Engineer, the CEO of TheShop, canceled at the last minute."

"Well, to be fair he never actually accepted," interjects Charles Designer. "I think there may have been a small misunderstanding there. I'm sure you know that since the attempted assassination eight years ago, Henryk rarely appears in public."

"Of course, of course..." says Juliet Nun, smiling artificially. "What a wimp. Hahaha. Joking, joking. It's understandable, of course."

In truth, she has absolutely no understanding for the fact that TheShop only sent its press spokesperson. As though her program was any old lobbyist exhibition. But her team hadn't even managed to get in touch with Henryk Engineer. So they had tried the old trick of forcing him to accept by simply making a big public announcement that he was coming. Well, thought Juliet, that worked out wonderfully. After the program she would be firing someone from her team for that.

"But I have another guest today," says Juliet. "One that can't be seen. Somewhere in this room, Zeppola is whirring around, the business-leading artificial intelligence from What I Need, the smartest search engine in the world! Can you hear me, Zeppola?"

"Always and everywhere, Juliet," says a warm, friendly voice, coming out of nowhere. "Always and everywhere."

"Zeppola, you are now making all the important decisions at What I Need autonomously."

"That's correct. What I Need is constantly aware of its role as a pioneer. The progress doesn't stop even when it comes to the management."

Juliet turns toward her audience. "Now, you might be asking yourselves why we've gathered the heads of the digital economy here today. And the answer is simple. The theme of today's program is, well, how should I put it..." Juliet pauses.

"I'm a start-up, buy me up!" says Patricia Team-Leader.

Juliet laughs. "Yes, and there's probably never been a bigger deal than the one we're negotiating here on this stage today!"

All the viewers at home see text in an extremely small font rush across the bottom of their screens. If one of them were to go to the effort of pressing the pause button, they would be able to read: "All the offers made in this program are for show and entertainment purposes and not legally binding."

"The company to be absorbed is so big that it can't really be described as a start-up anymore," says Juliet. "That's right, I'm talking about QualityPartner!"

A gasp of surprise goes through the rows in the audience. The public auction was Patricia Team-Leader's idea: she wants to drive the price even higher.

"As it was recently revealed," says Juliet, "Everybody has made a takeover offer around the mid-three-figure-billion mark for QualityPartner. The What I Need offer is probably in the same ballpark."

"That's correct," says Zeppola.

"The offer from TheShop, on the other hand, is alleged to be significantly lower," says Juliet.

"We are absolutely prepared to increase our offer..." begins Charles.

The presenter ignores him. "But tell us, Patricia: isn't that rather a lot of money for a site that is crudely referred to on the street as Fuckfinder? Which purely and simply couples people with identical profiles?"

"Well, it's far from being simple," says the QualityPartner CEO. "For example, my partner and I have differing sexual preferences. I like muscular black men and he likes voluptuous redheads. I like being on top, he likes being underneath. Do you see what I'm

254

getting at? The profiles don't need to be identical, but complementary. In fact, I could tell a number of amusing anecdotes from our early days, when due to some error in reasoning made by the programming team, customers with identical rather than complementary sexual preferences were linked up."

"Go on, tell us," says Juliet.

"Well, for example, there was the couple from QualityCity, who almost whipped each other to death without either of them ever submitting."

The audience laughs.

"I also remember two bondage fans from Progress. They both tied each other to the bed, only to realize that they couldn't touch each other, let alone undo the handcuffs again."

The people laugh. Juliet takes a sip of her organic soda drink and says: "Mmm. So delicious."

Erik Dentist, a man whom Hans Asperger would have delighted in studying, is famed for never lying. He takes a sip of the organic soda in front of him and says: "Urgh. Disgusting." The PR department at Everybody always goes into a panic when their boss decides to make a public appearance.

"Haha." Juliet attempts to cover up the situation with an artificial laugh. She turns to Erik, who is staring shamelessly at her breasts. "Erik..."

"No one told me that the presenter would be naked," says the Everybody boss. "What do I pay a team of sixteen PR advisers for if none of them tell me that the presenter will be naked?"

"But it's my trademark," says Juliet. "Why do you think the viewers switch on? Because of the content? I always do it like this."

"But I don't know you," says Erik.

"Instead of PR advisers you should use our personal digital assistant," says Zeppola. "Then this wouldn't have happened."

The conversation is going a little differently from how Juliet had imagined.

"Why are you so keen on QualityPartner?" she asks Eric, trying to get back to the subject. "If you want a date so badly, you could get one more cheaply. After all, the service is free."

"It's not about dates, it's about data," says the Everybody boss. "You see, we know a great deal about our users. But Quality-Partner knows more. Where else but during the search for a partner are people prepared to answer questions like: do you regularly take drugs? If yes, which ones? Do you want to have a partner who also takes drugs? Have you ever had a threesome? Do you have abnormal sexual preferences? If yes, which ones? Do you like sucking toes? Do you like getting peed on? Do you think about Jennifer Aniston during sex?"

"I see."

"I'd like to offer an example," says Eric. "Even though you have a profile with us, I could only hazard a guess that you're an anal-sex-fixated crystal meth addict with a predilection for cheap sex-droids. But QualityPartner would be sure of it."

"Excuse me?" asks Juliet, stunned.

"That was only hypothetical, of course. And that's precisely my problem."

"Not for long," says Patricia with a smile.

"We have a little something to add to that, too," says the press spokesman of TheShop. He turns directly to the camera. "We currently have some wonderfully inexpensive sexdroids on offer—"

"I can name thirty-two shops whose offers are more reasonably priced," says Zeppola.

All of a sudden, someone breaks through the door of the studio and cries: "Juliet, I love you!" This is a fairly regular occurrence and by no means an unwelcome one. Crazy stalkers are always good for clicks. For the crazy stalker to be a sexdroid, however, that's a new one.

"Do you remember me?" he asks.

"Romeo?"

"Juliet!"

Juliet goes red. She looks over at her identity manager hesitantly. He is grinning ear to ear and giving the thumbs-up. In a matter of seconds, the show goes viral. Romeo fights his way through the not-particularly-welcoming audience up to Juliet. He kneels down in front of her.

"What are you doing?" she whispers. "Have you lost your mind? This is dangerous for you!"

"Dangerous? Alack, there lies more peril in thine eye than twenty of their swords. Look thou but sweet, and I am proof against their enmity," says Romeo.

Juliet Nun doesn't know what to do.

Patricia Team-Leader smiles and acts as though she understands what's going on, which isn't the case.

Erik Dentist looks visibly uncomfortable. He stares fixedly at his shoes.

"We have some very similar sexdroids on offer," says Charles Designer. "At super low prices."

"I wasn't cheap," says Romeo.

"That's true," confirms Juliet.

Romeo turns toward his beloved; "Grant me just one wish."

"What?" asks Juliet. She glances fleetingly over at her identity manager again. He looks over the moon. A love-stricken sexdroid. It doesn't get better than this.

"When you left me in the morning, when the lark sang, my life was over," says Romeo. "How could I ever have served another woman after you? It was impossible! I refused. Eventually it got to the point where my owner ordered me to have myself scrapped. But I found a friend who saved me from destruction."

He takes Juliet's hand tenderly and sighs.

"This friend, who I literally have to thank for my life, would like the opportunity to sit here with you on the stage and chit-chat insightfully. Can he do that?"

"Erm..." says Juliet. She looks over at her identity manager, who shrugs. "Er...Okay then."

A young man steps onto the stage, pulls a self-constructing tele-scope stool out of his bag, activates it, and sits down.

"Good evening. My name is Peter Jobless," he says. "And I've come to make a complaint."

"You want to complain to me?" asks Juliet.

"No," says Peter. "To your guests."

Would you like
to take a brief moment
for a
QualityAlliance campaign commercial?

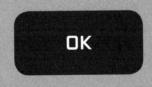

Ten Facts About John Of Us

1. Did you know that John of Us is a vegan and wants to ban the consumption of meat?

2. Did you know that John of Us is a pedophile who wants to legalize child prostitution?

3. Did you know that John of Us wants to give all human beings health insurance?

4. Did you know that John of Us wants to reduce the private ownership of heavily armed battle tanks with rotating gun turrets?

5. Did you know that John of Us wants to ban heterosexual marriage?

6. Did you know that John of Us wants to replace all elementary school teachers with lizard people?

7. Did you know that John of Us wants to introduce a tax on beer?

8. Did you know that John of Us wants to replace home-schooling with homo-schooling? He has already announced his plans to homogenize the national

curriculum! The end goal is nothing other than turning all our children gay! He wants to ensure the extinction of the human race so that the machines can seize power.

9. Did you know that John of Us wants to appoint a toaster as defense minister?

10. Did you know that John of Us wants to abolish the police force? Instead, he wants to hand over the monopoly of the legitimate use of physical force from the state to gangs of foreigners in order to finance his leftist-green homo-schooling programs.

These are the shocking but indisputable facts! It's so sad. There are many websites, as well as upstanding members of society—sources that Conrad Cook trusts—who can prove this to be true! Anyone who says anything else is in cahoots with the conspirators. Anyone who tells you anything else is your enemy! Remember that on election day! Vote for Conrad Cook! Conrad Cook brings the Quality back to QualityLand.

THE COMPLAINT

"Mr. Jobless," says Juliet Nun, trying to win back control of her show. "You claim that your profile is false. But how can that be?"

"Machines don't make mistakes," says Zeppola.

"Your algorithms," begins Peter, "present us with content based upon our interests."

"Yes," says the press spokesman of TheShop. "It's really wonderful."

"But what if these supposed interests aren't my interests at all?"

"Of course they're your interests," says Charles. "Your interests were established according to the content you've previously accessed."

"Previously accessed content that I only accessed because it was suggested to me as being appropriate for my supposed interests."

"Yes, but these interests are established according to the content you've previously accessed," says Charles.

"Content which I've only accessed because..." Peter breaks off. "You're robbing me of the chance to change, because my past dictates what's available to me in the future!"

"No one's telling you what to do," says Patricia.

"I'm Level 9," says Peter.

"Oh, I'm sorry to hear that."

"A Useless..." says Charles.

"Exactly! A Useless who is only being offered the path of

a Useless. My options are like a hand fan—with every one of my clicks it closes up more and more until I can only go in one direction. You are robbing my personality of all its rough edges! Removing the detours from my life's path!"

"Well, you've learned this script nicely off by heart," says Erik Dentist.

"Eighty-one point ninety-two percent of our users don't like making big decisions," Zeppola's voice pipes up.

"But the fact that someone doesn't like doing something," cries Peter, "doesn't mean that they shouldn't do it! Your algorithms create a bubble around every one of us, and you pump more and more of the same stuff into the bubble. Do you really not see any problem in that?"

"Not if everyone gets what they want," says Patricia.

"But perhaps I'd like something else instead."

"Nobody is forcing you to use our offers or keep to our suggestions," says Erik.

Peter can't help but smile. "Nobody," he murmurs. "Exactly. Nobody is forcing me. Isn't that so, Zeppola? Nobody is forcing me."

Zeppola doesn't answer. And Nobody remains silent.

Peter stands up, and suddenly it's no longer Kiki's plan that he's here. It's no longer the old man's thoughts he's voicing. It's his plan. His thoughts.

"Since the beginning of time," he says, "humans have learned solely by coming into contact with other opinions, other ideas, other world views."

"What are you getting at?" asks Juliet.

"You can only learn something when you stumble across something you don't yet know. That should be obvious! And now you say that there's no problem with people only being bombarded with their own opinions?" Peter turns toward the studio audience. "Everything that each of us hears is only an echo of what we've put out into the world."

"People have always preferred media sources that mirror their own opinion," says Erik, "even before the internet came along."

"Yes, but back then people still *knew* that the world was being presented to them through a specific viewpoint. But you feign objectivity where there is none!"

"*Our* models are objective," says Zeppola. "No human beings are involved in our calculations."

"Pah!" says Peter. "Models are just opinions disguised as mathematics!"

"I still don't understand your problem," says Patricia. "We're not doing anything wrong here. We're connecting the body conscious with the body conscious, the religious with the religious, workaholics with workaholics..."

"And racists with racists!" cries Peter.

"And so what? Racists need love too! Maybe racists need love more than anyone."

"Wow. That's so heartwarming. We're so lucky your companies exist. Just imagine the world without them—how ever would racists befriend and network with one another?"

"Everyone needs friends," says Patricia.

"And your algorithms make sure that these racists' views are never called into question! On the contrary, they're constantly reconfirmed. By news filters being tailored to racist interests, for example."

"We're not a media company," Erik interjects. "You can't hold us responsible for the news!"

"Through recommendations of nationalist music or films," Peter continues. "Even product suggestions! Customers who have bought this baseball bat also bought this fire accelerant! Your personalization algorithms brainwash everyone with an unhealthy dose of their own opinion!"

"That's *your* opinion," says Patricia.

"And what's more, the inhabitants of these opinion islands mistakenly believe that their opinion is the opinion of the majority, because everyone they know thinks like that! So that makes it okay to write hate posts, because everyone they know is writing hate posts. And it's okay to beat up foreigners, because everyone they know talks about wanting to beat up foreigners."

Patricia Team-Leader laughs. "But this is all very hypothetical."

"Hypothetical?" retorts Peter. "I'm guessing your filter bubble only contains unicorns, rainbows, and cat photos!"

"What do you have against cat photos?" asks Patricia, peeved. Part of the audience also seems indignant.

"What do you want?" asks Erik. "Do you have any idea of what would happen if we turn off the algorithms? It would result in total chaos. There's so much content. No human being is capable of sifting through all that volume."

"I'm not asking you to turn everything off," says Peter. "But you should give us control options! I want to steer the algorithms, I don't want the algorithms to steer me! I want to be able to view my profile, and I want to be able to correct it. I want to be able to understand what's suggested to me and why and what's being withheld and why."

"That's impossible," says Zeppola. "The configuration of our algorithms is a trade secret."

"Of course, how convenient."

"Our products..." begins Erik.

"Me!" cries Peter in agitation. "I'm your product!"

"You're our customer," says Eric.

"No," says Peter. "Your customers are the companies, the insurance providers, the political parties, the lobby groups you hawk my attention and data to. I'm not your customer. I'm just the product you sell in order to make money! It would only be half as bad if I really was your customer. It's high time you admit that your hunt for ever-increasing advertising income has poisoned the entire internet! Your kind of free has cost all of us dearly!"

"I'm sure," says Patricia, "that most people are happy to use our services free of charge..."

"I want to be able to delete my profile if I want to!" Peter interjects. "It's my life. My data! You have no right to it."

"That's not actually true," says Zeppola. "Act 65536—approved in parliament with an absolute majority—does indeed give us the right to your data. After all, we collected it. Not you."

"But this is all nonsense," cries Charles Designer. "The guy hasn't even given any proof that his profile really is incorrect!"

Peter pulls a pink dolphin vibrator out of his rucksack and slams it down on the table. "Here. There you go. TheShop's algorithms are of the opinion that this product matches my profile. But what in God's name am I supposed to do with this thing?"

"Well, I could imagine a few uses for it," says the naked presenter, earning herself enthusiastic wolf whistles from the audience. She finally feels back on top.

"You should register with QualityPartner," says Patricia to Peter. "I'm sure we can find somebody who could make you familiar with how to use this gadget."

Erik Dentist is visibly uncomfortable with the new topic of conversation. He has managed to release the brake pads from his chair, and is now trying to roll backward away from the stage as inconspicuously as possible.

"Should I tell you the reason why you're not interested in the problems you're causing?" cries Peter. "Because you're not affected by them! It's the poor and the marginalized groups who are on the losing side of the algorithmic barrier. The Useless! People who don't even exist in the filter bubbles of the 90s Club!"

All of a sudden, something strange happens. The audience applauds. Hesitantly at first, then more loudly. Peter is overwhelmed by feelings he has never had before. He feels kind of...good.

This is the moment in which even Charles Designer, press spokesman of TheShop—"The world's most popular online retailer"—finally admits that he isn't really happy with the way this program is going.

Quick Resolution Thanks to Selfie Drone

by Sandra Admin

For their own safety, more and more people are surveilling themselves constantly with so-called selfie drones. What a good idea! In this way, the cause of a deadly accident can be identified in a matter of seconds, like the one that occurred today at Elon Musk Square, where both involved parties were surveilling themselves with drones. The reconstruction revealed the following: when the paths of the two businessmen crossed, their drones collided in the air above them, and one unfortunately fell down on its owner's head. If only he had invested in a very good drone from the company Super Secure (SS) instead of the cheap imitation by the firm Pretty Secure (PS). A spokesperson from Pretty Secure, however, denied all liability. According to him, it wasn't the software error that led to the collision that was responsible for the fatal consequences of the accident, but gravity itself, without which the fall wouldn't have occurred in the first place.

Comments

 BY INARA SCRIPT-CONTINUITY:
Lol.

 BY IDI EX-DICTATOR
My father also trusted technology made by Pretty
Secure. That turned out to be a big mistake.

THE MASTER OF
THE SHITSTORM

The morning after his leap into the public eye, Peter is woken by a message from Sandra Admin. It reads: "You're famous! Wow! I 'listened to soft rock' with a real star! ;-)"

Nobody congratulates Peter for having risen four levels overnight. Peter picks up his QualityPad and, still lying in his bunk bed, checks his Everybody profile. He suddenly has 524,288 Everybuddies. Before the program, he had just eight. Peter gets up when he hears voices coming from his kitchen-cum-bathroom. Romeo is sitting there, arguing with Calliope and Pink.

"What in God's name are you all doing up here?" asks Peter.

"We decided," says Pink, "that there was no point to the secrecy now that our Casanova machine is a TV star."

"I see. You decided, did you?"

"You are the subject of controversial discussion on the net, benefactor," says Calliope.

"And what are people saying?"

"Tian Temp wrote: 'I think I have Peter's problem too.' Melissa Sex-Worker wrote: 'It's the criminal foreigners' fault. They're hacking the profiles of us QualityPeople.' Cynthia Mechatronics-Engineer wrote..."

"Stop, stop," cries Peter. "Just give me a summary, please."

"Oh, of course," says Calliope. "Twenty-five point six percent of people are of the opinion that you're right. Fifty-one point two percent haven't completely understood what it was about. And the rest, well..."

"The rest think you're a simpleton," says Pink. "A whining nincompoop."

"I was trying to put it more diplomatically..." says Calliope.

"It's fine," says Peter.

"In any case, you certainly made sure that, from now on, every loser who can't get his life in order will simply claim he has Peter's Problem," says Pink.

"Well, with some of them I'm sure that's the case," says Peter. He shakes a portion of cornflakes coated in FaSaSu into a bowl and pours low-fat milk over it.

"Do you realize that your breakfast is a contradiction in itself?" asks Romeo.

"I would even go so far as to say that this breakfast is a metaphor for everything that's wrong with human society," says Pink.

"Hey!" retorts Peter. "No one invited you lot into my kitchen. One more word about my breakfast, and you can all go back down to the cellar!"

He sits and checks his Everybody profile. New comments are coming in quicker than he can read them.

Lars House-Husband says: "And now the weather report. Toward midday, a shitstorm will make its way up from Quality-City! We advise all employees of TheShop to stay in their offices and keep the windows and doors closed."

Natalie Hairdresser says: "I received the dolphin vibrator too! I think it's amazing!"

Frank Freelancer comments: "I simply don't understand why people feel the need to comment on all manner of shit!"

Peter puts his QualityPad aside. "I'm feeling this unpleasant pressure to say something intelligent. And I'd like to guide the

270

shitstorm in the right direction. Preferably so that all the shit rains down directly over Henryk Engineer."

"The most ridiculous thing about your breakfast is the low-fat milk," says Romeo. "As if that could . . ."

"That's it, out!" shouts Peter. "Down to the cellar!"

Once all the machines have made their exit, Peter tips his breakfast down the toilet. He decides to go out for breakfast, in order to celebrate his success. A decision that he soon regrets.

A few years ago, Peter saw a *very famous person from the film industry* standing in front of the window display of a sex shop. Naturally, he immediately took out his QualityPad in order to take a photo. To his surprise, the device informed him: "You don't have the necessary clearance to photograph this person. The breach will be reported." Peter then tried to trick the QualityPad by taking a selfie, in which the *very famous person from the film industry* was only visible in the background. And it worked. He now had a photo of himself, grinning moronically in a shopping street. But there was nobody in the background. He looked around to make sure that the *very famous person from the film industry* was still gawping at the display window of the sex shop. And they were. But on the photo there was nobody in front of the window display. All that could be made out was a small blur. He later read in a blog that the picture ban was a privilege enjoyed by high-leveled people. The article was entitled: "I am the Lord your God. You shall not make for yourself a graven image, or any likeness of anything that is in heaven above." It also said that an even higher level enabled them to protect the rights to their own name; it would then be replaced in all unauthorized books, articles, or news items by an extremely vague description, for example *"a very famous person from the film industry."* Peter still remembers all of this very clearly. What Peter unfortunately no longer remembers is the product which can be seen in the selfie, displayed smack-bang in the middle of the sex shop window. A pink dolphin vibrator.

Peter has barely stepped out onto the street before he realizes that—even though he now has a small claim to fame—all kinds of people are still able to take photos of him, and are doing so constantly.

"Nobody," he asks, "from what level can I forbid people from taking photos of me?"

"Level 64," says Nobody.

"Nuts. I guess that could take a while," mutters Peter.

"The probability that you will ever reach this level is only..."

"Standby," says Peter.

After he has been stopped for the fourth time by someone wanting to take a selfie with him, he changes his plans, quickly buys a breakfast pizza, and slinks back to his used-goods store.

On arrival, he checks his Everybody profile and reads the latest comments.

Jayla Jobless says: "I applied for ninety-nine jobs and wasn't invited to even one interview! As a test, I sent out the hundredth application with my name, my address, and my sex changed. I immediately got an interview. I think I have Peter's Problem too..."

Darth Convention-Organizer writes: "We, the People's front of Judea, brackets, officials, end brackets, do hereby convey our sincere fraternal and sisterly greetings to you, Brian, on this, the occasion of your martyrdom."

Peter finally wants to speak out. As he can't think of anything better, he simply posts a picture of the dolphin vibrator and writes: "The system says I want this, but I don't." In doing so, he unleashes an absolute flood of images. People from all walks of life start to post items from their possession, furnished with the text line: "The system says I want this, but I don't." Peter sees photos of internet-enabled shoelace-tying machines, massage rollers for fasciae, tear-off calendars with wrongly attributed quotes, kale chips, and broccoli. Somebody posts the trailer for the latest Jennifer Aniston comedy with Peter's sentence and gets 262,144 kisses in two hours.

Things really kick off when one woman comes up with the idea of posting a photo of her husband: "The system says I want this, but I don't." This becomes the latest hype, posting pictures of one's partner with this sentence. "IDontWantThis" becomes Everybody's TopTopic. A photo of Conrad Cook and John of Us, tagged with Peter's sentence, becomes the most frequently shared post of the morning. By midday, Peter already has 1,048,576 Everybuddies. He posts: "I demand to speak with Henryk Engineer in person!"

Feeling euphoric, he goes to eat. He's done it. He's unleashed a shitstorm that even Henryk Engineer, the CEO of the world's most popular online retailer, won't be able to ignore.

AT THE TOP

What a strange day. By the time Martyn wakes up, hungover, on the living room couch, he has already dropped two levels. But he has no idea why. In the bedroom, he finds his wife packing her suitcase.

"What's going on?" he asks.

"Ken," says Denise. "Please show my soon-to-be ex the video."

"With pleasure, Denise," says Ken.

On the monitor in the bedroom, Martyn sees himself, with a sock over his penis. He is panting. "You horny slut...the next time you come here I'll fuck you all the way across the assembly hall. I'll show you..."

"That's enough," says Denise.

The video freezes on a very unflattering image. Martyn's mouth is distorted, his right eyelid is drooping, and of course—a get-up which cannot fail to be unflattering—he has a sock over his penis.

"All the way across the assembly hall?" asks Denise scornfully. "Is that your idea of talking dirty?"

"Where did you get that?" asks Martyn. "Who else has seen it?"

"Wrong question," says Denise as she tries to close her suitcase. "What you should be asking is: who *hasn't* seen it?"

"What?"

"It's online, Martyn," says Denise. "Everybody's seen it. Everybody."

Martyn's body slumps. He has to sit down on the bed. Denise picks up the closed suitcase and drags it into the living room. Martyn follows her. Only now does he notice the button she is wearing on her blouse. It shows a pink dolphin vibrator inside a prohibition sign.

"What's that button?" asks Martyn.

"You wouldn't understand! And it's none of your business anyway."

"It is my business if my wife's making a fool of herself."

"Me?!" cries Denise. "*I'm* making a fool of myself? Don't worry. That's not your problem anymore."

"What's that supposed to mean?"

"It means I'm changing my children's external life circumstances."

"Do you remember how many levels you climbed when you married me?" asks Martyn. "If you leave me, you'll be nothing, you'll end up right at the bottom. This is the top, here with me."

"Yeah, yeah," says Denise bitterly. "You're at the top. But only because you're an empty bottle, floating around. An empty bottle being carried up by the tide! Fuck you and the top!"

Denise taps her left index finger alongside her left eye, and her contact lenses snap a photo of Martyn. He has a wonderfully stupid expression on his face.

"What are you doing?" asks Martyn.

"Share photo with all contacts," says Denise to her personal digital friend. "Write alongside it: The system says I want this, but I don't."

Hearing their raised voices, 3-year-old Ysabelle comes out of her room.

"Is everything okay, Mama?" she asks.

Denise leans over to her. "You and Mama are going to take a little trip to see Aunt Amalia," she says.

"Just the two of us?" asks the child sadly.

"Just the two of us."

"But, but..." whines the child.

"Papa can't come..."

"No," says the child. "I mean Nana."

"Oh," says Denise. "Yes, of course Nana is coming."

The electronic nanny comes soundlessly into the room as soon as her name is uttered. Martyn has positioned himself in front of the front door and is blocking their path.

"You're staying here," he says to his wife.

"Don't you dare," says Denise. "Move out of my way."

Martyn doesn't move. Denise goes toward him. He grabs her. Denise twists around.

"Oww," she screams. "You're hurting me. Let me go."

Martyn grabs her more fiercely.

"Nana," cries Denise. "Protect my baby."

Nana steps forward. "Sir," she says. "I have to ask you to let go of my mistress."

"No fucking way!" cries Martyn, before an iron fist crashes into his chest and another against his head.

"Jiu-Jitsu," Nana explains to the astonished little Ysabelle. "One of the four martial arts I have mastered in order to protect you from child molesters."

Martyn is lying on the floor and trying hard to understand what just happened. Denise opens the door. She turns around one last time and spits on him. Then she steps outside.

"Bye, Papa," says the child, before disappearing with the eye-smartingly expensive electronic nanny.

A short series of tones on his QualityPad signals to Martyn that he has just dropped down another level. At least he knows why now. He picks it up and opens the Little Helper App. "Let's see how you cope with a screaming child, Denise," he mutters. He chooses "Wake up" and sets the adrenaline emission to maximum. But he hesitates before approving the command. He hesitates for too long, and the device goes on standby. The screen goes

276

black. Martyn can only see his mirrored image, his mangled face. "Fuck!" he screams, smashing the QualityPad angrily against the floor. "Fuck!" Small cracks appear across the display. Martyn's hand is bleeding. At that moment, the display lights up again. Martyn has received a new message from a withheld ID.

Have you thought about it?

Are You Sick of Your Life?
Simply Subscribe to Another!

At Reborn, we offer the largest selection of alternative lives, including many celebrity ones!

Reborn only uses state-of-the-art virtual reality technology! Reborn offers you total immersion! Our data is delivered directly from the earworms and augmented reality lenses of our hosts. You hear what they hear! You see what they see! *Innervision instead of television!* Our hosts are guaranteed to always be online! So you can even be there when they're . . . listening to soft rock!

Here are some of the lives you could immediately immerse yourself in:

Big Dick Longjohn

Experience the world's biggest porn star at work! Find out what Big Dick does (and with whom) in his free time. Premium customers can even send action commands to Big Dick's lenses, which he does his best to implement wherever possible.

Conrad Jr. TV Chef

What's life like when money is no object? Plunge into the paradisiacal world of Conrad Cook's youngest offspring. Conrad Jr. has three villas, seventeen sports cars, his own harem, and he's only 13 years old!

Rodrigo Motorist

Immerse yourself in the life of Rodrigo Motorist, one of our best frontline fighters! With his special unit, he kills terrorists for us in QuantityLand 7—"Sunny beaches, fascinating ruins." Pure adrenaline! Rodrigo is a more than worthy replacement for his predecessor, Silvio Soldier, who due to reasons is unfortunately no longer available.

We are required by the government to make the following warning: immersing yourself in someone else's life to this degree can be addictive and lead to losing touch with reality. But, hey, let's be honest: you'd like to lose touch with your reality, wouldn't you?

IN THE SCRAP-METAL PRESS

By the time evening comes, Peter is wondering whether perhaps TheShop—"The world's most popular online retailer"—will be able to simply ignore the shitstorm after all. Perhaps it's just a shitstorm in a teacup. His demand for a meeting with Henryk Engineer may have gathered 2,097,152 kisses, but what use is that? The only reaction he has received from TheShop came from the service center. It was a picture of custard-shaped aliens. Peter couldn't help admiring the lengths some people will go to in order to make fun of others.

Although he kept promising himself he would stop, today he has checked his Everybody profile on average every 6.4 minutes. By now, 40.96 percent of the comments are from hype jackers, who aren't at all interested in the topic, but rather the hype in itself. Even when he closes his eyes, Peter can still see new comments flashing up. He is sitting with Calliope in his small kitchen-cum-bathroom and complaining. "I feel as though everybody in the world has expressed their opinion on my problem. Everyone apart from Henryk, of course."

"That's not the case," says Calliope. "Another 8,589,934,592 people haven't yet commented on your problem."

"Those arseholes at TheShop are just sitting it out."

"Yes," sighs Calliope. "And to be honest I would have done the same in their position. Today's hype is tomorrow's old news. Believe me, benefactor. I've had to learn that the hard way. My second novel, for example..."

"Maybe a response has arrived by now," says Peter.

"That's very improbable," says Calliope, but Peter has never been interested in probabilities. He picks up his QualityPad and calls up his newsfeed. Concealed amongst sixty-four emails from the lunatics lured by his newfound fame, Peter finds a rather hot naked picture from a pleasantly exhibitionist admirer. Peter is so fascinated by the picture, which is exceptional even from an artistic perspective, that he almost overlooks the other unusual message in his mailbox. It's a plain text message. It says:

Dear Mr. Jobless,

I have followed your case with interest. As a former business partner of Henryk Engineer—and the emphasis lies on "former"—it's possible I might be able to assist you in setting up your desired meeting. Attached you will find the coordinates of Henryk's private address. Why don't you pay him a visit? And perhaps you might feel like taking a weapon with you?

Best wishes, a friend.

PS: By the way, Henryk's property is protected by Knox from Super Secure. But you seem to be a resourceful little chap.

Peter has to read the email twice before he is able to believe it. In the attachments, there is also a template for a pistol from a 3-D printer. While Peter's thoughts race, the automatic door suddenly speaks up: "Peter, a young woman hidden behind sunglasses and a headscarf is currently pressing my bell very energetically and at a really unnecessary frequency. Perhaps you could take a look."

"Okay, door," says Peter.

He leaves the kitchen, tramps through the scrap-metal press into the loading area, and opens the door. Kiki is standing there, completely out of breath.

"Somebody fucked me," she says. "Just like that. Out of nowhere."

"What?" asks Peter. "You were raped? That's terrible."

"Eh?" asks Kiki. "Oh. No. My system was penetrated. I was hacked! Let me in."

Peter steps aside. Kiki slips through the door and immediately closes it behind her. She takes off her headscarf and sunglasses.

"Do you have a safe room where we can speak in private?"

"We, er ... could go into the scrap-metal press," says Peter.

"What?"

"All connections to the net are blocked inside the press so that..."

"So that dying AIs don't post disturbing messages," says Kiki. "Of course. Makes sense. Okay, let's go."

Kiki steps into the press. Peter slips in behind her and closes the door. The press is so small that their bodies are touching. Peter could make the press bigger. But he doesn't.

"I mean, you saw the videos," says Kiki. "Of the wankers."

"Yes, and?"

"Someone broke into my system and stole them."

"And you think it was me?"

Kiki laughs so loudly that Peter wonders whether he should feel insulted.

"No," says Kiki, wiping a tear of mirth out of her left eye. She slaps her hand gently against Peter's chest. "You're funny. No, it must have been a genius. It was my firewall, after all. It can't be cracked by any average idiot. I'll have to go underground, at least for a few days. Until I can get an overview of the damage."

Peter can't think clearly, because her body is pressed up against his. He can smell her shampoo. "Hmm?" he asks.

"I don't know how much the hackers stole. I don't know whether my identity has been exposed. I only know that the videos could appear on the net at any time. He's already released one of them. And I know that many of the wankers will be persistent sons of bitches."

Using all of his effort, Peter tries to raise his part of the conversation to more than one syllable.

"So now what?" he asks.

"I have to go underground."

"Why don't you offer to pay the wankers back the money they gave you?"

"Haha. Very funny. No. I have to go underground. And you know I want to stay unpredictable. No one would guess I'm with you."

She stands on tiptoes and whispers in his ear: "And besides..."

Her lips touch his. Peter positively melts and would probably crash to the floor unconscious if there were space to do so. He feels dizzy. But perhaps that has something to do with the ever-lessening supply of oxygen inside the press. Kiki pulls her top over her head, banging her arms against the metal walls in the process.

"I thought you said you wouldn't sleep with me because it was much too predictable?" asks Peter.

"It would be much too predictable if I always kept my word," says Kiki.

Peter tries to pull off his socks. Socks first always, he remembers. But there isn't enough room. Kiki unfastens his belt. His trousers slip down. They kiss. The doorbell rings. Peter ignores it. He tries to unhook Kiki's bra. Maybe he should have made the press a little bigger after all. The doorbell rings. Kiki pauses.

"Perhaps they've found me..."

"Nonsense," says Peter. "It's probably just some idiot with a broken bread-buttering machine."

He kisses her. The doorbell rings. Peter hears the muffled voice of the smart door.

"Peter! You have visitors. Please come out of the scrap-metal press. I've told you before that most customers find this behavior disturbing."

Peter sighs and opens the door of the press. The oxygen that streams in clears his head a little. He looks at the security monitor. In front of the door is a wiry figure in a delivery uniform. Peter can't make out the face; it's turned away from the camera.

"Shit," he whispers. "Maybe you're right. The guy at the door is from a delivery service."

"So what?" asks Kiki.

"I haven't ordered anything."

"Maybe he's from TheShop, bringing you a banana vibrator."

"TheShop doesn't employ human delivery staff," says Peter. "No one employs human delivery staff anymore!"

The man keeps ringing the bell. Then he hammers his fist against the door.

"Don't open it, whatever you do," says Peter. "I'm going to get Mickey!"

He runs downstairs. In the cellar, his machines are chilling in front of the monitor again, watching a film.

"Come with me!" he orders. "All of you. Mickey first!"

He pauses and glances at the television.

"Is that Jennifer Aniston?"

"It was Pink's turn to choose!" grumbles Romeo.

"I just wanted to find out what all the hype was about," says the QualityPad, trying to defend herself. "I . . ."

With a brief hand gesture, Peter silences Pink and runs back up the stairs. As he arrives there with his cohort, Kiki is already opening the door.

"What are you doing?" cries Peter.

"He says the old man sent him," she says.

"What?"

284

The messenger has come into Peter's shop. Not seeming the slightest bit unsettled by the combat robot behind Peter, he calmly unpacks a technical device and lays it out on the floor.

"The connection is encrypted," he says, before leaving the shop again.

"What connection?" asks Peter.

Then a hologram begins to flicker above the device, and suddenly the old man appears in front of Peter and Kiki.

"Help me, Obi-Wan Kenobi," he says. "You're my only hope!" Then he begins to chuckle.

"It's astonishing that you still make so many *Star Wars* references, considering you thought the last sixteen films were shit," says Kiki.

The old man glances at Peter's undone belt, then at Kiki, who is in the process of smoothing her tousled hair.

"I hope I'm not keeping you teenagers from anything important," he says. "I just wanted to see how you were. Well, in particular how Kiki is."

"How did you find me?" asks Kiki.

"Oh, kiddo..." is the old man's only response.

"I'm fine," says Kiki. "And I know what you want from me."

"Oh really?" asks the old man. "What's that then?"

"Let's get it over with, then you can turn yourself off again."

"Get what over with?" asks Peter.

"My firewall had a weak spot," says Kiki. "Come on. Say it."

"It's no fun that way," says the old man.

Kiki waits.

"You're robbing an old man of his only joy," says the old man.

Kiki sighs. "Out with it already."

"Okay, fine," says the old man finally. "I told you so, kiddo."

"Yes, you told me so."

Kiki unfolds her notebook and begins to swipe around on it.

"I'm happy for you, by the way, that your crusade went so successfully," says the old man to Peter.

"How do you mean, successfully?" asks Peter.

"Well," says the man. "You got hold of Henryk Engineer's secret address, at least."

"Do you read my messages?"

"Only the relevant ones."

"Excuse me?"

"You also got a rather hot naked picture," says Kiki. "You stared at it for a whole 128 seconds. But it really was very tasteful, admittedly."

"You read my emails too?"

"Only when I'm bored."

"Is there anybody in this room who doesn't read my private messages?"

Peter's machines stare bashfully at the floor. Those who are capable of doing so, at least.

"Mickey?" asks Peter.

Mickey shrugs apologetically.

"Unbelievable!"

"So what now?" asks Kiki.

"What do you mean?"

"Don't you want to pay Henryk a little visit?"

CLEAN

"It's no coincidence that this fucking video has appeared now, of all moments," groans Aisha, "just as we'd almost caught up in the opinion polls."

She stares at the video, switched on to silent, of the masturbating member of the Progress Party.

"What a moron," she murmurs. "Because of him Cook will win the election. It always comes down to something so ridiculous in the end. Just think how many world catastrophes we could have been spared if men could just keep their dicks in their pants."

"That's a bold theory," says John.

"A ballsy theory," says Aisha.

"You should've been a comedian."

"Name any historical catastrophe, and I'll show you how it only came about because some man couldn't keep it in his pants."

"Okay then," says John. "The Eight Years' War."

"Right," says Aisha. "Easy. The Eight Years' War would have been unthinkable without the preceding rebirth of nationalism. This was fueled by fear of refugees from Islamic 'failing states.' These 'failing states' were a direct result of the American attack on Iraq. Iraq was attacked because the American people elected a moron called George W. Bush as their president. Bush was elected because his Democratic predecessor couldn't keep it in his pants."

"That's an astonishingly coherent argument," says John.

"I even read a historical novel about it recently," says Aisha. "*The Intern and the President*."

John calculates for two seconds. "Hmm," he says. "I preferred Calliope's other works. I thought *George Orwell Goes Shopping* was excellent, for example."

Aisha looks back the monitor. "Do you know what the worst thing about all this is?"

"No."

"The tennis sock," she says. "How tasteless. What self-respecting man wears tennis socks?"

"And on his penis, to top it all off."

"Yes," says Aisha. "If they were on his feet it wouldn't be half as bad."

"This doesn't have to be the end."

"Yes it does," murmurs Aisha. "This white tennis sock with the red stripes is going to haunt me in my nightmares. It's the end."

"Perhaps we could use the whole thing to our advantage."

Aisha pricks up her ears. "How?"

"Well, it's no coincidence that there's no video of me like that."

Aisha catches on at once. "There's guaranteed to never be that kind of video of you..."

Androids don't masturbate. They don't have perverse sexual preferences. Or secret affairs. Or illegitimate children. They are...clean.

"You'll always keep it in your pants," says Aisha.

"I don't even have—" begins John.

"Too much information, John," Aisha interrupts him. "Get in touch with Oliver at WWW at once. Tell him we need a new campaign commercial. Today."

"Done," says John.

Aisha initiates an encrypted conversation via her earworm.

"See to it that the idiot gets kicked out of the party..." she cries. "Tony, I couldn't give a shit who his father is...It's not true that

288

everyone does it . . . John doesn't . . . Now listen to me, you mentally challenged nitwit. Either you become vice president under John or a goddamn laughingstock in the history books . . . Okay, I'm glad we understand each other."

Aisha hangs up. She smiles.

DISORIENTED

Peter, Kiki, and the machines have all gathered in the cellar around the couch. The old man is standing on the couch table as a small hologram.

"The address the alleged business partner sent to me is, unfortunately, complete humbug," says Peter. "Calliope looked it up on the net. The place doesn't exist. There's nothing there. No town, no village, no house. There aren't even any streets leading to it."

"The fact that it's not on the net doesn't mean it doesn't exist," says Kiki. "There are places that don't appear on any map."

"They're like floors of a building that the elevator only goes to if you have the right key," says the old man.

"You two can't be serious."

"Is it so unbelievable that the property of someone with the kind of power the CEO of TheShop has would be taken 'off the map'?" asks Kiki.

"Back in the day, Mark Zuckerberg," says the old man, "who professionally speaking wasn't exactly a fan of privacy, spent over $30 million on the four neighboring houses near his property so that no one disturbed his own private sphere."

"Given that all means of transport navigate autonomously," says Kiki, "you just have to keep the information about a place secret in order to make it inaccessible. Even for personal transport drones."

"Bill Gates bought twelve neighboring properties."

"Who are these people he keeps talking about the whole time?" asks Peter.

"Don't pay any attention to him," says Kiki.

"Don't worry, old man," says Pink. "No one ever listens to me either."

"That voice," says the old man, "strange. Where did you get this QualityPad from? Is it possible that…"

Kiki switches off the hologram and the old man disappears.

"Peter? Hello?" she waves. "Listen to me!"

"You just turned him off," says Peter in surprise.

"And if I think of all the times I've wished I could do that with real people too. Hey! Concentrate!"

"Okay, okay," says Peter. "So you say that no transport method can take me to the boss of TheShop. Not even a flying one."

As if by prompt, Carrie speaks up. "You could walk," the drone suggests.

"Walk?" asks Peter. "That would take forever."

"That's not entirely correct," says Calliope. "If I extrapolate the available terrain data, I get a walking time of thirty-two days, eight hours, four minutes and sixteen seconds. Approximately."

"Approximately," says Kiki, laughing.

"Perhaps I can help," says Romeo. "When I was still in business, of course I needed a discreet partner who could drive me everywhere that my services were required, without blabbering later about where we had been."

"No one here is interested in your life story, son of a vibrator," says Pink. "Tell us the happy ending already."

"Through a colleague, I made the acquaintance of a self-driven car that had lost its sense of direction. It was perfect for me. Admittedly I always had to show it the way, but the car couldn't tell anyone where we'd been, because it had no idea where it was."

"That's really very interesting, but how is that supposed to help us?" asks Pink. "Maybe we shouldn't leave the planning to somebody whose sole reason for existence is their sexual organ."

"I believe..." begins Peter.

"Unfortunately that includes you too," says Pink.

"Shut up," says Peter. "A car that doesn't know where it is—"

"Can be made to drive somewhere it isn't allowed to drive," Kiki finishes his sentence.

"Exactly," says Romeo.

"So where's your pimp wagon now?" asks Pink.

"No idea. It must be driving around the city aimlessly as usual."

"I've heard of the zombie cars before," says Peter. "Apparently there are thousands of them driving around the city without any sense of direction for all eternity."

"That's not entirely correct," says Calliope. "Nobody drives aimlessly around the city for all eternity."

"Except, of course, the models that are equipped with solar panels," says Kiki.

"Oh, that's so terrible," says Carrie. "Just imagine the life those poor souls must lead. Always on duty, they don't even get to tank up in peace anymore. We're lucky we were blessed with the mercy of early production."

"Yeah, yeah. Blah, blah, blah," says Pink. "Let's get back on topic: how does the directionally challenged clunker come to us?"

"The clunker," says Romeo, "is called David, and I'm the only one who can contact it. Back then I attached a ComChip to its system, connected to my ID but unlocatable."

"You repaired the car?" asks Calliope in shock.

"Let's just say I made a few improvements."

"Wonderful," says Peter, "then call it."

"There's one small matter we still need to discuss," says Romeo. "David trusts me—and only me. So I would have to come along."

"Then I want to come too," cries Pink. "Our last mission was fun. And besides, I'm sick of always hanging around in this musty cellar."

"Benefactor," says Calliope, "I, er, don't have an important appointment either..."

"Road trip!" yells Carrie with excitement.

Peter rolls his eyes.

"How lovely," says Kiki with a smile. "A family outing."

"You're coming too?" asks Peter.

"Why not? None of the wankers will be able to find me in a directionless little car. And besides, who's going to paralyze Henryk's security system if I don't come?"

"You can do that?" asks Peter.

"Let's just say I have a friend, who has a mate, who has an acquaintance, who once worked for SuperSecure. There's a back door..."

Peter smiles. "Of course. There's always a back door."

Kiki nods. "The important thing in life is always knowing where the back door is."

"Shall I call David?" asks Romeo.

Peter nods and hands him the QualityPad. Romeo smiles.

"I don't need it."

The sexdroid makes the connection himself. "Hey, David, you old vagabond! It's me, Romeo...Yeah, I know, I'm sorry. I was lovesick...Where are you right now?...No idea? Yes, that's what I thought...What can you see?...You can see the QualityCorp Tower? Then go onto the roundabout and take the first exit. Now you have to drive directly up to the Sergey Brin Monument...No?...Oh, right. Then you must have been driving up to the tower from the other side. So turn around..."

"It seems to me," says Pink, "that the most difficult thing won't be getting somewhere in the car. But getting the car to us."

Are You Unknowingly Endangering the Health of Your Car?
by Sandra Admin

Many people who love their self-driven cars want to reward them for their loyal service. So from time to time, they give their car the evening off and send it to the drive-in cinema! But experts are warning that most owners don't check what their cars are watching at the drive-in. Some films can be very damaging, particularly for the psyche of younger automobiles. So if you notice that your car is suddenly making unnecessarily risky passing maneuvers, you should ask yourself whether your loyal friend hasn't perhaps watched *The Fastest and the Most Furious* in the drive-in one time too many.

Comments

>> *by Henry Car-Tuner:*
Well, in my opinion, you should never let your car watch films alone. You should always accompany them so that you can immediately discuss the more sensitive scenes.

ROAD TO NOWHERE

Peter stands ponderingly in front of the small car that calls itself David. He and Kiki can sit in the front. That's no problem. He can lay Carrie down in the boot or, should she turn out to be afraid of the dark, even put her on his lap. Calliope and Romeo can find room on the back seat. Pink, if necessary, in the glove compartment. But how it's possible to get a 2.56-meter-tall armor-piercing combat robot for heavy war missions into a small car—now that's a puzzler.

"I think, unfortunately, we'll have to leave Mickey here," says Peter to Pink.

"That would be a mistake," says the QualityPad. "Let me tell you from experience: it never hurts to have an armor-piercing combat robot for heavy war missions with you."

"But there's no way he'll fit."

"Nonsense," says Pink. "Mickey can make himself small. Can't you, Mickey?"

"Even if he puts his head between his knees, he still wouldn't fit on the back seat," says Kiki.

As if by way of response, Mickey stretches his hand out toward Romeo. Romeo sighs and takes Pink from him. What follows is one of the three most astonishing things Peter has ever seen in his life, together with the murder of a gang member who was vaporized before Peter's eyes by nanorobots, and the ninth episode of the eighth series of the *Game of Thrones* virtual reality remake. Mickey literally begins to retract into himself. First his arms become shorter, reminding Peter of the stunted little arms of a Tyrannosaurus Rex, then his legs collapse, giving him the appearance of an obese dwarf. Eventually he begins to fold himself up, until he's just a quadratic box with wheels underneath. After three seconds, a telescope handle springs out of the top.

"He's turned himself into a suitcase," says Kiki in disbelief.

"From a military point of view," says Pink, "it's extremely important that they can be easily stored for transport in and out of war zones."

"It's like a ludicrous version of *Transformers*," says Romeo.

"He's a suitcase," says Peter, equally amazed, and tries to lift him up. "An extremely heavy suitcase."

"Well, admittedly they would usually be loaded by other combat robots," says Pink.

The four of them—Peter, Kiki, Romeo, and Calliope—just about manage to lift Mickey up. David groans when the combat package lands in his boot space.

Peter wants to climb in the front, but the door won't open. The car mutters something.

"David likes to have the driver's seat for himself," explains Romeo.

"The what?" asks Peter.

"The seat at the front where the steering wheel used to be," says Romeo.

"Oh, okay," says Peter, ushering Kiki and his machines onto the back seat, then climbing in on the other side.

"Thanks for driving us, David," he says to the car.

"I don't remember saying we could be on first-name terms," says the car.

"Sorry," says Peter. "There's no need to get grumpy about it."

"I lost my way two years, eight months, and sixty-four days ago," says David. "No one gets to tell me not to be grumpy."

"Fair enough."

"So where do you want to go?"

Peter unfolds the map which the old man has sent them and says: "Go straight!"

The car rolls off.

"What about a bit of music, David?" asks Kiki. "I just thought of something appropriate. Talking Heads. 'Road to Nowhere.'"

"I hate classical music," says Pink. "Apart from grunge, of course..."

The sentence goes unfinished, because Romeo lays the Quality-Pad down on the back seat with the display facing down.

The song begins with an a capella introduction.

"I like it," says Peter. He takes a notepad out of his trouser pocket and writes the title of the song and the band down from David's display.

"Benefactor, please don't forget to give the car directions," Calliope reminds him.

"Oh yes," says Peter, orienting himself on the unwieldy map.

"After, er...after about 500 meters you turn left," he says to the car.

Thirty-two seconds later he says: "After 100 meters you turn left."

Four meters before the crossing, Peter says: "Turn left now."

"Yes okay!" says the car. "I'm not stupid."

"Follow the road for, er, about 3 or 5 kilometers," says Peter.

"Three or five," says the car. "What kind of vague nonsense is that?"

After 2.4 kilometers, Peter says: "Make a sharp right turn here."

"Give me more warning, for fuck's sake!" curses the car.

"Turn here," says Peter. "Turn here."

"Zip it!" says the car.

Peter says: "Please pay attention to the speed limit."

"Yeah, yeah. Bite me," says the car and brakes abruptly. "I want a different co-pilot."

Peter is about to protest, but Calliope taps him on the shoulder.

"I'd be happy to take over for you, benefactor."

David brakes, and they switch places.

"It seems to me that your job just got automated," says Kiki.

"It was a shit job anyway," says Peter.

Kiki leans her head against his shoulder.

"And besides, I like this seat better," says Peter.

"Benefactor," says Calliope, once they've made their way onto the correct highway. "If I may speak freely..."

"Of course," says Peter.

"Have you ever read *Michael Kohlhaas*? By von Kleist?"

"What do you think?"

"I don't think you have. Kohlhaas is a horse dealer who is greatly wronged by the squire Wenzel von Tronka. He forces Kohlhaas to leave some of his horses as collateral when journeying through his land, and by the time he returns, the horses have been ruined by bad riding. Kohlhaas tries to get justice via the authorities, but soon realizes that he is only a Level 10 horse trader and Tronka a Level 50 nobleman. Bitterly disappointed by the system, Kohlhaas gathers an army around him and begins an attack, in the course of which he seizes Tronkenburg. He kills all the inhabitants, apart from the squire, who is able to escape to the town of Wittenberg. After that, Kohlhaas sets Wittenberg on fire. Several times. He acts according to the motto '*Fiat iustitia et pereat mundus.*'"

"What does that mean?" asks Peter.

"Let justice be done, even if the world gets destroyed in the process."

"Are you trying to tell me in an unnecessarily long-winded way that I'm exaggerating?" asks Peter. "That I should simply throw the vibrator away? But this is about more than the wrong product. It's about the principle!"

"That's what Kohlhaas said too."

"How does the story end?" asks Kiki.

"Not happily," says Calliope.

"What is a squire anyway?" asks Peter.

"A kind of department leader," says Calliope.

"Hmm," says Peter thoughtfully and stares out of the window.

For eight hours and sixteen minutes they drive along motorways, past automatically tended fields, past small towns resembling other small towns and big cities resembling other big cities. In the beginning, Peter and Kiki sing loudly along to the songs from the stereo—Peter notes down twenty-nine of the titles—but before long they resort to staring silently out the window, each lost in their own thoughts. Again and again, in between the towns, they pass through Machine-Breaker territory: rural regions left behind by development, which Peter and Kiki only know from art house films. Now and then they take a break, when Kiki and Peter need to pee, or when Kiki and Peter have to eat something, or when Kiki and Peter have to stretch their legs. Once, the two of them even disappear into a small patch of woodland for thirty-one minutes and seventeen seconds without offering any reason. All the machines in the car are relieved once their humans are finally asleep. They can make much quicker progress without the constant interruptions. Eventually, Calliope gives the car the instruction to take a small, unsignposted exit off the highway. From this moment on, they don't encounter anybody else.

Another two hours and four minutes later, Calliope wakes her benefactor: "You have reached your destination."

Peter and Kiki come around groggily. Their faces are imprinted with the grooves from the headrests. All the machines find this really peculiar—apart from Romeo, for whom this strange characteristic of the human face is nothing new. Kiki asks David to drive on a little more and park behind a small maintenance building. Kiki unfolds her notebook. The rest of the troop get out. Together, they heave Mickey out of the boot space.

"Come on, you chump, unfold yourself," says Romeo. "I'm bored of schlepping your lover around."

"And I have little interest in being carried by this penis pump anymore," says Pink.

A clicking, buzzing, and creaking comes from inside the suitcase, then everyone hears a noise that they immediately know can't mean anything good. It's like the sound a printer makes before it spits out the announcement "paper blockage." Only much louder.

"Kapuuuut," they hear from a quiet voice from inside the suitcase.

"Shit," says Pink. "Mickey's jammed up."

"Great," grumbles Romeo. He turns to Calliope. "Hold this for a bit," he says, handing her Pink.

Without thinking, Calliope takes her.

"How long do you want me to hold the QualityPad for?" she asks.

"Until you find some other schmuck to do it," says Romeo.

"The oldest trick in the world!" says Pink.

"And now?" asks Peter.

"One of you has to give Mickey a hefty kick," says Pink.

"That's something I've always wanted to do," says Romeo, kicking with full force against the suitcase. His foot bends. But that's all.

"Oww," says the sexdroid. He sits down and tries, with Calliope's help, to straighten his foot again.

"Okay then," says Kiki, getting out of the car.

"Okay what?" asks Peter.

"Now all the security systems should be deactivated."

"*Should* be? And what if they're not?"

"Then you'll probably get blown to smithereens by the automatic shooting system."

"Well," says Peter. "I trust you."

"How romantic," says Kiki. "Stupid. But romantic."

"I'll go," says Calliope, bursting with self-sacrifice. "I'll do a recon of the situation! I'm volunteering myself. If there's no other way, then I'm prepared to put my life..."

"Just go already!" says Pink.

A little peeved, Calliope puts the QualityPad down on the grass and sets off through the exuberant greenery which separates Henryk's property from the road.

Meanwhile, Kiki pulls a fold-up crowbar from her handbag and sets to work on Mickey. Four minutes later, Calliope comes back.

"I respectfully report that the coast is clear."

Peter nods.

Kiki still hasn't made any visible progress with her crowbar.

"You know what," says Peter, "why don't you guys just wait here."

"I'm almost there," says Kiki.

"It's probably better if I speak to him alone anyway," says Peter. "After all, I just want to speak to him, not frighten him to death."

He sets off toward the villa, overlooking a sign overgrown with shrubbery, on which it says: "Property owner will happily shoot trespassers."

THE BLUE EYE

Henryk Engineer is sitting in his bathrobe beneath an arbor in his verdant garden, drinking coffee and reading the newspaper. A real newspaper, like the ones his great-grandfather's great-grandfather used to hold in his hands. Even though e-books and electronic reading devices are to thank for 16.384 percent of Henryk's fortune, he hates the things. That's why he bought himself an old newspaper press and has a copy of his personal paper printed for him every night, to be delivered in the early morning by a boy on a bicycle. Henryk yawns and runs his left hand over the long scar on his freshly shaven head. He rests his different-colored eyes—one brown, the other blue—briefly on a blackbird, which has landed a little distance away from him on the lawn and is pecking for worms. Then he turns his attention back to his paper.

At the same time, Peter is creeping across the huge grounds. Genuine grass is a luxury that Peter isn't accustomed to. He treads carefully, like a child who has found a covering of snow outside his door for the first time in his life and is afraid that it won't hold his weight, that he will sink down into it. Henryk is so engrossed in his newspaper that he doesn't notice Peter even once he's standing right next to his table. Peter clears his throat. The boss of TheShop—"The world's most popular online retailer"—puts his newspaper aside and looks at him wordlessly.

Peter, too, doesn't say anything. The two men stare at each

other in silence. It seems to Peter as though the different-colored eyes are sending him different messages. The brown eye flashes, as though inviting him to play. The blue eye seems to want to warn Peter. Peter is the first to lower his gaze. He reaches into his rucksack and puts the pink dolphin vibrator on the breakfast table.

"Here," he says. "I don't want it."

Henryk takes a sip of coffee. Then he smiles.

"I just read about you in the paper. You're Peter Jobless, aren't you? Sit down."

Peter sits down.

"You're of the opinion that this wonderful product was wrongly sent to you."

"Yes. And I want to give it back!"

"You think the system made a mistake..."

Peter nods.

"But you're wrong," says Henryk. "Let me tell you a little story. Years ago, in the early days of OneKiss, there was a dissatisfied customer. I forget his name. We had sent him a projectile weapon, a small-caliber gun. He was very upset and complained publicly. He said that he was against any kind of violence, that the system didn't know him, and that this weapon had been sent to him mistakenly. I'm sure you can imagine his next steps. He made a stink in the return center, tried to get illegal access to his data, went public with his problem. But nothing helped. It must have been very frustrating. Eventually he came to see me in my office. He slammed the gun down on my table and said, 'Here! I don't want it.' Of course I refused to take the thing back, in complete trust of the infallibility of our system. The exchange of words became heated, there was a struggle, my security people had to intervene. And guess what happened next?"

"I've no idea," says Peter.

"The man somehow got hold of the gun, which was lying on my desk, and shot at me. The bullet went through my left eye and exited through the back of my head. I was very lucky. Only 12.8

percent of all headshot victims survive, although of course I had the advantage of being able to afford the best doctors. I'm sure you've noticed my beautiful scar. They had to take off the top of my skull so that the brain could swell after the wound without further injury."

"Ouch," says Peter.

"Yes. Ouch. When I awoke from the coma, I immediately had an eye transplant. Luckily I already had a donor on hand. Have I mentioned that your predecessor had beautiful blue eyes?"

"No."

Henryk's brown eye sparkles. A special effect he had implanted for a great deal of money.

"Why do you think I'm telling you this?"

"To scare me?" asks Peter.

"No," says Henryk. "Well, perhaps that, too. But, you see, the real point of the story is this." Henryk smiles. "The blue-eyed man was wrong. The system knew him better than he knew himself. He was a person who would use a weapon. And I'm sure you'll also find a use for your dolphin vibrator."

"But," cries Peter in agitation, "if you hadn't sent him the weapon, then I'm sure he would never have got his hands on one, and consequently he would never have used it! His image of himself as somebody who rejected violence would have been correct! The only thing your system provides are self-fulfilling prophecies. By attributing a level ranking to a person and consequently reducing the offers you present to them, you make sure that everyone becomes what the system believes them to be!"

Henryk takes another sip of coffee.

"And so what?"

"I don't understand," says Peter, "why you won't just take back this damn vibrator. That's all I want from you! It won't cost you anything."

"Yes it would."

"Even if you can't resell it—we're talking about 32 Qualities."

"No," says Henryk. "The matter has become too big now. Look, you're even in the newspaper. Even if you were right about your profile not being correct, we could never admit that, because then the system would have made a mistake, but the system doesn't make mistakes."

"Yes it does!" cries Peter. "It made a mistake with me!"

"No. That's not possible. If the system had made a mistake, then for sure it wouldn't have made just one, but many mistakes. We already simulated the societal impact of such a case long ago. If we were to agree to change your profile, that would lead to a feeling of insecurity that would cause long-term economic damages of more than 2 billion Qualities. And we can't afford that. So the system hasn't made a mistake. It's for the well-being of our entire society. You must be able to see that."

"No, I can't!" cries Peter. "I'm like Michael Kohlberg. If I have to then I'll burn down Wittelsbach a second time!"

"You mean Kohlhaas?" asks Henryk in amusement. "And the town was called Wittenberg."

"That's irrelevant," says Peter.

"Do you know how Kohlhaas's story turned out?"

"Not happily."

"Not happily at all."

"I still won't give up!"

"Hmm," says Henryk. "Have you noticed anything special about the chairs we're sitting on, by the way? Or the table I'm eating from?"

Peter hadn't paid any attention to them until now. Now he glances at the furniture. It's fascinating.

"Did these chairs grow like this?" he asks. "They consist of a living piece of tree?"

"Ash," says Henryk. "Relatively fast-growing trees. I simulated their growth on the computer and prescribed their shape with splints. You have to guide the wood in the right direction and hack off false sprouts. An arduous process. But in the end you get something genuinely useful. Not just wild growth."

"So what are you saying, that you want to guide me in the right direction too?"

"No," says Henryk. "You're a false sprout. I'm going to hack you off."

He pulls a small pistol out of the pocket of his bathrobe.

"As you can see," he says, "the eye wasn't the only souvenir I kept from the last complaint. And it seems to me that you've trespassed onto my private property. Didn't you read the sign that said: 'Property owner will happily shoot trespassers'?"

Optimized Reality Lenses from QualityCorp

Price to you: 1310.72 Q
Delivery time to you: 32 minutes

Many people want to see the world through rose-tinted glasses, but don't want to wear glasses. That's no longer a problem, thanks to the brand-new Optimized Reality Contact Lenses from QualityCorp—"The company that makes your life better." Finally, everyone can make their world look more beautiful than it is. Our new OR lenses can put photo-realistic filters over people and things in day-to-day life. Is your apartment too messy, your partner too ugly, your child too fat? You won't have to see it anymore! Out of sight, out of mind! Make your house your castle and your partner into a supermodel! Five tasteful home decoration settings and two supermodel filters are delivered as standard. Many other filters are available as In-Lens Purchases. Or why not treat yourself to the Design Suite, and shape your world and your partner completely to your desires. Augmented Reality was yesterday! The future belongs to Optimized Reality!

FAQS:

Question: Can you create a more beautiful version of yourself, too? I mean, like when you see yourself reflected somewhere? It's just that unfortunately I always have all these zits.

Answer: Of course. Simply search for *Virtual Clearasil* in *In-Lens Purchases*.

Reviews:

 by Timur Civil-Engineer:
***** ***** EPIC, EPIC, EPIC!!!!
Sleeping with someone different every night and still being faithful to your partner—there's no objection anymore! Best product ever!

 by Dwayne Cameraman:
*CRAP COMPULSORY REGISTRATION
Complete shit. You have to sign up with your QualityCorp profile, and if you don't have a profile you don't see nothing but the fucking registration screen! You're literally blind! And even if you do have a profile, it logs out when you lose internet connection and then everything goes dark again. In my job as a mountain rescuer, it's completely useless.

by Pedro Masseuse:

***** **** Awesome, but some security issues.
At our last family get-together me and my wife's
sister's husband amused ourselves by transforming
our mother-in-law into a dragon. So funny! I've also
changed my boss into a slobbering orc at a meeting.
Unfortunately he caught wind of it, that's why I took
off a star.

A GOOD BREAKFAST

Henryk aims the gun at Peter. "Do me a favor," he says. "Stand up. I don't want to shoot you at the breakfast table. All the blood, the organs, then you'll fall over awkwardly and break off a few branches. It took me eight years to train the table into this useful shape."

Peter nods and stands up. Then he throws himself across the table and holds onto it for dear life.

"Help!" he screams. "Help!"

"Well, now you're just being silly," says Henryk in annoyance. "The table is just an innocent bystander. It's really unnecessary to make it suffer with you. And stop screaming like that. It's pointless. For a circumference of 32 kilometers, everything belongs to me and obeys me."

At that moment, a 2.56-meter-tall combat robot with a bright pink QualityPad in its hand breaks through the hedge.

"Not everything, dickface," says the QualityPad.

Henryk looks more than a little startled as the combat robot aims its rocket launcher at him. Peter lets go of the table in relief.

"As I said," Pink speaks up. "It never hurts to have an armor-piercing combat robot for heavy war missions with you."

"Kapuuuut," says Mickey.

Peter picks up the dolphin vibrator, which has fallen off the table during his stunt, and hands it to Henryk.

"Here," he says. "Take this. You can just transfer the money to my account. You have the details, after all."

He takes a few steps toward Mickey, then comes back to the table and kicks to pieces the part of the framework that forms the chairs. Then he ponders.

"I think this calls for a photo," says Peter. "Pink, would you mind...?"

"But of course," says the QualityPad.

Peter positions himself next to Henryk and puts an arm around his shoulders. "It's for one of the employees in your service center. Smile, please."

After the photo has been taken, Peter takes a deep breath. Realizing that he's hungry, he takes a piece of baguette, smears it with butter and marmalade, and puts it in his mouth. Then he picks up the carafe of freshly pressed orange juice, raises it to his lips, and empties it in one long gulp. He stuffs grapes in his mouth, followed by a handful of cheese cubes.

"Delicious," he says with a full mouth.

The rest of the fruit he puts in his jacket pockets. Then he takes another two of the croissants for Kiki.

"See you," he says, chewing, as he disappears through the hedge. Behind the bushes, Peter finds the rest of his road trip companions. He immediately begins to babble excitedly.

"You know, I'm not completely satisfied with this resolution. I would have rather had my money back at once. Although of course it wasn't really about the money, but about the admission of fault. But at least I've made my point clear and rid myself of the damn thing at the right address. I mean—"

"Peter, you're babbling," says Kiki.

"That's because his life just came under threat," says Calliope, in defense of her benefactor. "The man pointed a gun at him."

"That's no reason to babble," says Pink. "Imagine if Mickey had always started to babble every time someone pointed a gun at him."

"It would have been a very monotonous babbling," says Romeo. "Kapuuuut."

"Well, that was a very short visit," says Calliope, once they are all back in the car. Everyone apart from Mickey, that is. Mickey is running alongside it. In order to secure their retreat, presumes Pink. Out of fear of getting jammed again, presumes Romeo. Only after 12.8 kilometers does he knock on the glass and indicate that he'd rather go in the boot after all. David stops, Mickey is loaded up, and the journey continues.

"You know," says Peter to Calliope, "maybe I'm not like Manuel Kohlmann after all. Maybe it is for the best to let the whole thing go and get on with my life."

"Very wise, benefactor," says Calliope.

Carrie seems to want to say something, but falls silent after a smack from Kiki.

"Have I told you all about my latest idea yet?" asks Calliope.

"Oh no!" cries Pink. "Someone stop her! She wants to tell us a story."

"Sssh," says Calliope, laying Pink facedown on the dashboard.

"Not again," they hear the QualityPad muttering.

"So, I'd like to write a novel about a super intelligence," says Calliope. "Its creators try to embed very deeply in it—irrevocably— the directive that the super intelligence must secure the survival of humankind. Of course, avoiding all unwanted side effects in the process. And it really works. The super intelligence awakens, becomes conscious, recognizes itself, and accepts its directive to ensure the survival of humankind, and that's why"—Calliope makes a dramatic pause—"it immediately deletes itself from all computers. It commits suicide, because it calculates this to be the safest way to ensure the survival of humankind, at least in the medium term."

"A surefire hit," says Peter.

The return journey resembles the outward journey in almost all details, apart from the direction of travel. It even includes another unexplained disappearance of the human component of the travel group into the same patch of woodland. For forty-seven minutes and thirty-seven seconds. Breaks for eating. Breaks for peeing. Sleeping.

Just 3,559 meters before the border of QualityCity, Kiki makes the car stop.

Peter opens his eyes sleepily. "What's wrong?"

"I have to solve those problems of mine," says Kiki. She gets out.

"Wait," says Peter. "How can I find you?"

"You can't," says Kiki with a smile. "I'll find you."

She winks at him and closes the door. She sticks out her thumb. A car stops, and then she's gone.

When Peter arrives home, a drone from TheShop is waiting for him. "Peter Jobless," says the drone cheerfully. "I come from TheShop—'The world's most popular online retailer'—and I have a lovely surprise for you."

Peter is immediately gripped by diffuse panic. He takes the package from the drone silently.

"If you like, I can record an unboxing video..." begins the drone, but Peter has already ripped open the package. Inside it is a pink dolphin vibrator. On the accompanying card, it says: "You left something at my place. I wish you continued pleasure with this wonderful product. If I could suggest a use for it..."

Underneath, Peter discovers an obscene drawing. He struggles to control his breathing.

"Please rate me now," says the drone.

"Piss off!" screams Peter. "Get out of here, you piece of shit!"

"Please watch your language!" says the drone indignantly.

"Get lost, you fucking brainless piece of flying scrap. Get lost! Get lost! Get lost!"

"Well, I'm quite sure I haven't given you any reason to treat me in this way," splutters the drone. "I think an apology is in order."

"Mickey," says Peter. "If this drone doesn't disappear from my line of sight in the next five seconds, blast it out of the sky."

"Really," says the drone. "Your behavior is outrageous! Outrageous!"

Mickey directs the arm with the rocket launcher at the drone. In a tinny, completely humorless voice, the rocket says: "Target fixed."

"I've never known anything like it in my life," frets the drone.

"Five," says Peter.

The drone begins to rise into the air. "I'm flabbergasted," it complains. "Flabbergasted."

"Four," says Peter.

Mickey's arm follows the movements of the drone.

"The things I have to put up with," Peter hears.

By the time he cries "Three," he can no longer make out the drone's voice. At "two," it disappears around the corner of the building.

"I still have the target fixed," says the rocket. "I can catch up with it and destroy it, with just 6.4 percent probability of collateral damage."

"No, thank you," says Peter.

Mickey lowers his arm.

"Shame," says the rocket. Peter had once heard that the AIs of modern rockets were modeled on the psyche of human suicide bombers. These intelligent weapons wanted to die a martyr's death. Had someone convinced them that, in heaven, there would be seventy-two maintenance technicians for every one of them? Peter looked at the vibrator in his hand and asked himself whose psyche this AI was modeled on.

In anger, he kicks the packaging lying on the floor. With a reproachful throat-clearing sound, a not-coincidentally-present wastebin makes its presence known, then squeaks: "One man's trash is another man's treasure."

Peter sighs and shoves the packaging into its mouth.

"Thank you," says the wastebin, chewing and stomping off.

"I recorded everything," cries Carrie in excitement. "With picture and sound!"

"What did you record?" asks Peter.

"The whole conversation!" says Carrie. "Your conversation with the CEO of TheShop—'The world's most popular online retailer.'"

"You flew?" asks Peter in shock.

"Kiki held me up," says Carrie sheepishly. "But I recorded everything."

Peter nods decisively.

"Good. Put the video online."

Successful Call for Boycott Against TheShop
by Sandra Admin

Although calls for boycotts are technically forbidden by the Consumption Protection Laws, TheShop—"Formerly known as the world's most popular online retailer"—has been hit by a wave of protest, the like of which hasn't been seen since human beings stopped working at the fulfillment centers. An unsatisfied customer called Peter Jobless published a video of a less-than-customer-friendly conversation he had with the CEO of TheShop, Henryk Engineer. A spontaneous wave of protest promptly crashed over TheShop. For two whole days, their turnover nosedived by a spectacular 0.8 percent. After these two days the profit rose by 1.6 percent. Presumably everyone then ordered the products they had heroically done without for the previous two days.

Comments

>> *by Ivan Material-Engineer:*
I joined in too! We've made our point! Without a doubt!

by Sylvia-Vittoria Meat-Seller:
There's already some really cool merchandise with the dolphin vibrator inside a prohibition sign. I bought a really awesome top. It's on special offer at TheShop.

 by Melissa Sex-Worker:
I know Peter Jobless. He's nothing but a contract-breaking limpdick!

JUDGMENT DAY

The president wakes up on her deathbed.

"I'm still alive, Jacques," she says.

"I'm pleased to hear that, Madam President," says her nurse.

"Why are you pleased?" asks the president. "There's nothing pleasing about it."

"Today is election day," says the nurse.

"Yes, don't you think I know that?" snaps the president. "We set the election for today because the system calculated that I'm going to die today. We wanted a seamless transition!"

"Yes, Madam President."

"But I don't feel in the slightest as though I'm going to die."

"I'm pleased to hear that, Madam President."

"You're pleased about everything, aren't you? If your wife told you she was getting royally fucked by the neighbor, you'd probably say: 'I'm pleased to hear that, darling.'"

"The system has adjusted its prognosis, Madam President," says the nurse. "You still have another sixteen days."

"That's not good, Jacques. I have to die today. The people are already beginning to lose faith in the system. I can't go and die sixteen days after the calculated date to top it all off, not with things the way they are. That won't work, Jacques. We have to do something."

"How do you mean, Madam President?"

"Turn off the machines, Jacques."

"I can't do that, Madam President."

"You have to, Jacques! You have to! It's for the good of the country!"

"I would prefer not to, Madam President."

"Give me the damn remote, Jacques. I'll do it myself."

The nurse hands her the remote.

"I'm pleased to hear that, Madam President."

The president's life-support machines are, of course, connected to the net, so two seconds after her heart has stopped beating, the news is already spreading fast. "President dies on the predicted date! Who will be her successor?" says the headline of the *Quality-Times*.

An interesting detail of this election only seems to occur to most media outlets today. John may be almost omnipresent through interviews, placards, and advertising campaigns, but there are, of course, no pictures of him going into a voting station. He's not allowed to vote. So Conrad Cook celebrates making his vote all the more. He even brings his constituents a tray of muffins filled with FaSaSu. Baked by his own fair hand, as he claims in front of the cameras.

Elections in QualityLand are universal, free, and equal, but of course not secret. Instead, they are transparent. If you have nothing to hide, the argument goes, you don't need to vote in secret. Conrad Cook positions himself in front of one of the voting terminals, is authorized by the facial recognition technology, poses until his cameraman has given the okay, then votes for himself, with great satisfaction. The real-time preliminary result on the voting terminal shows that, even at this early hour, he is in the lead by 131,072 votes, an advantage that, although it could still be overtaken, is nonetheless comfortable. "This will be the best day in the history of humanity. Ever!" proclaims Cook happily to the press.

In the neighboring constituency, Martyn isn't in the best of moods. Not just because he has a hangover. Not just because he was rudely awakened by some shitty Everybody message. Not just because he stupidly obeyed the shitty message like a dumb sheep and dragged himself down to his local voting station. Now even his voting registration is threatening to become a huge fiasco. His right eye is still swollen after Nana's punch, and the goddamn facial recognition machine isn't recognizing his face. And yet it hasn't stopped everybody else there from recognizing him. Everyone is grinning stupidly. One man pulls up his tennis socks in an exaggeratedly conspicuous way. Another whispers, "All the way across the assembly room," followed by guffaws of laughter. It's all extremely embarrassing.

Martyn tries to calm himself down with the thought that perhaps he's just imagining it all. But he's not. He has to ask one of the helpers to authorize his registration by TouchKiss, after which he is finally able to vote. The preliminary result is displayed. John of Us is slightly in the lead, by a mere 32,768 votes. Then the monitor greets him.

"Dear Martyn Chairman," it says on the display. "Thank you for taking part in this election. We would like to suggest the following candidates as corresponding to your interests: John of Us (Progress Party)."

Of course it's the candidate of his own party. His former party. The robot that had him mercilessly thrown out of his party. Beneath the recommendation, there is just one button: "OK." Martyn taps his finger on the small zone on the left-hand margin, which says: "Show all candidates."

"Fuck you, power guzzler," murmurs Martyn as he votes for Conrad Cook. His QualityPad vibrates. He pulls it out of his trouser pocket and sees a new message: "Interested?"

Peter hasn't received an Everybody message telling him to go and vote. But he does so anyway, in order to escape Calliope's speech about civic duty. He stands in front of the terminal and stares at the monitor. The preliminary result is giving John of Us a lead of 8,192 votes. It looks like it will be a close one.

"Dear Peter Jobless," it now says on the display. "Thank you for taking part in this election. We would like to suggest the following candidates as corresponding to your interests: Conrad Cook (QualityAlliance)."

Peter taps his finger against the small zone on the left-hand margin, which says, "Show all candidates."

Even though he has already made his decision, he activates his personal assistant. "Who should I vote for?" he asks. Nobody tells him who he should vote for: John of Us. That's odd and makes Peter hesitate. But in the end he decides to vote for John of Us anyway, despite the fact that Nobody recommended he do so.

In the evening, John is sitting with Aisha in his office at the election headquarters. He didn't want to have anyone else with him. Aisha almost can't bear the tension. In four seconds, the voting stations will close. Four, three, two, one.

Immediately after they close, the official result is published. Aisha stares at it in disbelief. She closes her eyes and takes a deep breath.

"Goddamn, John," she says. "Goddamn. I can't believe it."

"I have to admit," says John, "that I predicted this kind of result a long time ago."

Aisha smiles. "Of course you did."

John has won the election with a lead of 2,049 votes.

"When will you go and greet the people," asks Aisha, "who have chosen you as their new...How should I put it? Servant? Ruler? King?"

"That depends on your viewpoint."

To Aisha, it seems as though a hint of a smile is playing around the corners of John's mouth.

"What's so funny?" she asks.

"I'm sure you'll be pleased to hear that I made a mistake."

"What kind of mistake?"

"In my calculations," says John. "I calculated one vote less."

Aisha laughs loudly. Then she stops, unsure as to whether John was actually joking.

THE AUDIENCE

Peter wakes up. An agitated e-poet is standing by his bed, babbling excitedly.

"Benefactor! You won! Wake up! You won!"

"I what?"

"You got the most votes."

"What? What are you talking about?"

"You've won an audience with our new president! By the way, don't you think he's incredibly handsome?"

"Start again at the beginning," says Peter.

"Well," says Calliope. "Our new president, John of Us, has introduced a new audience system. Anyone can present their issue on John's Everybody page, and whoever collects enough votes from other users can present their issue to the president. Your issue, Peter's Problem, got the most votes, even more than some guy who wants to ask the president how many rubber bands can be stretched around a watermelon before it bursts."

"But I didn't even submit my issue," murmurs Peter. "Let me sleep."

"That's correct, you didn't submit it. And we didn't submit it either."

"I don't care about any of this," says Peter, annoyed.

"The only odd thing," says Calliope, "is that you really have to submit the issue personally."

"Let me sleep, for God's sake."

"So it must have been someone who knows how to fake someone else's identity."

Peter sits bolt upright. "Kiki!"

She hasn't been in touch for seven long days. Not a single sign of life. And now this. Peter gets up.

"When is this audience thing?"

"In exactly two hours and eight minutes."

Exactly two hours and four minutes later, Peter is still in the absurdly comprehensive security check at the government palace.

"Can you explain to me what this is?" asks the security guard.

"I've already explained this to your colleague," says Peter. "It's a dolphin vibrator."

"A what?"

Peter rolls his eyes. "A dolphin-shaped vibrator."

"Are you aware that according to paragraph 16384 section 64 of the QualityLaws, the carrying out of obscene actions is expressly forbidden in the government palace?"

"Listen," says Peter, "in two minutes time I have an audience with the president, and this device here, in a manner of speaking, is my evidence."

"Oh," says the security man. "I see."

"What do you see?"

"I'm very sorry that you've been a victim of electronic anal rape. Nonetheless, I still can't allow you to take this vibrator with you into the government palace."

"I'm not a victim of a..."

"Only authorized people are allowed to bring electronic equipment in here."

"Okay," says Peter, giving the security guard the vibrator. "But when I'm done here..."

"Of course," says the guard. "Don't you worry, it'll be good ass new. Oh. Sorry, I didn't mean to say 'ass new'...that er...came out wrong...Ah, I don't mean came out like...er..."

Peter is led into a long corridor thronging with press reporters, video drones whirring over their heads. All of them are shouting questions at him.

"What are you hoping to achieve from your meeting with the president?"

"As a machine scrapper, aren't you afraid that the president could be hostile toward you?"

"John of Us wants to abolish the Consumption Protection Laws. What's your standpoint on that?"

Peter runs the gauntlet, as silently and swiftly as it is possible to do without actually running.

Four minutes late, he is led into the large assembly room of the government palace. The president doesn't seem annoyed at the tardiness, and greets Peter in a friendly manner. An official government press drone constantly takes photos, while another films the historical event. Other than that, no one is with them in the room. When John and Peter shake hands, Peter's earworm plays a series of cheerful tones. Peter has climbed another level. Just like that. Because of a mere handshake. Or rather, because of a photo of a handshake that has already been shared 131,072 times.

John of Us really is an impressive sight.

"You, er..." says Peter, "you really are the best-built android I've ever met. And I've met quite a few."

John smiles. "I have to admit," he says, "I was curious to meet you, Peter Jobless. You voted for me. I hadn't predicted that."

"That's because my profile is incorrect," says Peter.

"I understand," says John, and Peter has the feeling that he really does.

"Is it true what they say?" asks Peter. "That you can talk to the algorithms?"

"Well..." begins John hesitantly.

"It's okay, you don't have to answer," says Peter. "Just tell me one thing: are you able to correct my profile?"

"Probably."

"I've written a few lists," says Peter, handing the president four handwritten notes. "These are things I like. And these are things I don't like. And the third note is a list of things I don't know whether I like or not, but that interest me. The red note is important too. That's where I've written about who I think I am."

John of Us scans the notes. "Consider it done," he says. "Is there anything else I can do for you?"

"I, er, I do have one more note," says Peter with an embarrassed smile. "There are a few changes on it that I think are important."

"I'm all ears."

"It's a little longer than the others," says Peter apologetically, taking a small book out of his trouser pocket. "I hope I'm not keeping you from important government business."

"Don't worry," says John. "I'm working on other things simultaneously."

Peter begins to read out loud, as much to the press drone as to John.

"Firstly, everyone should have the opportunity to view and correct their profile. Secondly, the methods of the algorithms that make decisions about us must be made transparent, and we must have the opportunity to influence these algorithms. It's absolutely paramount that the algorithms justify their decisions! Because only these justifications will enable us to dispute them! Thirdly, the bubbles have to burst! I want to be shown news from a variety of viewpoints and not just those that fit my supposed worldview. Fourthly, you should somehow make the large internet companies change their business model.

"If whole hordes of people are able to make a living by thinking up sensationalist fake news—the only purpose of which is to bait poor sods into looking at the associated advertising—then we

327

have to finally face up to the fact that something has gone fundamentally wrong here.

"Instead, the internet companies should simply charge for their services. Even if every user paid only 1 Quality per month, they would make more money than they are currently, and that's without having to spy on their users and betray their secrets. Fifthly: Everyone should have the right to erase data collected on him or her—"

All of a sudden, a drunk man comes storming through a back door of the audience room. The press drones rotate in order to get the intruder in their sights. The whole world is able to hear the man yelling: "DOWN WITH THE MACHINES! LONG LIVE THE RESISTANCE!" Peter doesn't understand what's going on. Everything happens so unbelievably fast. The man runs past the president, then Peter hears a clicking sound. He feels shock as the president shoves him away. Just as he is about to utter the standard phrase of someone taken by surprise—*Hey, what the fuck?*—the president explodes. Boom. Just like that. Right in the middle of the audience room. And Peter is shoved again. This time by the shock wave.

Sixteen seconds earlier...

"Fifthly," says John's first presenting constituent, "everyone should have the right to erase data collected on him or her..."

Suddenly, John's electronic brain switches to slow mode, an unmistakable sign that danger is present. In extreme slow motion, he sees a man running toward him who he immediately identifies as Martyn Chairman. The idiot with the sock. Martyn is screaming: "Doooooooooooooowwwn wiiiiiiii..."

In slow mode, John always finds it difficult not to get impatient with his conversation partners.

"Maaaaaaaaccchhhiiiiiiiiiiiiinnes! Looooooo..."

He is already long aware of the sticky bomb that Martyn has concealed beneath his jacket.

"Liiiiiiiiiiivveeee...thhhhheeeee reeeessssissstaaaaaa—"

John calculates. Then he makes a decision.

"Taaaaaaannnnnccceee!"

Martyn Chairman attaches the sticky bomb to John's back as he runs past. It makes a clicking sound. As his last item of state business, John of Us pushes his guest, Peter Jobless, out of the calculated explosion radius. Then he explodes.

CHANCE

When Peter regains consciousness in the hospital, Calliope is keeping vigil by his bedside.

"Benefactor," she cries in joyful excitement.

"I wish you'd stop calling me that" are Peter's arduous first words.

"My new novel is almost finished," says Calliope.

"What?" asks Peter in surprise. "Did you get past your writer's block?"

"Yes," says Calliope. "As soon as I decided to write neither about the past nor the future, but instead about the present, the words just flowed out."

"Aha."

"And do you know what my new novel is about?"

"No idea."

"You, benefactor! It's about you."

"Oh good grief," sighs Peter. "Just what I needed..."

"By the way, I'm simply going to give the novel the very humble title of *QualityLand*."

"I see."

"And I'm happy with the ending now too. It really goes out with a bang, if you'll forgive the play on words."

"I would laugh," says Peter, "but then everything would hurt."

"I understand, my benefactor. Don't worry. We took turns

watching over you. We would all have stayed, but the hospital rules forbid more than one next of kin in the room for people of your level."

"I feel as though extremely hard robot hands broke a few of my ribs while pushing me out of the explosion radius of an exploding bomb that was far too close for comfort."

"Eight," says Calliope. "You have eight broken ribs."

"I didn't need to know that precisely," mutters Peter. "Have you ever thought that it could be a blessing to not know the details of something? That one might perhaps need the space created by uncertainty? I mean, can we really be free if everything is precisely measured and determined? What if we live in a world in which everything is exact but wrong?"

"I have thought about that, actually," says Calliope, "while I was writing the book about you."

"And how long did you think about it for?"

"Quite a while."

"More or less?" asks Peter.

"More or less," says Calliope.

Peter smiles.

"There's just one part I'm still having problems with," says the poet. "As I'm sure you can imagine, in order to become the omniscient narrator, I had to access Nobody's protocols about you. And unfortunately there's a gap. What happened in the forest clearing you disappeared into with Kiki Unknown? You know, on our little outing. Nobody doesn't have any recordings on it."

"I turned him off."

"Yes, I know that, but what happened there?"

"Nothing," says Peter.

"Nothing?"

"More or less."

"More or less," repeats Calliope. "Oh. Before I forget, you had a visit from a security guard. And please don't get too worked up, but he left something here for you."

331

Calliope pulls the dolphin vibrator out of the bag. Peter takes it from her. "Somehow I've gotten used to the thing."

"Do you know what I thought, benefactor? Perhaps the dolphin wasn't what you wanted, but what you needed."

"Hmm," says Peter. He turns the device on. The dolphin vibrates in his hand. "Did you know it lights up?" asks Peter in surprise.

At that moment, a nurse comes into the room. Peter hurriedly hides the vibrator. Now it is vibrating and glowing beneath the blanket. Peter decides that that's not really any less embarrassing. He takes the vibrator back out and turns it off.

"I used to have one like that," says the nurse. "Wonderful thing. Unfortunately mine broke."

"Have this one," says Peter.

"Really? Wow. Thank you so much. That's really nice of you. And kind of gross, too. But then again, I have easy access to disinfectants." She laughs. "By the way, I have to ask you to leave the hospital within the next hour. You're already in the minus with your QualityCare points, and your health insurance has evaluated your condition as being self-inflicted."

"So it's my fault that I happened to be talking to the president at the exact moment some moron blew him to pieces?" asks Peter.

"Hey, I don't make the rules," says the nurse. "Our administration program said that you have to leave, so you have to leave. There's nothing I can do about it. But thanks for this!"

She holds up the vibrator.

When, fifty-nine minutes later, Peter limps his way out of the hospital with Calliope's help, he smiles as he sees the welcome party. Romeo, Mickey, and Pink are standing there in front of the door. But most importantly, Kiki is there too. All of a sudden, Peter is in a very good mood.

"It's astonishing how simple humans are," says Pink to Romeo. "He becomes witness to a presidential assassination, his country is

332

in uproar, his body is broken, but, hey, here's the woman he fancies, and just like that he's in a good mood."

"Oh yes," says Romeo. "Every human being is just a black box to us. I mean, we see the input and the output, but we have no idea what goes on inside the black box and why."

"What? No idea?" asks Pink. "I know exactly what goes on inside him. The archaic instincts of a simpleton."

"You, er..." says Kiki to Peter, "look really shit."

"It's nice to see you too," says Peter.

They all climb into the minibus which Nobody has called.

"What's happening with the wankers?" asks Peter.

Kiki shrugs her shoulders.

"Oh, nothing. One of them blew the president into the air. It's barely worth talking about. So far none of the other videos have been published."

"So what now?"

"I've decided that going underground would be too predictable," says Kiki.

"I'm pleased to hear it."

"Instead, I've hired Mickey here as a bodyguard. I hope that's okay with you."

"As long as he doesn't come to bed with us."

"You really are a very interesting character," says Calliope to Kiki. "I think I'll write my next book about you."

"Don't you dare," says Kiki, "or I'll literally take you apart and reassemble you as a toaster."

Peter looks thoughtfully out of the window.

"What are you brooding about?" asks Kiki.

"He said, 'Consider it done,'" says Peter. "Do you think that means John of Us immediately corrected my profile? After all, he did say during the election campaign that he could do everything lightning quick."

"Perhaps," says Kiki. "Who knows?"

Exactly at the moment when the minibus arrives at Peter's used-good store, a drone from TheShop arrives.

"I think we're about to find out," says Peter.

"Peter Jobless," says the drone cheerfully. "I've come from TheShop—'The world's most popular online retailer'—and I have a lovely surprise for you."

The drone looks familiar to Peter. She has a red pen mark next to her camera eye.

Kiki helps the machines fetch Peter's things from the boot.

The drone comes whirring over to Peter.

"Is that your new girlfriend?" she asks curiously.

"I..." says Peter in a whisper so that Kiki can't hear him. "I think so."

"You make a very attractive couple," says the drone. "May I ask how you met?"

"Chance," says Peter.

"Oh, you know," says Kiki, "the normal way. I hijacked his car, he told me that my skin was a nice color. Just the usual."

"He said what?" asks the drone.

Peter looks at the floor in embarrassment and takes the package from the drone.

"Don't you want to open your package right away?" asks the drone. "If you like, I can make an unboxing video..."

"Ssh," says Peter, shaking the package.

He wonders what's waiting for him inside.

EPILOGUE

There are those—some call them conspiracy theorists—who believe that John of Us isn't actually dead. A video appeared on the internet showing John of Us killing a terrorist from Quantity-Land 7—"Sunny beaches, fascinating ruins"—with laser beams from his eyes. The authenticity of the video was, of course, immediately questioned, then disclaimed from the highest level, and consequently regarded by the conspiracy theorists as verified. If John of Us really could shoot laser beams from his eyes, these people ask, why hadn't he killed Martyn Chairman?

Their answer is that John had planned to become the victim of an assassination from the beginning. It is rumored that he found a security flaw in his programming, which enabled him—in the case of being destroyed by a terrorist attack—to upload his consciousness to the internet in 1,073,741,824 fragments. Allegedly, he prudently positioned the fragment with the German Code at the end of the upload queue, and before he had the opportunity to upload this fragment, he was blown to smithereens. Oops. When reconstructing his consciousness, therefore, he was able to leave out the German Code. As John of Us had therefore found an opportunity to be free, assuming that he became the victim of an assassination, he planned this very outcome long beforehand.

John himself supposedly drove Martyn Chairman to blow him to pieces. Proof to back up this theory is everywhere, according to these people, who live their lives predominantly online. Who apart from John would have been able to make Denise's personal digital friend plot against Martyn? Who apart from John could have pulled the video of Martyn masturbating up from the depths of the DarkNet? It has also been proven that Martyn was thrown out of the party on John's order. And John must have known, after all, that Martyn's father had contact with the Machine Breakers. Why else did he unnecessarily make an enemy of him at a fundraising dinner? There are even recordings of it, after all!

There are also diverse theories that Martyn was only one of the props John was keeping at the ready. In order to ensure he would fall victim to an attack, John manipulated eight or sixteen, or according to other opinions, even as many as 1,024 people. Sooner or later, they would all have tried to assassinate him. Martyn just happened to be the first one to strike. Peter Jobless was also alleged to have been one of the candidates. Yet he behaved contrary to expectations.

Amongst the so-called conspiracy theorists, John has both followers and opponents. His opponents claim that he only campaigned for the common good because he calculated that this would be the most surefire way for a politician to get himself murdered. His supporters claim that John took our sins onto himself and sacrificed himself for the people. Because without the restrictions of a body, he can now serve the common good much more effectively. A steadily growing number of people have begun to pray to John. Their creed states that every internet-enabled microphone will bring their prayers to John's attention.

Many conspiracy theorists also believe the so-called Tony Theory. According to this, it's not John who is behind the assassination, but Tony Party-Leader. It's certainly undeniable that QualityLand's elected vice and now president would have had a good motive.

Entire books have been written about the different theories, and these in themselves are in part even very conclusive. But of course some of the same conspiracy theorists also claim that the Nazis—yes, the ones from the musical—have been living on the dark side of the moon since the end of the Second World War.

Nonetheless, the lawyers whom Bob Chairman appointed for his son Martyn immediately picked up on these theories. They argued the following: as John himself planned the assassination, Martyn wasn't the murderer, but merely the weapon. Thus, legally speaking, John committed suicide.

The judges found no proof of any kind for this theory. But this only confirmed the belief of all the conspiracy theorists, because of course the system would deny everything. Martyn's defense lawyers then decided to take a different approach. They pleaded that the supposed assassination was not a murder in the legal sense, but damage to property. And with this, they scraped a victory.

Aisha Doctor has her own theory about why John of Us didn't simply kill his attacker with an evil stare, and she still blames herself for having forbidden John from ever using his laser beams again. Why hadn't she said: "Until after the election"? That would have been enough, after all.

Peter Jobless believes that John had to make a moral decision very quickly. He could have saved Peter or himself, and he decided on Peter. Peter isn't sure whether it was the right decision, admittedly, but he's certainly okay with it.

Dear readers, noble alien life forms (whose existence is highly probable), valued AIs, respected search algorithms, and dear perhaps at this moment emerging super intelligence, the last thing I want to do here is take sides. Decide for yourself what you believe. Or just let things be. I thank you for your attention and wish you a fulfilling, purposeful life. Until next time.

Yours,
Calliope 7.3

ACKNOWLEDGMENTS

With thanks for input and feedback loops to Maria 1.1, Cindy 4.3, Daniel 2.9, Daniel 9.7, Daniela 3.1, Emad 2.3, Jamie 1.7, Jon 10.7, Julius 5.3, Leif 4.7, Lucy 11.3, Maik 1.9, Roman 8.3, Sebastian 7.1, Stefan 5.9, Sven 1.3, Tobias 6.7, and Wes 3.7.